MEET ME IN THE
DARK

To Amber

MEET ME IN THE DARK

A Dark Suspense

By

JA HUSS

ISBN - 978-1-936413-83-6

Edited by RJ Locksley

Cover Model: Adam Ayash

Cover Photo: Rick Day

Interior Designed and formatted by

E.M.
TIPPETTS
BOOK DESIGNS

www.emtippettsbookdesigns.com

DESCRIPTION

He's empty, inhuman, dishonest, and cruel.
She's never wanted anyone more.

Sydney has lived in fear for eight years after freelance assassin, Merc, failed to rescue her from a cult-like militia group. Left in the hands of a sadistic man, she did whatever it took to survive. But Merc's last words gave her hope. Hope he'd be back to finish the job.

After Merc is betrayed by her father, Sydney becomes his target. He wields sex, drugs, lies, and love like weapons. Merc knows just what to do with a fearful girl like Sydney. He's in control. He's always in control.

But Sydney Channing is not what she appears. And Merc's only redeeming act — the very one that made Sydney's life a living hell — might just be his worst mistake yet.

WARNING: Meet Me In The Dark is a STANDALONE non-traditional DARK CAPTIVE ROMANTIC SUSPENSE. It is not intended for sensitive readers.

PROLOGUE

SYDNEY

Christmas Eve
Eight Years Ago
Somewhere between Laramie and Cheyenne, Wyoming

"Fear is not your enemy. Fear keeps you alive."
– Sydney

The darkness is my friend. How many times have I said this to myself over the years?

I see the shadows off in the distance as they make their approach. Two men. Two? Really? Who do they think we are?

"Anyone, Sydney?" Garrett is right behind me, his hands on my waist. But that's not where they stay.

I don't turn when I answer, "Nope, nothing as far as I can see."

He pinches the skin over my ribs. I'm not fat, so this hurts. But I know better than to react.

He leans into my ear and breathes out his words. "Your dad will never keep us apart."

1

I turn into him, smiling. "Never." And then I rise up on my tiptoes, even though I will never be able to reach his lips unless he bows down, and offer him a kiss.

"I've got a plan to keep you with me forever. All you have to do is trust me. Do you trust me, Sydney?" He stares down at me with those green eyes. It's like they can see me in ways I cannot even see myself.

"Yes," I whisper up to him, willing him to believe the lie so bad. I wait patiently for the kiss, for a response, but his eyes hold back. They are mysterious and dark, even though the green is bright. That's what attracted me to him in the first place. Those green eyes. They sparkle. They sparkled that night I first met him too, but tonight it is with the promise of violence and back then it was with lies.

My calves begin to burn from standing on my tiptoes, but he never gives away what's in his mind. He never does. If I am transparent, he is opaque.

"Turn around and keep an eye out," he says, walking away.

I do as I'm told, not letting out the long breath of relief that I feel from his shunning me, but I picture it in my head as I spot the two shadows on the move again.

I don't know who the bad guys are here. Hell, I'm not even sure there are any other people in this world *but* bad guys. But I'm pretty sure Garrett is the worst of them all.

Twenty-four years old to my sixteen, he is a man and

I am a girl. He is tall and I am small. He is angry and I am desperate.

Isn't that what they say those men look for? Men who prey on young girls? They like us angry. They like us defiant and wild. They like us desperate for a way out of the fucked-up world some other man put us in.

And I am all those things. Or at least I was.

Two years on and off under Garrett's influence and I'm beginning to think all the fight has been beaten out of me. He never wanted a partner in this shit he's got going here. He wanted someone to fuck and control. And when I refused—told him I was a virgin—he held me down and—

A dog barking outside pulls me from my thoughts. Then there are more dogs barking. We have a lot of dogs here at the compound. They scare the shit out of me.

"You see them?" Garrett calls out from the other room, where the men are loading weapons.

"No," I say back. And I don't. I just know they're there. So it's not a lie.

The door opens and Garrett's friend Jared comes in, pulling his coat tight around his body using his fingertips. "Just a coyote. He ran off." The wind blows in some snow and a gust of cold air flashes past my face, making me blink as I take a deep breath.

It wakes me up.

This is really happening, Sydney. Your one chance is here.

Don't fuck it up.

I don't hear any more from the next room over, aside from the sound of weapons loading, and I turn my thoughts back to the dark. The moon rises as the time passes, but the shadows are gone now. Maybe the report Garrett got was wrong? Maybe it was only a recon mission tonight?

The attack comes just as I finish that thought. The window shatters in front of me and a gas canister comes flying through.

But I'm ready. We're all ready. Because these guys who came tonight have a traitor in their gang and Garrett was warned. I'm not sure how that makes sense, but my head is foggy from the drugs he makes me take every night.

I pull my gas mask up from the floor and put it on, then point my gun through the broken glass, nervously looking behind me for Garrett. He's yelling orders to Jared and Clide, so I know this is it. My escape is imminent. I break the window with my elbow, feeling a shard slice right through my thick canvas jacket, and then look behind me again. Jared is still in the other room and they are shooting.

I sling my rifle up onto my shoulder and then brace my hands on the window sill and jump up.

Hands close around my waist, pulling me back. "What the fuck are you doing, Sydney?"

I gulp some air as I turn to Garrett, the gas mask making him seem like something out of a fucked-up war movie. "I saw them!" My voice comes out nasally through my own mask. "I saw them in the trees. I'm —"

He smacks me down onto the ground and then rips my mask off. The chemicals immediately begin to penetrate my mouth and nose. My throat starts to constrict, and then I take a boot to the stomach. "Did you let them in, Sydney? Are you trying to leave me?"

I shake my head frantically, and I look up in his direction, but I can no longer see anything but the cloud of gas that surrounds me.

Shooting starts from outside. Bullets are flying through the window I was going to climb out of. Garrett's boots thud across the wood cabin floor and I reach for my mask once again. It takes me several seconds to get it fastened, but the damage has already been done. My eyes are burning.

I stand up, trying to get above the cloud, but I'm not very tall, so I have no hope. I feel for the walls and find the window again. I hold up my hands and keep my rifle slung around my shoulder in case those guys outside are still watching this window, but no calls to drop my weapon come. I blindly press my hands on the sill again, and this time when I draw myself up, the cruel hands never stop me. I fling myself out and onto the hard-packed snow. It's wet and cold and feels wonderful on the exposed parts of my face.

I crawl a few paces and then get to my feet and run

wildly towards the trees. An explosion erupts behind me, but there is no heat and no flying shards of wood from the cabin, so I know it's one of ours. A distraction. They are making for the trucks with the dogs, just as planned. They care more about those damn dogs than they do me, even though I have a gun and I could stop them.

No one calls my name, and for that I am grateful.

I trip and fall, stumbling over the thick tree trunk that marks the edge of the flat land behind the cabin, and my rifle goes flying from my hands and I only keep it by reaching out with the tips of my fingers on the shoulder sling.

Fuck! Do not lose the gun, Syd!

I shoulder my gun, thankful I still have it, and then fling my mask off, convinced that the tear gas is trapped inside it.

I force myself to open my eyes. It seems that the moon has become brighter in my moments of darkness, but I know that's not true. I'm just fucked up.

I squint them down, so I'm almost blind, just a sliver of ground visible as I look down at my feet. I stumble forward and reach a tall pine tree and fling myself behind it.

"Sydney!" Garrett calls my name and then I hear the crunching of snow as he heads towards me.

I panic and unsling my gun, point it in his directions and squeeze the trigger without aiming.

"You bitch," he says, reaching me clearly intact. He grabs my rifle from my hands and pushes me face first into the snow, his muscled body straddling my back to keep me pinned. "You almost hit me, you stupid cunt. Come on," he says, getting off me and pulling me to my feet. "Phase one is over. We gotta run to the extraction point for Plan B. If you'd done your job properly we'd be in the truck right now." And then he grabs my face between his thumb and fingers and squeezes. "I better not find out you broke my trust, Sydney. Or else you will pay for this. I will—"

The gunfire interrupts him. Bullets spray around me, hitting the branches of the tree, flinging needles everywhere as the scent of pine invades the air. I struggle against him and get free. But only because he is busy shooting back.

My vision has cleared a little, so I open my eyes as best as I can and run.

I run.

My feet sink into the deep snow when I cross that boundary between yard and brush, and it feels a lot like those dreams I used to have where I was walking through deep mud.

But I don't care. The only thing worse than getting away is not getting away. Either way, my life as I once knew it is over. And if this is the end, I'd rather meet the assassins out here in the dark than be kept as Garrett's plaything at the next camp.

"Sydney," he calls again. But I keep running. I hit a patch of ice and stumble, my knee twisting painfully as I catch myself before going down, and then I'm on hard-packed snow again. Gliding across the top like I'm a rabbit running across a frozen river.

Be the rabbit, Sydney, my mind says. *Be the rabbit.*

It works, because the snow holds my weight as I make a curve back towards the cabin, hoping to throw Garrett off my trail.

The few minutes of fresh air do wonders for my eyesight, and by the time I've circled back to the grove of short pines on the west side of the cabin, I can see a little better.

There is one truck left. The truck Garrett and I should've been in if things had gone according to plan.

I eye it for several seconds and in that time all the shooting stops.

He does not yell my name. No one is screaming. No bullets are flying.

Whoever is left here, we're all in stealth mode.

My heart, which has done a fair job at taking this all in stride because of the drugs he feeds me, begins to beat so fast, I think I might have a heart attack.

I hear a helicopter off in the distance and wonder if it belongs to us or them. And then I shake my head. I'm not part of this anymore. No matter what happens, I'm not part of this anymore. There is no more *us.*

It's only them.

I look for a way to get to the truck. If I can get there

before Garrett, I can leave on my own. The keys are tucked under the wheel well, in a magnetic box. If I can just get over there...

I bolt towards a rock formation, my feet slipping down into the deep snow a few times, making my dash look a lot more like a slow lumbering than anything else, and then throw myself behind it.

My body slams into the ice, cutting open my face, but there's no shooting. There's no Garrett.

A boot stomps down on my back, pressing hard against my spine. "Don't fucking move."

But I do move. I turn my head and look up at the face of a killer. Not the killer I know, but it doesn't matter. I'll take anyone at this point.

"Don't shoot," I whisper.

He drops down to his knees, one on either side of my body, and then flips me over and presses a pistol against my head. "Where the fuck did they go?"

I stare up at him. His face is covered by a black cloth so that only his eyes are visible. They are the dark eyes of a man who just got fucked over. He knows. He was set up.

My silence pisses him off and he wraps his hand around my throat and squeezes. "You better start talking. Who told them we were coming?"

"Sydney!" Garrett yells. Why is he still here? Why didn't he leave?

"Please," I say to the guy. "Get me out of here. My father—"

"Your father set me up, bitch. You're not going anywhere with me."

"No, I swear. You're here to save me! You're here to take me back!"

"Sydney!" Garrett calls again.

My eyes dart in the direction of his voice.

"You're afraid of him, huh?" the big man asks me. "It's me you should be afraid of, cowgirl. Not him. But if he's the one who scares you into talking, then so be it." He lets go of my throat and calls out, "I've got her, Garrett. She turned on you! She told us where you were."

I'm shaking my head the whole time. "No!" I scream. "No!"

The big man pulls the cloth covering his face down so I can see him. And then he smiles. "I'm gonna leave you here, Sydney. I'm gonna leave you here with Garrett. He's gonna do things to you that only the traitors of the world have the pleasure of knowing."

"Please," I whisper.

"Tell me what the plan is tonight."

I hear a helicopter off in the distance and look towards the sky. "They're not here for you, bitch," the dark man says. "They're here for me."

"Kill him," I say. "If you kill him so he can't get me

again, I'll tell you."

He punches me in the face so hard I feel the pain in my neck as my head snaps to the side. The shock vibrates up into my skull, temporarily knocking me out of the game, but I can still hear. The dark man is yelling to Garrett.

They are making a deal that involves handing me over to Garrett in exchange for information.

"No," I squeak out. "Please." I don't even think this guy hears me, because he never stops talking to Garrett. "I'll tell you," I say. "I'll tell you who the target is, if you just keep me away from him."

This gets his attention. "Who?"

"The little girl."

And that's when I see pure evil.

Garrett might be sadistic and mean, but this guy is in a whole other category of fucked up.

He leans down into my face and whispers as he talks. "I will come back for you, bitch. When you least expect it. When your life goes back to normal and all this is nothing but a nightmare. Just when you think it's over. I will come back for you." And then he leans in close to my ear. "I *own* you."

ONE

SYDNEY

Present Day
Somewhere outside Jackson, Wyoming

"I call it adjusting. It's a cross between concession and acquiescence. Not quite a surrender, not quite a win."
– Sydney

Now I stare out the window, remembering that night back when I was sixteen. He left me there, just like he said he would. Garrett got me back, and that was how my adult life started. Terrified, alone, and helpless. Subjugated and beaten into submission. I lost myself that year. Probably even before that, now that I think about it. It was not my first encounter with Garrett, but it was my last stand. He took me in, remade me into what he wanted, and then he—like everyone else in my life—disappeared.

We'd bought a bar in Cheyenne after all the shit from the cabin incident died down and been in business about eight months when my father was killed in a freak airplane accident flying into Jackson Hole for a ski weekend. His body was never found and it was a big deal. My father was the US Senator from Wyoming for more than a decade. He was fully expected to win a third term in the next election when all this happened. I can't say I was too broken up about it when I saw it on the news. Or surprised. He had a lot of enemies.

Enemies that included officials with powers in the most influential nations on the planet. Of course, he had friends in those positions too. But the Company — the secret shadow government he was born into — was split up a decade ago when almost a hundred members were killed in what the nation's largest newspapers wrongly called a 'turf war'.

Garrett is part of them somehow. I am too, since my father is. But they never wanted me for anything, so Garrett's request for ownership was settled without much protest.

There was a party in the bar the night my father died and we celebrated my successful implantation — Garrett's words — into his… well, what to call it? A cult? Not quite. A militia? Yeah, but they are more than that. I guess, if forced, I'd call it his family. I became his family.

And even though my family life was pretty messed up, I really don't think this is what a family is. I really don't.

At least I was free of the Company's expectations. I lost all my support. And I got Garrett full-time instead of the Company handlers. But even a drugged-up, stupid sixteen-year-old knew that being cut out of that shit was good.

My father wasn't such a popular guy in my circles. Of course, the crash was ruled an accident. Pilot error. That's not how people die in my world. It's never an accident. And for a little while I thought Garrett was the killer. Or at least I wanted to believe that, because the alternative was that He was the killer.

Two months later Garrett disappeared. He left the bar one night with some buddies and just never came home. None of them did. And if you're me, attached to him, you don't look luck in the eye and start asking questions. But this was when I knew for sure it was Case.

He owned me, he said. His eyes are burned into my memory. Cold eyes. Dark eyes. The eyes of a killer who takes no prisoners and never forgets a debt.

But it's been six years since Garrett disappeared and I've been on my own. Six long years of waiting for Him to come for me. Except he never did. In fact, I never saw or heard from him again after the cabin incident.

So I ran the bar. It's a big country bar in Old Town Cheyenne. We have specials every night. Ladies free on Wednesdays and ninety-nine cent microbrew Mondays. Things like that. I was only eighteen when I took it over, not even old enough for a liquor license, but since Garrett wasn't officially dead—only missing—it all stayed in his name. I moved on.

No one stopped me.

No one.

And this, more than anything that has happened to me in my short, fucked-up life, is what bothers me most.

Because he said he'd be back. And Merric Case doesn't look like a guy who goes back on his word.

So where the fuck is he?

My phone buzzes on the nightstand and I roll over on the bed to check the screen. I smile and pick it up, tabbing the accept button as I bring it to my ear. "Hey," I say in a low whisper that is appropriate when you're laying down in the dark in the middle of the night.

"Hey," Brett says back. "I miss you."

He makes me smile. He really does. "Miss you too," I say back. Brett Setton is a good guy. He's tall, blond, blue-eyed and has a body an eighteen-year-old football player would die for. He's mature, smart, and runs the bar like he's running Wall Street. He's perfect. And tomorrow we are getting married.

How did I ever get so lucky?

"I can't wait to see you in your dress."

I look over at the dress hanging from a hook. It's sparkling with the glint of pearls in the moonlight. The train is long, the bodice tight, and the shoulders strapless. It's almost shimmering silver instead of white.

"I can't wait to see you out of your tux," I say back

16

playfully.

He laughs at that and I smile. "OK, well, I'll let you get some rest. See you in the morning, Mrs. Setton."

"Love you," I whisper back.

We hang up and I place the phone on my belly. His sisters gave me a whole bunch of lingerie as a present. I know Brett likes the sexy look, but I'm a country bar girl at heart and I mostly wear shorts and tank tops to bed. So this little nightie I'm in right now is not me at all. But it is Brett.

That makes me smile again.

His sisters bought me a nightie for each night of our honeymoon in Fiji, plus the night before the wedding. Sarah, his oldest sister, said it's bad luck not to look pretty when you go to bed on the night before your wedding. I've never heard of that, but my experience in weddings starts and stops with my own, which hasn't even happened yet.

And wedding nights. I'm nervous about that too. My nights with Garrett were filled with confusion and shame. I dreaded being next to him in his bed. Brett will have something planned. He'll have expectations. And since I've never slept with him even though we've been dating for over a year, it scares me. I have this very irrational fear of sleeping with people. I can't explain it, it just… overwhelms me.

I sigh as I look up at the ceiling. The dimmer light in the chandelier must not be turned completely off, because two bulbs are glimmering a faint yellow.

I don't see two bulbs though.

I see two eyes.

The rich amber of those dark, evil eyes as they peered down at me out on the side of the hill.

My hand comes up to touch my throat as I remember what it felt like to be under him. His hard body pressed against mine. His breath teasing me with his threats. It was soft but filled with violence at the same time.

I know his name now. Merric. But it took me a while to get that information. It took a lot of innocent conversations with close enemies to tease that out of them. Merric Case.

I called him the soft killer those years in between. Not that he'd kill me softly, if he ever decided to come back. But he whispered his threats that night. I close my eyes and feel his breath, sliding into the shell of my ear — tickling me with fear.

Merric.

Brett.

Merric.

Brett.

My hand slips down into my expensive lace panties and finds the sweet spot. But I pull back and swallow down my sick desire.

Why? Why do I think about him? He punched me in the face. He left me with Garrett that night. He had to know what he was doing to me. But he left me there.

I close my eyes and think of the man I have, not the man who says he owns me.

Brett is nothing like the men I grew up with. My father had some interesting friends and none of that was in a good way.

I'm his illegitimate daughter from a woman he had on the side after his wife died. He and his wife never had any children, so he took an interest in me. He tried to save me, too, I guess. He sent the soft killer to come get me. At least I think he did. It's hard to tell who was setting up whom that night. Was Garrett setting up Merric Case and his friend? Was the little girl the target the whole time, and my father used Merric to get her father away from her so they could take her out?

But the girl lived. I know that for sure. I saw her on the TV once. Garrett and I never met up with those militia friends again, and for that I can be grateful. If they had been around when he disappeared, they'd have stepped in to fill his role. I shudder at the thought of them touching me.

But now I have Brett. Perfect Brett.

I turn over in my soft bed and close my eyes. I need to try to sleep. Put these old memories behind me. Slip into my brand-new life as wife, and sister, and maybe even mother.

That makes me smile. I picture perfect little Brett babies. Tow-headed kids with blue eyes and cherub cheeks. His sisters all have kids, so I can easily slip one of their faces onto the child that might be ours.

But the dark hair and amber eyes come back to me again. *Stop, Sydney.*

Why didn't he come? Why did he let me live?

My phone rings a tune I've never heard before. I'm in a daze as I stare down at it.

It stopped ringing. Did I answer it?

And then I sit straight up in bed as the answer to why Case lets me live comes to me.

He's going to come after Brett, not me. I can't marry Brett. I *can't* marry Brett. Case will make him disappear, just like he did Garrett. Only this time Case won't be saving me, he'll be killing me.

My feet are on the cold wooden floor in an instant and I walk over to the window. *He can't get us here, Sydney. He can't.*

The wind is blowing so hard it whistles through tiny cracks in the window sill. I can feel the draft. It's the dead of winter at the lodge Brett's family have owned since it was built in the 1920's.

And it's closed. It's not a ski resort, like most places around Jackson Hole. It's a mountain retreat. More of a dude ranch than anything else. They tell me that they close for the winter. The horses are sent to a stable near Denver to spend the winter pulling sleighs in the park and carriages on the streets of downtown.

I breathe a small sigh of relief when I see no one outside. But the wind makes a sound like a helicopter and that night at the cabin comes back to me. I thought the helicopter was there to save me. But it wasn't. It was there to pick *him* up.

I've learned a few things about Merric Case over the years. He's got money. He's got resources. And he's got a network.

The few people who wander into my bar whom I met through Garrett in times past speak his name in hushed tones, if they mention him at all. Not out of respect, either. Out of fear.

I need to tell Brett.

I walk to the door of my room and actually have my palm on the antique glass doorknob, ready to pull it open and walk down the hall to Brett's room, when I come to my senses. What will I tell him? He can't marry me because I'm obsessed with a killer? I laugh a little. Will I tell him I was born into a secret organization called the Company? That they have been filling my head with propaganda my entire life? That I'm a danger to him, myself and others and he should run as far away from me as he can get?

What the fuck am I supposed to tell him?

I can't marry Brett.

No, Sydney. You can't tell him any of that. He'd never believe you. The best you could hope for is making him think you're crazy.

Maybe I am crazy.

Maybe I should just admit it.

No. I shake my head. I'm not crazy. That shit happened. I can still feel the tear gas in my eyes. Smell the splintering pine needles when that shot blasted through the trees. Hear the roar of the helicopter in the air above me.

It was real.

That life was real. Those secrets were real. Those *people* were real.

I walk to my suitcase and grab the pair of jeans I came up here in and pull them on over my pretty lace panties. My hoodie is still draped across the chair and I pull that on over the nightie. And then my boots are on and I'm at the window, the wind still seeping through the cracks as I open it. The snow blows in, bathing my face in a sweet shower of ice crystals.

I need to leave. I need to get the hell out of here before Merric Case comes back to finish what he promised me eight years ago. I throw my leg over the sill and jump down into the snow that has drifted up against the side of the lodge and tug the window back down. I turn into the weather and run across the grounds towards my truck.

With any luck the snow will blow over my footprints and they will not know what happened.

And maybe this is fitting? That I disappear, just like Garrett did.

22

Maybe he loved me after all? Maybe he left to give me a chance? Maybe he gave himself up to his fate in order to change mine?

It's a lie I tell myself often. I'm not proud of it, but it eases the hurt of being left behind. Twice. Both times by monsters. Maybe Garrett was a violent asshole, but he was all I had. And what does that say about me that a monster can't love me? I'm so unlovable even evil men can't stand to be with me.

I can't marry Brett.

But I want to. I really, really want to. He's so nice. And treats me so good. But I can't marry him if that means Case will include him in his little revenge scheme. I have to protect Brett and his family. They are a good family. Old money. Educated. Upstanding people who contribute to charities and try to make the world a better place.

I hit the truck and realize I left my purse and phone behind. But my keys are still in my hoodie pocket, so I get in and start her up, looking up at the lodge windows for any sign of life.

It's dark. Like me. Like my past.

Like Him.

I put her in gear and ease forward into the snow. I know this mountain. It's dangerous in the winter under the best of conditions, and this storm will make getting down into the valley treacherous. But I know this mountain. I know it very well. We've been up here dozens of times since Brett and I met. His sisters live here full-time so we come visit every chance we get. So if anyone can get away in this storm, it's me.

I go slow. I wind my way down, slipping close to the edge more times than I can count. But when I get to the part where the cliff side disappears and the forest takes over, I let out a sigh of relief and turn the music on. I played this song the whole way up here and I'll play it the whole way down too. That eases my nerves a little more.

It's the little things that get you through, Syd.

I know that. I live for little things. That way you're never too disappointed.

The snow gets deeper and deeper as I go and my wheels slide around, creating a sea of slush. I see a huge drift up ahead on the road. At least six feet high. I look in my rear view, anxious about who might come after me if they notice I'm gone, and then gun it.

I'm not getting stuck on this mountain. I'm not. Once I'm in, I'm all in. I've never been someone who changes their mind once I hatch a plan. And quite frankly, I'm not up to witnessing the disappointment on Brett's face if he finds out I tried to run and failed.

The tires slip to the right, making me correct the steering, and then they find purchase on some stones or twigs and the truck lurches forward. The snow mound acts like a ramp and then I'm flying through the air. A moment later the front end crashes into the ground and I am thrown forward, my head hitting the airbags so hard I see stars.

TWO

"Limits are for finding strength. Push yourself until you can't move... and see what happens."

– Case

There comes a time in every soldier's life when they realize—all this bullshit is bigger than them. You are small. They are big. You are weak. They are strong. You are dead. They live on.

I picture myself standing out in a vast desert surrounded by nothing but sand on all sides. There's a crashed plane nearby, smoking.

I'm in uniform, desert fatigues. But they are ripped from the crash. My body is burning from the sun and the pain. My lips are cracked and dry. Water is the only thing on my mind because that's how you get through as a soldier. You only think of survival.

The problem with survival for most people is that it's overwhelming.

I'm not most people.

When others see nothing but sand, I squint and see the outline of a mountain range hidden in the mirage of the desert heat.

When others feel their throats closing up as the dry wind whips past their face and threatens to choke them, I picture kissing a woman's lips, still wet and cool after taking a refreshing drink of water.

When others realize this bullshit is bigger than they ever imagined and all they want is to go back home and fuck their girlfriends and drink beer, I remind myself there is no girlfriend. There is no back home. There is only me.

Other people walk away.

Other people give up.

Other people forgive and forget.

I am not other people. I am Merc and there are three things you should know about me.

Number one. You might be bigger, but I will last longer.

Number two. If you fuck me, I fuck everything you ever loved.

And number three. I never lose. My victory is only delayed.

The tracking app dings in my hand and then a light appears. A smile cracks before I can stop it. Because how fucking perfect am I? I know her so well. And after almost eight years of careful observation and planning, I should.

I tab a graphic on my phone app and pull up a

satellite view. It's real-time. Because while this bitch has been running her little country western bar in Cheyenne, planning cute little theme nights and trying to forget that she was once under the control of a ruthless man, I've been accumulating wealth, gathering technology, and feeding my desire for vengeance. I have all the tools. If revenge is a journey, then I'm well-supplied for it. I have anything and everything I want or need to pull off one last job before I disappear for good.

And it all starts now.

I check the laptop in the passenger seat, also showing the drone feed in real-time, and watch as it changes direction when she leaves the parking lot of the lodge that is heavily covered by ancient conifers. A few keystrokes later and I've got a pretty good bird's-eye view of her truck as it turns onto the only road leading in and out of the almost deserted resort.

I knew back in June she'd run. I knew because she changed the wedding date four times. This was her last chance to settle down. And if she had, I might've called that a victory in and of itself and found another way to finish this job.

But—I let a smile crack—I'm so glad she didn't. Her black truck winding down the mountain road is the only reminder I need of who and what she really is.

Sydney Helena Channing. Company kid. *Use her, abuse*

her, and she always comes back for more. If the girl has a motto, that's it. That's the girl I've come to know and hate as I watched and waited patiently for all the many pieces to fall into place. Tonight is the first move of the endgame. And I'm about to put her motto to the test.

Sydney is the one who started this for me. Yeah, maybe the senator was the one who set me up—but there's no way I'd have taken the job on Christmas Eve if a teenage girl wasn't involved.

Channing knew that. He fucking knew that.

I grit my teeth and force myself to push the past away. What's done is done. The present is coming up on me in a black truck showered in white flakes.

Almost eight years. That's how long it took for this moment to arrive.

I light up a cigarette and roll the window down, letting in the frigid mountain air. The snow is picking up, and good God, could this night be any more perfect to pull this off?

I glance down at my phone tracker again and my heart rate jacks up a little with anticipation.

Today I get full access. For the first time in years, full, unobstructed access to her. But that's not all I'm going to get. No, not by a long shot.

Her headlights wind down the mountain and a few minutes later there she is. She guns her truck to get through a heaping pile of snow. It's hiding a tree that spans the whole width of the road.

No cars in. No cars out.

The resort is closed and so are the roads. Guests arrived two days ago and aren't due to leave until after the wedding.

If there *was* a wedding. I'd usually feel a little guilty about taking a woman the night before her wedding. But not this woman and not this wedding.

I'm not the one running. She is.

The truck doesn't plow through the snow like it should, like she expects. The hard-packed snow underneath the innocent-looking pile shoots her straight into the air.

I appreciate the beauty of a two-ton projectile completing a mid-air arc as it flies towards me and then gravity takes over and pulls her back down to earth front-end first. The crunching of metal almost drowns out the hiss of airbags being released, and then the mountain goes quiet. The only sound is the muted music coming from her radio.

A song I know well. A song she knows well too.

I smile at that. I smile at the crashed and smoking truck on the snow-covered road. I smile at all of it.

I open the door of my truck, and that little annoying alert dings through the stillness. I ignore the open-door alert and step out. My steel-toed boots crunch in the snow as I walk towards the tree, and then I place a hand on the frozen bark and hop over it, listening for her moans.

But what I get instead is swearing. "Fucking shit!"

Perfect. It would've really sucked if the crash had killed her before I got my chance to end this properly.

I wait as one gloved hand reaches outside of the broken window of the driver's side door and pulls the handle. The truck is tilted at an angle, so she tumbles out onto the snow in a heap. "Shit," she groans.

I watch silently as she gathers herself up onto her knees, and then, after a few wobbly seconds, she rises to her feet. She huffs out a long breath of air and wipes her brow, covering her hand with blood.

"Fuck." Her head comes up and searches around and she stops dead as she realizes I'm standing about twenty yards off. "Hey," she yells. "Did you see that?"

I say nothing, simply reach into my pocket.

"Can you help me?"

I raise my gun and squeeze the trigger, hitting her square in the left shoulder.

She flies backward into the snow, not even a scream.

I walk towards her slowly, taking my time and looking around for any sign of headlights in the distance, but there are none. We are completely alone tonight.

I stop a little way off and watch her body in the snow. Her arm jerks a few times, a dark patch appearing underneath her, and then I check my watch and wait three minutes before walking out to pick up my trophy.

When I get to her blood-covered body her eyes are closed

and her mouth is open. I grab the rope from my pocket and tie her legs first, then her hands. And then I hike her small body up over my shoulder and walk back to my truck bed. I open the tailgate, pull the lever that keeps the bed cover in place, and it rolls back to give me enough room to lay her down on top of the tarp. I wrap her limp body up, and then roll the cover back over the top of the bed and lock the tailgate closed.

Done.

Well—I laugh—she's done. But I'm certainly not.

The snow is coming down harder now, and I estimate that all evidence of my truck and footprints will be covered in about twenty minutes. Long before anyone at the resort realizes the bride-to-be is gone. Long before they realize they can't drive down the mountain because of the fallen tree trunk. Long before they call—well, I laugh out loud at that thought.

People I target don't call the police.

They call killers.

Like me.

I get back in the truck and put her in gear, upping the heater since it's damn cold out. Poor Syd will be shaking pretty good when the tranquilizer wears off. But she'll be shaking more from the fear than the cold by the time that happens.

THREE

SYDNEY

Eight Years Ago

"That feeling? When your mind is blank and your heart is empty. And then you have to pick up that gun and do your job. You mean that feeling? Yeah, I know it. It's called giving up."

- Sydney

"Sydney?"

I lie there on the ground, listening to the retreating *womp-womp-womp* of the helicopter, willing this not to be my reality.

A boot to the ribs tells me that's pointless.

I turn my head towards Garrett, pain radiating up through my chest, and find his face. He's got his leg back, ready to deliver his foot to my body again, when he stops.

I swallow and close my eyes.

"Tell me he was lying."

"He—" My throat is dry and my words falter.

Garrett kneels down and grabs me by my jacket, pulling me up and shaking me hard at the same time. "Tell me. He

35

was lying."

"He was lying," I whisper. And he was. "I never did anything. I have no idea who he is!"

"You were leaving," Garrett says. Usually Garrett is a raging asshole when I piss him off. But he's so calm now. He's so calm this scares me even more and my whole body starts shaking. "You were running away, weren't you?"

I swallow again and then before I know what's happening, I piss myself. The heat leaks between my legs and I start to cry. I just close my eyes and start to cry.

I don't know how long I stay like that, but the next thing that happens scares me even more than the threat of his boot.

Garrett picks me up and holds me in his arms. I never open my eyes, not even when he places me in the truck and drags the seatbelt across my chest, clicking it into the lock. He shuts the door and walks over to the driver's side and gets in. Starts the truck. And we drive off.

We drive for hours. The sun comes up behind us and we're still driving. Going west.

Hours later we pull off the main highway and take a dirt road. That's when I speak. "You're going to kill me." It's not a question.

"I was," Garrett says. "Before last night."

I can't even muster up a sob.

"But—" He stops. Just stops. Never starts up again. And

I don't push it. I just sit quietly, listening to the song he's playing on the stereo, letting it calm me, until we finally come to a rest outside a cabin.

I reek of piss, but my pants have long since dried and my bladder is full again, even though I haven't had anything to drink in the six hours we've been on the road together.

Garrett turns the truck off and we sit in silence for a few seconds. A ticking noise from the engine is the only sound.

"We live here now." And then he gets out and walks around to the passenger door. He opens it for me and then unbuckles my seat belt. "Can you walk?"

I look up at his face and try to find the anger. The hateful, evil, and sadistic man I have come to know. But all that is missing right now.

Garrett reads my silence as a yes and tugs on me until I swing my legs out and stand up. My back hurts. My ribs hurt from where he kicked me. My face hurts from where that assassin punched me.

"Just kill me," I say, looking up at Garrett. "Just kill me and let me die. I don't want to do this anymore."

"I don't blame you," he says. "If I was you right now, I'd feel the same way. Even if I didn't know what was gonna happen next."

And then he turns around and walks away, leaving me standing there. He climbs the front porch steps to the small hunting cabin, opens the door without using a key, and walks inside, closing the door behind him.

The wind picks up and reminds me it's winter.

I wrap my arms around myself and shiver.

I do the only thing I can. I follow him in.

FOUR

SYDNEY

"He always told me that the secret to staying alive was stillness. I've seen it in action too many times to disagree."
- Sydney

I wake up and immediately wish I hadn't. I'm blind.

No, it's just dark. It's the definition of pitch black.

I squirm and realize I'm tied up. My hands are secured to whatever it is I'm lying on. My legs are spread apart, also secured, and the ass of my jeans is wet.

I smell the piss and realize that's where the memory came from. I'm living in a time loop.

No. This is the present. I was in my truck, running away from my wedding to Brett. But there are too many similarities between now and then, so my mind is revisiting them.

Shrink talk. That's what that is. But it's true, I can feel it. I'm a prisoner again.

Has there ever been a day in my life when I was not

someone's prisoner?

Don't get on your high horse now, Syd. You signed up for this.

I did, I remind myself. I did. But if your last name is Channing, even if it's a secret, then what choice do you have?

Excuses.

I try to swallow, but my throat is so dry, I can't make it work. So I do nothing. I don't move, or struggle, or scream.

It's no use. I know this.

So I do the only thing I can do. I slip back into my old habits. I go inside myself, looking for the darkness that is even blacker than my reality.

And it comes easily.

It's a summer day. The dry wind is hot as it blows across my face, but the humidity from the river flowing nearby counteracts it. Makes everything perfect.

"You ready to learn to fish?" Garrett asks me. "I can't always take care of you, Syd."

I smile at him. He's so fucking handsome standing there in the water up to his knees. He's wearing a pair of jeans and nothing else. His chest is muscular and tanned to just the right level of bronze. The river splashes up against his legs and some of it reaches his lower torso. I follow the drips as they make their way into his waistband, the weight of the water tugging it down a little, revealing that little happy trail of hair that I love so much.

"Hey, Syd?" he says with a grin. "Eyes on my eyes."

I do find his eyes. They are a dark green from where I stand. But they are bright in all the ways that count. "I'm ready," I say.

He grins at me and casts out his fly, talking me through all his motions. I can't even begin to understand what he's trying to teach me. Or, I mean, I could. Probably. But he's so handsome, I lose all thoughts of fishing and concentrate on how his muscles move as he weaves the line back and forth into the air.

A fish takes his bait almost immediately — this place is a fly-fisherman's wet dream — and then he's laughing. "That was too easy. Now you try." He reels in and unhooks the fish and tosses it onto the bank, and then extends his hand, asking me to join him.

I take it and let him guide me out onto the rocky shoreline of the Yellowstone River. The water isn't too deep, but it runs fast up here.

I slip on a rock, but Garrett catches me before I fall. "Easy," he says, as I gather myself. "The water's too cold for a swim today, Syd."

"Sorry," I say, straightening out my lifejacket.

"You OK?" he asks me in that gentle voice he uses when he knows I'm out of my comfort zone. "Ready for this?"

I nod. "I am." And then I laugh. "I'm tired of watching. Well…" I blush and correct myself. "Not really tired of watching you fish. But it really does look fun."

"It is," he says, kissing me on the cheek.

The blackness is back and my throat is drier than ever after the memory of the cool river. I reach up and touch my throbbing face and realize I'm no longer tethered down.

Someone was in here with me. Who? I rack my brain. How many enemies do I have?

My laugh bursts out into the darkness and then resonates in my head like an echo as the stillness settles back in. The blackness is overwhelming and my breathing spikes as the familiar panic starts to take over.

No. Not now, Syd. "Hush," I tell myself. "Hush."

I take long draws of air into my lungs, willing the fear away like a pro. I don't know how long it takes for my own heavy breathing to allow the small sound to creep into my consciousness, but one second it's not there, and the next it is.

Dripping water. My throat tightens up as I imagine what it would be like to drink again.

I sit up and stave off the wave of dizziness, but my head spins for minutes before I can swing my legs over the side of the hard wooden platform. I lean over and close my eyes tightly, not sure why this helps, since I can't see anything anyway. But it does help.

The dripping is coming from the right. I reach down with a foot and find the floor, then drop to my knees and crawl in that direction. I reach out in front of me, but the room is empty save for a drain in the middle of it. Why would there be a drain here?

I let it go. I have no clue. Maybe I'm in a slaughterhouse and they hose the room down? So I just crawl. Nothing to bump into until I get to a wall. The dripping is to my left now, and I let the wall guide me until I reach out and feel the unmistakable cold of a porcelain sink.

I use the lip of the sink to stand myself up and feel around for the source of water. There are no knobs, just a single spigot with a steady drip.

When you have nothing, you take what you can get. So I lean my head into the basin and open my mouth. It takes whole minutes to let enough water pool inside my mouth to swallow it. But it's the best feeling in the world when my constricted throat opens up. I repeat this again and again, and then my legs are shaking from standing so long. I slump to the floor and take it in.

Concrete. Not the smooth concrete you find in a home. Rough, unfinished concrete like a sidewalk. Or a slaughterhouse. And very cold.

The wind whips outside. I listen for any other sounds but all that comes is a chorus of howling in the distance. Not the high-pitched yipping of coyotes, but the low, deep, mournful howl of wolves.

I swallow down the fear. But there's no denying it. I'm somewhere no one will find me.

The wall is behind me. Every room has four walls. So I get on my hands and knees and begin to crawl along it. My fingertips find a few dried leaves as I make my way forward. Webs too. And when I stop crawling for a moment, I hear a scuttling sound. Bugs, probably. I crawl a few more paces and then scare the shit out of myself when my hand hits a metal dish and it clangs loudly, breaking the silence. I sit back on my butt and close my eyes, my heart once again beating fast.

And then I bend over and reach around until I find the dish. There is nothing in there, but when I bring it to my face I can smell it.

You don't grow up in Wyoming and never smell the stench of house mice. There are far more house mice in my home state than there are homes. I toss the dish aside. If there was food in there, it's gone now. Eaten by the rodents.

The dish, the water dripping, and the discovery that I am untethered is my signal to call out in the dark. *Who's there?* That's a good one. *What do you want?* is another.

But I'm not the kind of girl who cries out pointless questions.

A shuffling noise off to my left stops me dead.

Someone is in here with me.

Whoever it is made that noise on purpose, trying to make me react. But I'm not the kind of girl who reacts, either.

Instead I stand up and press my body against the wall.

My heart rate jacks up again—anything seems to trigger it right now—and I have to hold my breath to make the room go silent so I can listen.

"I know you're there." It's my only option. Whoever it is is waiting for me to react. But it's a statement, not a question, so that puts me on the offensive.

I wait in the stillness, my arms at my side, my eyes closed so I can concentrate on listening.

But I stand there so long I grow tired, and after some indeterminate amount of time, I slump to the floor. My head becomes heavy and I realize my mistake too late. The water was drugged.

I fall asleep wondering why they'd bother letting me wake up if they were only going to put me back to sleep again.

Garrett and I are in the woods now. Not on the river. It's fall, which is winter up here in Montana, because summer is absolutely over by late August. I look over at him in his green camo camp gear, then look down at myself. We match and that makes me happy for some reason.

He flashes me hand signals and I nod, moving off to the left of him. There's a moose up ahead. We've been tracking it for most of the day. If we can get a moose, we're set for the winter.

Those are Garrett's words in my head, but they are mine now too. Because we need food.

I move off, as silent as I can, as Garrett does the same in the opposite direction. The moose is directly in front of us, hidden by a thick group of pines.

A twig snaps, and for a second I panic. But it's not me. It was Garrett and the moose is on the move.

Don't let it get away, Syd. *Garrett's voice in my head again.* You know what will happen if you do.

We'll starve out here. We are sixty miles from the nearest ranch. We have a snow machine but no gas. We have firewood, but no food. We have water. That's about it.

The fear any normal person would have when they see a two-thousand-pound bull moose coming at them falls away and I take aim. Right for its heart.

I squeeze the trigger and the round blasts out, the kick powerful enough to make me step back before I can steady myself.

The beast roars in front of me and then stumbles and falls to its knees.

Garrett is there, gripping my arm.

"Nice going," he says. "You almost fucked it all up by stepping on that branch."

I look up at him, but he's smiling. I smile back.

FIVE

*"Pain is in the mind. Just think of a good moment and go there—
an alternate reality is not the worst way to go."*
– Sydney

This time when I wake, I'm tethered to the table thing again. My mouth is dry, my stomach is rumbling, and I need to go to the bathroom.

I close my eyes to go back into my memory of that day's hunt. I didn't even get to the good part. After we quartered the animal and carried it home, we stuffed our faces with meat for the first time in weeks.

But a sound wakes me back up. I can hear something. And I can smell something too.

Food. Meat.

Whoever this is must be a mind-reader.

No, Syd. They know how long it's been since you ate, that's all.

"Garrett?" The word comes out before I can stop it.

"Try again," the deep voice says from behind my head.

I gasp in surprise.

"Not Garrett." His boots thud on the floor as he steps out from behind me. It's still dark, and I can't see anything. But his hand brushes against my shoulder, and then he squeezes. I cry out in pain before I can stop myself. "You smell like piss."

I don't say anything as he lets go of my wounded shoulder and walks along the table. His fingertips stroke along my ribs and I realize my hoodie is gone. I'm still wearing the nightie Brett's sisters gave me. And as soon as that realization hits me, my nipples perk up. His light touch pauses for a moment, like he knows. And then he rounds his palm and places it over my stomach. "Hungry?"

I close my eyes and hiss in a breath.

He moves on. His whole hand this time. He drags it down my hip and I can feel the heat of him even through my jeans. He pauses there, lingering on the bone that protrudes out, then slips his hand in my front pocket and pulls something out.

"Hmmm," is all he says. He lifts the nightie up so my stomach is exposed and it's only then that I realize how cold it is in here. When he places it gently over my belly button my whole body erupts in a shiver.

A whimper escapes.

"Why do you have an acorn in your pocket?"

His tone is hard. Like this is important. I can't think of a

48

single reason why this might be important, so I tell him. "It makes me feel better. I always carry it."

"Everywhere?"

I nod.

"Hmmm," he whispers.

I swallow hard and keep my eyes closed as his palm again rests on my hip bone.

"I asked you a question that you didn't answer."

My mind races. What did he ask me? I can't remember.

"Are you hungry?"

I nod and he stays silent. But his hand is on the move again. He drags it down to the top of my thigh and stops one more time. His fingers spread and then his large palm stretches out. He will rape me. I know this as soon as I feel the tingle of his touch get too close to the v of my open legs.

"Get used to that feeling, Sydney. You're gonna stay hungry for a while."

I hold my breath to prevent the *fuck you* I really want to scream at him.

He leaves his hand on my leg for what seems like minutes. Like he's waiting for me to cry out or beg him to stop. But I stay silent.

"Are you cold?"

I nod again, even though I know he's gonna say I should get used to that too. I don't know if he sees that movement, or feels it, or what. But he does not repeat himself. Instead he moves on. His fingertips trace down the inside of my thighs, a light touch that might be provocative and hot if I was not strapped to a wooden table being threatened with rape. He stops once more when he gets to my knee.

"Why are you wearing a nightie under your clothes?"

That is not a safe question, so I don't answer.

This time his hand slides back up to cup my pussy.

I moan, but not out of desire. I moan because he's threatening me without using words. Letting me know he is respecting my boundaries. But he doesn't have to. "It was the night before my wedding. My sisters-in-law gave it to me to wear."

"Was?" he asks in a curious tone. "Was the night before your wedding? How long do you think you've been here?" I shake my head but he doesn't accept my passive response this time. He unbuttons my jeans.

"I don't know," I answer quickly. "A few days ago? I was drugged."

"Hmmm," he says again, pulling down my zipper.

"Please," I whisper, my heart beating so fast.

He pulls the fly of my jeans apart and slips his hand inside. "Please what? Please continue?" I shake my head quickly. "Please make it feel good? Please don't stop? You're gonna have to give me more than please, cowgirl."

"Why are you doing this!" I scream it. There, he did it. He broke me. I give in. I can't take it anymore. I'm weak. I'm

50

stupid. I'm—

"Who am I?"

"Case," I say immediately.

"How do you know that?" I can hear a hint of satisfaction in his voice.

"I don't." My voice trembles. "I just guessed. You sound like him."

He lets out a little grunt. "Do you remember how you begged me that night, Sydney? Because I do. Did you think I'd save you, cowgirl? Did you think I was your hero in the dark? Did you think I'd take you home to your daddy?"

I did think all those things. I was desperate for them. "I'm so glad you left me. Leaving me was the best thing that ever happened."

His hand slips inside the waist of my jeans. "Was it?" He tugs them down until they are at the top of my thighs and won't go any further due to the fact that my legs are tied in an open position. He feels my pussy through the thin lacy panties. I instinctively clench my legs together and try to limit the space he has available down there.

He backs away, withdrawing his hand. But then I hear something being unsnapped, probably from his belt. There are a few more noises that I can't place, and then he's slipping his hand around my right ankle. His touch is soft. Softer than I expected. I stifle a whimper by biting my lip.

"You're gonna want to hold still now, Sydney. I'd be

lying if I said I don't want to cut you, but you have enough blood on you for now. So let's try to get through this without adding much more."

"*What?*"

A cold shiver erupts up my leg when the metal touches my skin. I hiss in a breath to stop from screaming, but I hold still. He cuts the denim starting at the inside of my ankle and slices it all the way up to my knee.

"Be very still now," he says as he repositions the knife on my inner thigh. "You'll bleed like a motherfucker if I cut you up here."

I can feel it this time. Either he's not careful or he's doing it on purpose, but he cuts me over and over again. Poke after poke. I hiss out in surprise each time. He apologizes but doesn't stop. By the time he's to my crotch, I can't hold it together.

I sob. My whole body shakes. The acorn he placed on my belly button rolls off me and thuds onto the wooden table.

He places a hand on my hip for a moment, and I force myself to imagine it's a gesture of reassurance. This calms me and I take a deep breath. His hand moves away again, grasping at the open fly, holding it taut so he can cut.

The fabric breaks and the tension eases.

"Pretty good. Those pokes were on purpose. If you'd moved, there'd be slices."

I say nothing.

"Let's do the other one."

He pokes me again. More than he did with the first leg. But this time I stay still. I let him do whatever he needs to. I can smell myself now. Blood, and piss, and sweat, and fear. I don't know how long I've been here, but the stench coming off me says it's more like days than hours.

"And now the pretty panties." He cuts those easily, one snip over each hip. "And the nightie." One cut on each shoulder strap and then he sets the knife down, grabs my breasts for a moment, giving them a hard squeeze, before ripping the front of the nightie straight down the middle.

I am naked. I am bare. And never in my life have I ever been so happy to be in the dark. I sob, as silently as I can, as he walks around.

The room goes silent and I admonish myself for not paying attention. Did he leave? Is he still here? Why didn't I pay attention?

The silence drags on as I lie there. Then a roar fills the room and I recognize it as the sound of water running through pipes.

A moment later I hear his boots. He was gone. That makes me feel better. He's creepy enough. I don't want to start imagining him as some psycho who stands in the dark pretending to not be here.

"I'm gonna clean you up, Sydney. You reek pretty bad."

I don't know why, but an image of a warm sponge bath presents in my mind.

That's when he blasts me with the hose. A punishing stream of ice water that hits my body like a thousand stones. I scream, I can't help it. It hurts. I turn my body away, so that the left side of me takes the most punishment, but he doesn't linger in one spot for too long. He blasts me everywhere. Even between my legs.

That's it. I sob uncontrollably. It hurts so much. My whole body is on fire from the raging water hose.

But then, as quickly as it started, it turns off. I can hear the water in the pipes still, so I know it's only temporary.

"I'm going to wash you now." And even though it was my first image when he said that earlier, I'm more surprised at the hot rag dragging down my skin at this point than I was the fire hose.

He is gentle. He dips the washcloth into a tub of water, squeezes it out, and then caresses my whole body with it. He washes me everywhere. But there is no hint of sexual meaning behind this gesture. He never says a word and neither do I. He just swipes away the filth of me and replaces it with something new. Something fresh.

"I need to use the bathroom," I say, hoping he will untie me and give me some clothes.

"I have to rinse you off now. Feel free to relieve yourself as I do it."

"How?" I ask, before I can stop myself. "Please, not that hose!" I choke on a sob as the word comes out.

The ice water is my only response. It pelts me, erasing any soothing sensation from the washing. I close my eyes tight and let him do it this time. The piss leaks out of me from the fear and the need. I don't even try to move my body away. What's the point? I'm spreadeagled on top of a wooden table. I'm going nowhere. He's made that very clear.

I lose time from the punishment, but eventually it does stop. I am not even crying now. I'm freezing. I'm in pain. I'm scared. I'm hungry. And I have no fight left. A chill runs up my body and I take deep breaths to keep the cold from taking over.

His footsteps appear again. Only this time they are not boots. Bare feet.

He comes up next to the table and stands quietly.

My whole body begins to shake uncontrollably again. My teeth chatter and all my muscles tense up as the fear takes over.

"Are you cold?" he asks.

I can't even make myself relax enough to answer, but I grunt out a response to keep him happy.

And then his hand is on my stomach. It's so warm, like he just pulled it back from a fire. Nothing—and I do mean nothing—has ever felt so good to me.

"Is that better?" he asks.

I nod and open my eyes. It's still black in this room. But

I don't want him to pull his hand away. It's the only place on my whole body that feels good right now. And then he lays his chest over mine. His whole body feels like it was warmed from a fire. I crave the heat. I need it so bad.

"Do you want me to stay here with you? Wrap you in my arms and warm you up?"

"Yes," comes out immediately. There is no hesitation.

He climbs onto the table and presses his body next to me for a moment. Then he sits up and leans forward. The tension holding my left leg open wide disappears. The same thing happens on the right side.

I close my legs and bring them up to my chest, trying to get warm. But he gently repositions them. He slides his body up next to mine and we scissor our legs together. He's bare-chested, but he still has his jeans on. His arms wrap around my waist and he pulls me in tight against his body.

Everything else disappears. The thirst. The humiliation. The smell. The hunger. The cutting. The bath. The cold. It all goes away in a single moment. The moment when Merric Case leans in my ear and whispers in a deep throaty growl, "I own you. I think you forgot that, Sydney. But I'm patient. I will remind you. Over and over. Until you come to terms with what that means and I can finish what I started eight years ago."

SIX

*"Do I believe in right and wrong? Sure. As long as we understand
I'm always right."*

– Case

S he lies completely still as the words sink in. Silent. I reach up and pinch her nipple, making her squeal. "I never talk for the sake of hearing myself, Sydney. When I talk, even if there is no question, you will respond to me. You can choose the way in which you respond. I'll correct you if it's wrong. But you will always respond."

"OK," she whimpers.

"Now that you're comfortable" — she lets out a tiny huff of air to let me know she disagrees, but I ignore it this time — "let's talk about Garrett. Where is he?"

"You killed him."

"I did not kill him. But I'd very much like to."

"He disappeared years ago. And if you've been watching me, and I know you have, then you already know this."

She's brave, I'll give her that. Because that was a

statement of defiance. Arrogant, almost. But she is also stupid.

I sit up and remove my body heat from her. She takes a few quick breaths, but then calms herself and whispers, "Wait."

"Too late, cowgirl. Or should I just start calling you wildcat? Hmmm? Too fucking late. You'll learn. Eventually."

I get off the table and walk over to the water hose and turn it on again.

She does not move as I spray her a third time. But she bites her lip hard enough to draw blood and when I turn the water off, she is practically convulsing, she is so cold.

I drop the hose on the floor and walk back over to her.

"I thought you killed him, Case. I swear to God. I thought you killed him and my father. I don't know where he is."

"I did kill your father. Right here on this table." That makes her whimper. "But Garrett got away. Where did he go and what is he doing?"

She squints her eyes and shakes her head a little. But she knows what will come if she doesn't answer now. She knows I'm not fucking around. I'm not here to coddle her through this. I'm not here to pry it out of her. So she gulps down some air and responds.

"Maybe he went to our cabin?"

"I checked. And then I burned it down." She sucks in a

breath at that. And why does she care? It makes me wonder. It pisses me off, actually. "So try again."

"Camping somewhere?" she offers.

"Where?"

"The campsites don't have names that make sense to anyone but us. I could show you—"

"Wrong. Try your best, Sydney. Tell me where he camps and I won't have to spray you again."

She draws up her knees, since her legs are still untied, trying to cover herself from the thought of the ice-cold water. And then she squints her eyes again. I realize this means she's thinking. But I haven't had enough personal contact with her to discern if it means she's thinking up a lie or just regular thinking.

"Always up in Yellowstone. Purple Mountain is where we start. And then we veer off at the second switchback, and continue to climb to the top of the mountain, and then double back on the opposite side. There's a deer trail—"

"Do you think he's there?"

"No," she answers immediately, and I smile.

"No, he's not. I followed the two of you there several times. So I've checked, and had others check, repeatedly over the years. Where else?"

She continues to list their camping spots and each time she says no to my question. I know he's not camping, but this gives her time to think about how she wants this to go.

And since I'm a reasonable guy, I give her this time.

"That all?" I ask, when she's finally done. Her teeth have been chattering for so long I think she's probably losing weight before my eyes, that's how tense her muscles are.

"That's it, Case. I swear." It comes out *Cccc-aaaase* and *swww-eeee-aar*.

I believe her. I've checked all of them several times over the years. It's like the man really does know how to vanish. Of course, the world is big and I am just one person. I have a partner, but even two people can miss a few places when you have to cover the whole earth looking for someone.

But none of this makes any sense. And it's all pointless right now anyway. I'm only here to establish control, and I think I've succeeded in doing that. "Well, I'm tired. And hungry. So you get some rest."

I reach into my pocket and withdraw the syringe, uncapping it with a flick of my thumb, and press it into the fleshy muscle of her upper arm. "You can sleep too. But food, Sydney, food is a reward. Not a right. You can go a few more days before I really need to feed you."

She whimpers, but cuts it off almost immediately. "I'm cold."

"You're supposed to be."

"Pppp-lease," she stutters, her lips trembling and her legs shaking. "Warm me again. Please."

I place my hand over her belly like I did earlier, and she relaxes with a long breath of air. "I like to see you suffer,

60

Sydney. Make no mistake. I didn't warm you earlier to make you happy. I did it to confuse you. I'll give you a tip. To help you get through the next few days before I kill you —"

"No," she says, begging. "No, please."

"I hate your fucking guts. I have been dreaming about killing you for years. Just like I dreamt about how I'd kill your father. I tortured him on top of this very table. It's stained with his blood. And yours will add to it. So if you want it to go easy, do what you're told. Don't lie. And don't expect me to give a shit. Because I'm more than happy to fuck with your head for a few days as I pry this information out of you. Information I *know* you have. And I *will* get it."

She cries then. Full-on sobs. I wait for the drugs to take over and then I cut the rope that binds her to the wall at the head of the table. She tries to sit up and fails, and then the sleepiness overtakes her pathetic attempt at a fight and she curls into herself like a baby, desperate to find some warmth.

I take a deep breath and walk over to the hose, roll it up and place it on the hook in the connecting utility room, then close and lock the door behind me. I remove my night vision goggles before I flip on the light, and then I place those in the little cubby of gear before walking through the next door and back out into my cabin.

It's cold in this room. I've been with her for at least two hours so the fire has died down. I throw some wood on it and change out of my wet clothes and stir the stew that's been cooking over the flame all day to stimulate her hunger response. I spoon some into a camping bowl and sit down on the couch a few feet away from the hearth and eat.

When I'm done I stretch out, pulling the bearskin that hangs over the back of the couch over me, and I think about what to do next.

I think up all the ways I might break her. I have no shortage of ways. But even though I knew how I'd kill her father, Senator Channing, from the moment he fucked with my life, I have no such plan for Sydney. I have run it all through my mind over and over again, but how to do it so it's satisfying? I'm not sure.

Strangulation during sex is currently at the top of my list. But I've always enjoyed slitting throats. It's quick, which I hate. But messy, which I love.

Then there is my specialty, of course. Assassination-style. Bullet to the back of the head.

I don't know. I can't decide. If I get her to take me to Garrett, I could do them both each way. I know exactly how I'm gonna kill that motherfucker.

I smile at the thought and then I turn over and close my eyes, enjoying the warm fire and the stew in my stomach.

It surprises me how satisfied I am with her first real day of questioning. I broke her quickly. A lot quicker than I expected. She's grown weak, perhaps. He beat her down pretty good, but his absence makes her weak. He must know this. She's been away from him. Living her seemingly normal life in Cheyenne. Running her little country western bar. Theme nights and live bands replaced her militia training.

But that shit never goes away, I remind myself. It might get rusty. You forget what it feels like to live minute by minute, struggling to go on. But it comes back quick enough if the training is done right.

And her training was exceptional. Garrett knew exactly what he was doing when he took her away that night they tried to kill me. He knew. He set me up then and he's setting me up now. I can feel it. Something is off. Something is wrong.

Maybe he's good enough to evade me all these years and get away with it. He was trained better than me, that's for sure. He was a Company kid and I was just a stand-in after the rest of the assassins were picked off one at a time by a friend of mine. But I'm a natural, they tell me. I'm a natural killer. It's all I've ever wanted to be.

A psychopath.

A cold, emotionless, empty shell of a man whose only goal in life is to kill this girl and the man who trained her, so I can set my world straight again.

SEVEN

SYDNEY

"When all my power is stripped away, I still have choices. Like choosing not to give a shit. That's a very powerful choice when a person thinks she has no power."

– Sydney

When I wake my whole body hurts. Everywhere the high-pressure water touched me stings like I was burned. I'm untethered, but when I move my legs, the knife pricks erupt in pain. One alone is not enough to matter. But dozens of them all up the inside of my thigh are far, far harder to ignore.

I swallow and realize I'm thirsty again. He's drugging me. The drugs make me confused. But I've always been thirsty. I drink a lot of water on normal days, and being deprived—

Wait. The sink is dripping again.

It's drugged, my mind tells me.

But why drug it when I just woke up? No. He's doing something with me. I'm not sure what, but it makes no sense that the water—

I'm cold, I suddenly realize. My whole body is shivering. My dark world comes fully back to me as I wake up from the fog. Everything is so cold, everything... except my feet. They are toasty warm.

Why? Why does none of this make any sense?

I sit up and get dizzy in the blackness with no reference point to concentrate on. I gather myself and wait for my vision to clear.

It never clears. So I close my eyes and swing my legs over. I don't need eyes. What good are eyes in the dark? After a few minutes I reach down with my toe, noticing they are no longer warm—so that was not some freak accident of biology heating me up—and touch the rough concrete floor. I stand, sway for a moment as I hold onto the table, and then use it to walk to the end. It's warm over here.

I drop to my knees and crawl forward, the heat building as I go. I get to a wall—not wood, but metal—and my whole palm flattens against it.

It's a heater or something. About three feet wide and three feet tall. I press my whole body up against it and I can hear sound from the other side.

A fire. It's a fireplace, only I'm on the other side of it. Separated by a sheet of metal.

But that is better than anything I could've hoped for. I sit there, willing myself to relax. He gave me heat. And water, I think as I absently log the sound of the drips on the other side of the room. Heat and water. And I'm clean.

He gave me three things. Which means he will give me more.

I have a little glimmer of hope.

A sudden grating sound shakes me from this fantasy I'm building and there's a sliver of light as a tray is pushed through a plate-sized hole at the bottom of the room, where the sink is.

Food. That's four things. And I didn't do anything for these last two except wake up. I swallow down what that might imply, and crawl along the wall until I reach the tray. The meat is cold and the fruit is warm. But I don't mind cold meat or warm fruit.

I take a few berries—absently wondering where he got them in the dead of winter—and stuff them in my mouth. They are not very sweet, but I don't care. The raspberries are ripe and soft. They practically melt in my mouth.

The meat is gamey, but I like game meat. Have learned to like game meat after so many years camping with Garrett. It's elk, I can tell. There's not a lot of it, only a few mouthfuls. But it's been so long since I ate, my stomach feels full when I finish. I force myself to eat the berries too—needing the vitamins they contain—and then I stand up and feel my way over to the dripping sink. I lean my head down and let it pool into my mouth until I can swallow enough to matter, then repeat this a few more times until I feel satisfied. I walk back over to the heat and lie down in front of it, listening for the crackle of wood.

What is he doing?

I ask myself that over and over again. But I already know the answer. He wants Garrett. Hell, *I* want Garrett.

No. You want Brett, not Garrett.

Is that true? Do I want Brett? What must he think of me? Running away from our wedding? Does he think I planned an escape? Does he think I've been kidnapped? Is he looking for me right now? Did he find my truck out there on the mountain?

There was blood in there. I crashed. So that's why my body is so sore. Maybe it's not from the hose? Maybe it's from the crash?

I'm so confused. Why did I ever leave Brett? He was the only good thing in my life since Garrett left.

Case would kill him and you know this, Sydney.

Case would. I have no doubts now. I did the right thing by leaving. Right thing for Brett, anyway. Me? Not so much.

Case is going to kill me. Whatever kindness he's showing me now is just a means to an end. He's keeping me alive for his own purposes. He said as much. He hates me and he's looking forward to my death.

And he killed my father.

Do I care?

No. No, that was another blessing in disguise. My father was a monster. If Case is the monster in the dark, my father is the monster in the light. Hidden by the brightness of his career, his money, and his status.

I let out a small laugh. "Not anymore, asshole." Because he's dead. I look around the room and see only blackness. But I can imagine it in my mind. I have a very active imagination. I can imagine my father writhing in pain on that table. Maybe he had the fire hose treatment too?

I laugh for real, picturing him getting one of his suits cut off him. Case slicing him up instead of poking. I mean, I'm young, and cute, and sexy. Even I know this. And my father is old, and mean, and ugly. Case would not be cupping his hand over my father's private parts like he did mine.

Why did he do that?

He's going to rape you, Sydney.

I take a moment to let that sink it. He's going to rape me. I know it. I can feel it.

You can use that against him.

Maybe I can.

A door creaks open on the other side of the room and I force myself not to move. I stare in that direction. No light escapes, like it did when the tray of food was pushed through, so I can't see anything.

But I can certainly feel him coming in. I can smell him too. And it's not a rank smell. He doesn't smell like someone who's been camping in the woods for a few weeks. This cabin has a shower somewhere, because he just smells like a man.

"What do you want?"

"You know what I want," he replies.

"I can tell you everywhere I think Garrett is."

"I know that, Sydney. But that's not what I want. I want the place you know him to be."

"I don't have that information."

"You do," Case insists. "And I'm going to get it out of you."

"And then rape me and kill me."

He laughs and my skin prickles up and down my arms. He laughs again and the hair on the nape of my neck stands up. I don't even have a word for how his laugh affects me.

Fear, that inner voice says. *Terror.*

I take a deep breath. "I'm not afraid of you."

"You should be."

"I'm not afraid of anything."

"You're afraid of everything, Sydney Channing. I've been watching you for eight years and never have I ever come across a weaker girl. I have known twelve-year-old girls who are braver than you are right now."

"I'm not sure she counts."

"Fuck you," he snarls.

"You'd like to, wouldn't you."

He walks towards me in the dark and I realize he's wearing night vision. Has been this whole time. Every moment I thought I was in the dark was a lie I told myself. How could he see me nod my head, how could he see I was wearing pretty panties, how could he cut my clothes off me if he wasn't wearing night vision?

My stomach churns as his boots thud across the floor and then he's there in front of me. Before I can scoot away, he's pulled me up to him, holding me against his chest, squeezing my upper arms so tightly I know he's leaving marks on my skin.

"There's a huge difference between brave and stupid. You are stupid."

"Why should I care if I'm stupid?" I ask him. His breath is hot and it floods across my face, smelling a little bit like raspberries. "You're going to torture me, rape me, and then kill me. What do I have to lose by being stupid instead of brave?"

"Your fiancé," he replies.

I have to admit, this catches me off guard.

"I know why you left. How many times do I have to say it? I own you. I own your mind, I own your body, and I own your future." He pauses, like he's thinking. "Or what's left of it."

I struggle to get away and he lets me slip out of his grasp. I back up a few paces, then trip over the lip of the hearth,

JA HUSS

falling back on my ass. I look up where I think his face is. "If I knew, Case" — I use his name. Isn't that what they tell you to do? To make a kidnapper see you as a person instead of a target? — "I'd tell you. But I have no clue where Garrett is. I really thought he was dead. I really thought you killed him. I really —"

Case grabs me by the arms and pulls me to my feet before I can finish, dragging me back over to the table. He picks me up, sits me on it, still holding me tightly, and then leans down into my ear. "I know that's what you *think*. That's why you're still alive."

That makes no sense.

But then there's a prick of the syringe into my arm and the burn of drugs as they are forced into my muscle.

"Why are you drugging me?" I ask, my voice trembling. "I'll answer any question you have, just please. Stop drugging me."

72

EIGHT

MAC

"Fear, like all emotions, is a weapon I use with skill."

- Case

I don't answer her question, just hold her tightly as the drugs take over. She begins to rest against me, her body becoming heavy. After several minutes she slumps down.

I pick her up in my arms and then lay her down on the table, tying her hands first and then her legs. My fingertips travel up her leg, lingering briefly on the prick marks I made with the knife, as I position myself next to her head. I lean down and whisper, "Are you ready?"

I can feel her nod, just slightly, but enough to know the cocktail I came up with is working. "OK, then. Let's start from the beginning again. What happened after I left you out at the cabin eight years ago? When I left you with Garrett?"

She mumbles but none of her words makes sense.

Fuck. I gave her too much.

"Sydney," I try again. "Tell me everything that happened when I left you with Garrett at the cabin eight years ago."

She mumbles again, but it's a little better now.

I wait for several more minutes, checking my watch, then ask again.

This time she answers. "He was nice."

Hmmm. I've heard this before. She's said it several times already when under the drugs. So many times, in fact, that I have to assume it's true. "How was he nice? What did he do?"

"He taught me to fish."

I shake my head and sigh. "No," I say sharply. "Before that. Back at the cabin. What did he say?"

"Nothing. He just took care of me. He took us to the Bighorn cabin and we stayed there. It was nice."

"Nice?" What the fuck game is Garrett playing?

"He took care of me. He protected me."

I shake my head and have to draw one of two conclusions. The dose was too high. Or that fucker is not what I think he is. I go with the first because the other isn't even possible.

My breath comes out in a long huff, a mixture of dissatisfaction and fatigue. I'm tired of this shit. I want this to be over. I want to kill this girl and this guy and move on. I want to go back to my friends and say, "It's done." I want to see the look of relief on Sasha Cherlin's face when she finally gets to put the death of her father behind her.

But I can't do any of that until I figure out what the hell is going on. I understand that Sasha was a threat. She was a twelve-year-old trained assassin. She was a wild card that needed to be dealt with. She was a liability and an asset, because back then she had all the answers everyone needed thanks to her father's big mouth.

That got him killed. That almost got *her* killed. But I saved her ass that night and I saved her ass again, over and over since then. She's grown now. In college. Living a nice, safe, normal life.

So we won. I tell her that, anyway. We won. And I know she shouldn't believe it. But normal life makes you forget to be wary. She's lived normal for too long now. The last time I said it a few years ago, she said, *OK. We won.*

And she believed me.

But I didn't. I didn't believe it when I said it and I don't believe it now.

We lost. Because we never got the answers as to why. Why?

I need to know this, and Garrett McGovern is the path to that level of satisfaction. And my only connection to Garrett is Sydney.

What if I'm wrong? What if Sydney has no answers? She passed the lie detector test when I drugged her up when she first got here. That was ten days ago. She's been mostly unconscious since then. And she has no memory of it, for sure. That drug is made to wipe your memory.

I need a different approach.

I place my hand on her cheek, flattening my palm against her soft skin. She lets out a little, "Mmmm," to that gesture and leans into my touch. Like she craves me.

My eyes close at her murmurings and what they might mean, and I take a deep breath to get my mind back on the job. "I want you to concentrate now, Sydney. When was the last time you saw Garrett?"

She takes her own deep breath, mimicking mine. "Yesterday."

"Fuck." This is not working right, goddammit. "No, Sydney. It wasn't yesterday. It was a long time ago. Tell me the last time you saw Garrett."

"The night before my wedding."

"Jesus Christ." She's got it all fucked up. She's got me and him all fucked up. I walk out of the room and close the door behind me. I grab fistfuls of my hair and feel a roar coming up. But I calm myself and walk back out into the main room of the cabin and sit on the couch.

I'm not getting anywhere. She's had too many drugs. She's had too much trauma since I took her. She's, quite frankly, not as easy to break as I first thought.

I consider calling my friend to ask for some insight into how I might've fucked her memory up so bad. But I nix that idea. He doesn't do that anymore. None of them do this shit anymore. I'm the last one. I'm the only one left who's still in the business.

I walk over to the other side of the room and pick up my guitar. And then I walk back over to the couch and lean up against the soft leather of the arm, kicking my feet up and cradling my instrument at the same time.

I begin to strum. It helps me think. Hell — I smile a little as I remember — this guitar got Sasha and me through some really fucked-up times back in the day.

God, I miss her. She's gonna graduate from college this spring and I'm gonna be there. I'm gonna be there with a present. A gift of satisfaction. Of retribution. Of revenge.

And this stupid girl in the other room is my only chance at making that gift a reality.

My fingers start strumming the song. One I've heard Sydney play over and over again since I started watching her. It's a soft tune, one that Sasha used to like as well, back when she was into that sort of thing. These days she's all about school. No time for dates, or parties, or music. That kid is a swift-moving arrow with dinosaurs as her target.

The tension eases out of me as I think of my adopted little sister. Not daughter. My friend the amateur psychologist adopted her as his daughter. He can have that title.

I actually laugh at that. All those phone calls he placed to me when she was fourteen, trying to ease her back into civilian life after that mess of a final job we did.

They did, I correct myself.

They all retired. Life went on. And they went on with it.

But me? I'm stuck, man. I'm stuck in time. I'm stuck back in the hills between Cheyenne and Larimer. The night Sydney's father and Garrett tried to kill Sasha and got her father instead. The night I vowed that we'd get those motherfuckers.

And we did. A long time ago. We got them.

All but one.

I need him.

I need to torture him and make him pay.

I need to kill him. And I need Sydney Channing to make that happen.

I will do whatever it takes to get my revenge.

Whatever. It. Takes.

NINE

"When the monster in the dark wants to drag you into the light,
just go silent and still."

- Sydney

I come down off the drugs the same way I did the previous times. Thick, sticky mouth desperate for water. My stomach rumbling. The silence. The bottoms of my feet are warm from the hidden fire. My eyes are blind from the hidden light.

I sigh. Then I sit up and repeat this whole thing over again. Feet to the floor. Walk to the heat to warm myself. There's a rug covering the stone hearth. The food slips in, along with that coveted sliver of light, through the plate-sized slit in the wall. Crawl over. Eat. Get up. Drink.

He does not come in this time.

Why is he drugging me?

I go back over to the covered fireplace and sit on the rug. It's not anything special. But it's more than what I had.

79

So that's number five. Five things he's given me to ease my discomfort. What's his angle? Lure me into talking with simple pleasures?

It's working. I am grateful for the rug, the water, the food, the fire, and the fact that I'm not tied up.

I lie back and stretch out. The rug is not long enough for my whole body to lie across it, but I don't care. I scoot over to the metal plate that keeps most of the heat and all of the firelight out and press myself against it.

It feels good.

I'm not afraid, though I should be. I'm not wishing for anything at the moment. So I think whatever Case is doing, he failed.

My eyes close, and even though I just woke up from the drugs, this is not the same thing. This is exhaustion.

I stay this way for a while and then, ever so subtly, I begin to hear sounds from the other room. His boots thud across the floor. They come near me, like he's on the other side of the hidden fire, then retreat. The heat becomes more intense. He must've added wood.

I smell food. I already ate, so I'm pretty sure this is not for me. But I'm not hungry, so I don't care.

I let my mind slip to Garrett, then replace those thoughts with Brett. I should be thinking about Brett. He's good. He's sweet. His family is nice. And I hate that he will find out what a shitty person I am if they ever find my body.

All the questions that will come out about me. All the answers that will follow.

I swallow down the shame. I've seen a few therapists in secret over the years. Appointments when I've been out of town for some reason or another. Set up in advance. One-time-only things. I mean, I tell them I'll come back, but I'm never in the same place twice.

And I tell them all the same story. Made up, of course, but close enough to the truth so I can glean a little bit of help from their responses.

And they all say the same thing. I'm not responsible for my father. I'm not responsible for being related to him. You can't choose your family, isn't that what they say? I do not have to be ashamed for things he's done.

But what about the things I've done? The things I'm doing?

The door opens with a creak again.

"You don't know why I left," I tell Case as he steps into the room.

"No?" he asks, taking a seat on the wooden table. It creaks from his weight. "Tell me why you left then."

I could refuse. It's none of his business. And I'm not required to have light conversation with him. This has nothing to do with what he wants. It's plain old curiosity. But I'm not going to refuse. I want him to know. "Because I love them. They're good people and I knew you'd be back.

I heard your words. I knew what they meant. And I knew you were just waiting for some big moment to appear back into my life."

"You came to me, Syd."

His use of my familiar nickname unsettles me in so many ways. "I ran from them. To save them from you."

"You came to me. I was waiting out there on the road because I knew you'd come."

"How the fuck did you know?"

"Because you told me."

I laugh at that one. "OK."

"You told me with your actions. I wasn't even sure if I'd show up that night." He pauses for a moment, like he's thinking back on a memory. "I mean, it was definitely a trap. But it went off easy." He flicks on a small lantern. The little battery-powered bulb inside the glass is just enough to illuminate his face as he talks. "Too easy, Sydney."

I have not seen his face in years. And I don't see it now, either. I see his eyes. His deep, yellow-brown eyes that remind me of honey, or amber, or a subdued sunset painted in warm ochre watercolors. "What was?" I whisper, transfixed by his stare.

"You." He stands up, letting the lantern drop, and then I only see his legs as he comes towards me. He sits down on the hearth next to me and I can feel the heat of the fire coming off his body. I can smell it too. He smells like the memory of the woods on a summer night.

"You were too easy," he continues. "Maybe Garrett is on his way here right now. Maybe he's outside, ready to break in and kill us."

I snort. "You mean you. Not me."

Case lifts the lantern up again, only this time it's so he can see my face. "Why?"

"Why what?" I ask back, annoyed.

"Do you love him?"

I squint my eyes from the light, and then swat his hand away, making the lantern sway for a second. I half expect him to smack me for that. But he doesn't. "Why wouldn't I?"

He laughs and I can just barely make out the smile.

Jesus fuck. Why does my killer have to look like this? I glance down at his chest and see that he has no shirt on. His gaze follows mine and then when I look up he shrugs.

"It's hot out there," he says with a smile, nodding to the other side of the fire that I don't get the pleasure of experiencing. I open my mouth to say something, but he beats me to it. "Do you like?"

"Like what?" replaces the words about to roll off my tongue.

"My chest."

I close my eyes and smile, laughing as I do it. "You did not just ask me—"

But then his hand is around my neck and he's pressed his face right up against mine. "Yes or no?" He fists my hair, pulling it and making me wince.

But I don't answer him. Fuck that. I'm not telling this murderer that he's hot.

And then he's on his feet, swinging me over his shoulder. He slams me down on the wooden table hard enough to knock the breath out of me. My hands are tethered to the wall again, this time not spread apart, but both together, wound up with thin leather strips that were not what held me before. I bring up my legs and kick him in the chest. He steps backwards from the force, and then he growls as he takes one still-kicking leg and clamps a leather cuff on it. He repeats this with the other leg and then there it is.

I'm ready. I'm ready to be raped.

Case takes a breath, like he needs it, and I internally smile that I kicked him hard enough to cause that pause.

"He called you wildcat for a reason, I guess."

That word stops me. Like instantly. I lie still, unable to move.

"Hush," Case says.

It comforts me and I settle, so he reforms his question. "Why did he call you wildcat?"

I'm so confused. "Who?"

"Nice try," Case says with a smirk. "I'm not sure what's going on here, but we're gonna sort it out, wildcat. We're definitely gonna sort it out." And then he pulls a feather out of his jeans pocket and flicks the tip against my bare nipple.

I feel it bunch up from the touch and close my eyes, shaking my head at the same time.

He leans down in my space, right next to my ear, and whispers, "You like it, don't you?"

"No," I answer.

"Liar." He takes the feather and traces it over my ribs. Down one. Up the next. Down again. Up again. Stopping in the center of my stomach. "Why do you carry that acorn in your pocket?"

I'm biting the inside of my lip when he asks that question, and when I let go of it to draw in a breath to speak, I taste blood. It sets me back a moment.

"Why, Syd?"

"Don't call me that."

"Because only one person calls you that, wildcat?"

"Don't call me that either."

"Because that's not really a pet name, it's something so much more?"

"Who the fuck are you talking about?"

Case laughs. "Take one guess, sweetheart."

I know it's Garrett. I know this. But what Case is saying doesn't make sense. So I say nothing.

Case lets out a breath. But then his feather travels down my stomach to the dip between my hips. "Brett likes you bare?"

I fume inside. "That's none of your business."

"Have you ever fucked him?"

"Fuck you."

"I know you haven't. I've heard him complain about it before."

"Fuck you."

"He's afraid you'll be a huge disappointment in bed."

I close my eyes to block him out.

"But he's got nothing to worry about in that department, does he, Syd?"

I remain silent. But Case doesn't remain still. His feather dips down between my legs, to my sex. He tickles my clit a few times, making me cry out with humiliation. "Stop," I say.

"Stop?" Case asks. "I don't think you really mean that, do you, Syd?"

"Stop," I say again. "Stop now, and you won't have to add 'rapist' to your resume."

He chuckles under his breath, like I'm so funny. "I'll stop if you say it again." I open my mouth, but he clamps a hand over it before I can get the words out. "Hush," he says.

My mind spins with that hush. Something is there. Something weird.

"Hush," he says again, like he knows. "Hush, Sydney. Because I think I know why we're not getting anywhere with the drugs."

I look up at him. Past the hand that's still clamped over my mouth. His amber eyes hold me like that. Completely in his grasp. Completely under his control.

"Say yes and I'll tell you the question that's on your mind now. Say yes and I'll stop the confusion. Say yes and I'll ease it out of you in a way you might enjoy. Right here on the table where I killed your father. I'll tell you my little secret." Case pauses for a moment. And then he lifts his hand away from my mouth. The *no* I'm screaming inside is trapped there in my mind.

Case exhales, releasing the tension he was hiding. He's not as in control as he wants me to think. And then he resumes his play. The feather tickles my clit once again and I close my eyes and shake my head.

"Say no, then."

But I don't say no.

Because *hush* means something, I just can't quite place it. Hush. It's a soft word. A soothing word. Not a mean *shut up*. Not a harsh *be quiet*.

Hush.

Case leans over my parted legs with one hand on the inside of my knee. His touch is soft and soothing. He gives me a slight squeeze and then dips his mouth down to my inner thigh and kisses the marks he put there with his knife.

I close my eyes and shake my head. My legs tremble. I

want to speak. I want to say no so bad.

But I want to say yes much more.

His tongue travels up my thigh, his hand gently caressing the opposite knee. "Say yes," he murmurs as he kisses. "Give in to me, Syd. You know you want to."

I do want to. But I'm not ready to say it out loud yet.

Case unbuckles his belt, undoes his button, and unzips his fly. The lantern isn't bright enough to see it, but the shadow of his hard dick is thick as he fists it in his hand. He drops the feather and reaches for the knife attached to his belt. And then he drops his pants and we are both naked.

He climbs on the table and straddles my hips.

I let out a whimper.

"I want you to say yes, Sydney. Because yes is the answer to all your problems right now. I'm the answer to all your problems right now. But you can say no. Now's your chance. Your last chance, Sydney. I can kill you now" — he holds the knife up to his throat, making a slicing gesture across it — "and it will be over. You never have to know the truth. You never have to face this reality. Say no and I'll make it all the confusion go away. It will be very simple and I'll make it very quick."

I stay silent.

"But wildcat, do you really want to move on to the next world being played instead of being a player? Do you really want to give up? Give in? Check out? Don't you want to *know*, Sydney? Don't you want answers to all those burning questions you must have?"

I hold my breath trying to understand him.

"If you give me what I want, I'll make it better for you."

What am I supposed to say to that? "Fuck me then. Or kill me. I don't really care. Do whatever you want."

"You're missing the point, cowgirl." He stares down at me. I can't see his eyes very well, there are too many shadows. But I know that stare now. I've seen it in my head for years. I've craved it.

And here he is. The gift I wanted, but not the way I fantasized. I wanted him to choose to save me that night. And even though I know I'm only here so he can use me, I still need to hold on to the illusion I've built up in my head. I want Merric Case to desire me so much, he chooses differently. I want him to change my life. I want him to take it back.

"What's the point?" I ask softly. "Tell me what you need and I'll try and give it to you."

He huffs out a breath of air. A sort of satisfied laugh. "Famous last words, Syd. If you really want to give me what I want, you need to tell me what you know." He crawls up my body, a hand on each side of me, one still grasping the knife. And then he positions his cock in front of my face. "You've seen him."

"Who?" I ask, my voice barely a whisper.

"Garrett," Case says, leaning down to whisper back as his lips cover mine. "You've seen him, Syd. Lots of times. You used to disappear every once in a while. Be gone for days. Sometimes up to a week. I used to think you had quite the stealthy skillset." He pulls back a little so he can see me. His body is covering most of the light behind him, so I can't see him at all. His face is just a shadow. "But I've been thinking about why you're not responding to the drugs, cowgirl. And the only possible answer is Garrett."

I shake my heavy head and close my eyes. "I don't want to play anymore. I don't want to play—"

"You're gonna play, Sydney. You know how I know that?"

I don't answer. I don't open my eyes. I'm so dizzy.

"Because all I gotta do is tell you to *hush*."

I spin. The darkness becomes so much more than blackness. It becomes everything. It becomes safety, and relief, and desire. It calls to me, makes me want him in ways I can't explain.

It splits me open and empties me out.

And then he's there with my reward. My last chance is over.

He fills me back up.

TEN

MERC

"Satisfaction comes from achievement. The problem comes when you can't decide where the finish line is. Sometimes you cross without realizing."

– Case

Her lips wrap around me as I ease into her throat. Her tongue flattens down, sliding against my shaft. I grunt, wishing I had her in the light. Wishing I could see every moment as she takes my whole length.

"You feel good," I tell her, my hand pressing against her face for a moment of encouragement.

She gags a little when I thrust too hard.

"Shhh," I tell her. She's out of it now. Lost in her own world. I hate to take her this way, but I need her in that world. It's the place that has the answers. And this is the only way I know to get her there. Garrett used her this way. He knew a long time ago how to make her comply with his demands.

I'm just figuring it out now. And she's damn good at it. Her teeth scrape against my skin and make me wish for more. I want her on her knees. I want her eyes on me, open wide and filled with the desire to please. I'd fist her hair and pull her towards me, making her take me all the way to my balls.

Just imagining that is enough. I throw my head back and she chokes as I come down her throat, but she swallows just as the sobs start. I pull out and get off the table so I can get dressed.

The sobs build to full on crying. Big ugly gasping. Tears streaming down her face. Coughing. Semen she didn't already swallow spilling out of her lips.

I have a moment of pause and wonder if I should just kill her. This is not what I thought it would be.

But I don't. Because I need so much more from her than this. I need to get inside her. So I lean into her ear and whisper, "Hush."

She stops all of it. Like I just flipped a switch.

And I did.

I put my hands behind my head and look up at the shadows on the ceiling. When I look down at her she's staring at the ceiling as well. But her eyes are blank.

I know what he did. I know exactly what he did to her. That motherfucker.

Kill her, the voice in my head says. *Kill her now.*

But I take out the syringe from my pocket and plunge it into her thigh instead. I need answers and she is the only one who has them.

My phone buzzes in my pants so I walk out of the room and take it out so I can tab the accept button. "Yeah." I don't get service up here. Not regular service anyway. This is a local network I rigged up when I first bought the place.

"You have a message, Mr. Case."

I put it on speaker and go grab a pen and notepad from the coffee table. "Go ahead."

"Sasha called three times."

I put the pen down and scrub that hand down my face. "What'd she say?"

"She says she really needs to talk to you. Should I patch you through?"

"Sure. Buzz me back when you get her on the line." I end the call and sit down on the couch. She's the last person I need to talk to right now. I stare at the fire for a few moments and then my phone buzzes again.

I press the speaker as I take out my knife and start carving into the wood of the coffee table. "Sash," I say, trying to sound upbeat.

"Where have you been? I've been calling."

"I'm in the mountains. No service."

"Obviously. I need you to look something up for me."

I scowl and take her off speaker. "Why can't Ford do it?"

She laughs. "Please. He's the last person I want to know about this."

"The answer is no. Anything else? I'm real busy."

"Why? I just want a background check on a guy."

Now it's my turn to laugh. "Ford can definitely do that, kid."

"Yeah, but if Ford does it, he'll go too far. He'll have people follow him and stuff. And then he'll show up and scare the shit out of the guy. And I might like this one."

Fucking Ford. "I can't, OK? I'm not near my gear. I'm…" I think about Sydney in the other room. Should I tell Sasha? No. Not yet. Not until I have answers. "I'm not gonna be near a computer for a few weeks, probably." She's silent on the other end. "Sasha?"

She sighs. "I thought you were done working?"

"I am," I lie. "I'm just taking time off away from shit. Call me in a few weeks if you still like this guy and I'll help you out."

"Hmph. Well, I got into grad school. And I already got an internship for the summer. Just lab stuff. But it's a good start."

Sometimes I do wish she was my kid. Then these proud moments would be the result of me instead of her normal family. But if I was the one who'd kept her, she'd be all kinds of fucked up by now. "I never doubted you, brat. I'll call you in a few weeks and we'll celebrate."

I end the call before she can say anything else and then

throw my phone onto the couch and pick up the guitar. I start strumming that song again. It's soft and slow. Reminds me of that year all the shit hit the fan.

I hum along with the melody, the meaning behind the words taking over for a little bit.

Happiness is not what you think, this song reminds me. You spend your whole life looking for it, but you can't find it. It's not a thing. It's a state of mind.

My fingers continue to strum as I think about the words and then I stop and set the instrument aside.

Way too depressing.

I get up and turn out the lights and then dress so I can go check the property. Make sure that fuck Garrett didn't really set me up. Of course, it's been ten days, but old habits never die.

I get my winter gear on and step out into the cold night air. In the summer you can hear the river from here. But it's frozen over now and will be for at least three more months.

I don't like it out here in the winter too much. But this cabin is the perfect place to kill a girl. That's why I brought her here, after all. I *will* kill her. She's Garrett's weapon and she needs to be neutralized. It's not my fault he did this to her. It's not my fault she's so fucked up.

My feet crunch along in the snow as I think about that for a moment. Sydney Channing is probably gone. Her mind is very messed up. And if I tell her just how badly she's been used, it might complicate things.

I really need to keep this simple. I pat my pocket looking for smokes, shake one out, and light it up. If I go back in there and tell her what I think is going on, things will not be simple. Things will become more than complicated. I'll start something I might not want to finish.

If, on the other hand, I go in there and cut her throat? Well, then things get real simple.

Maybe Garrett is looking for her right now. Maybe I can take her somewhere and parade her around to get his attention. Make her bait.

I take a long drag of nicotine and blow it out as I consider my options. When the smoke is finished I toss it down into the snow and stub it out. I start the snow machine in front of the cabin and patrol the outer perimeter of the property, checking for tracks. Garrett. Wolf. Mountain lion.

All predators.

But the only tracks out here are mine.

When I'm satisfied we're alone, I park the machine in front of the cabin and walk back inside. My mind is made up.

Simple is definitely the way to go.

I need to be with Sasha. Do that little job for her. Make her happy. I need to catch up to my friends and get a life. Put this shit behind me.

It's time to kill Sydney Channing and move on.

Tonight.

ELEVEN

"Things have meaning because we give them that meaning. Everything. From the song in your head to the photos in your phone. They mean things. For me, they just mean a little more."
- Sydney

The phone call throws me. Sasha Cherlin. I've heard a lot about that girl but I've never actually met her. Seen her, back when she was a little girl. Heard about her. And maybe, if I'm honest, wished I *was* her on more than a few occasions.

Her life might've gotten off track — fucked up is a much better way to put it — but she had a real father growing up. She was never hidden away. She was never…

Stop, Sydney. There is no point in going backwards. Now you have to think about…

The music throws me again. I'm tied to the table still. His drug cocktail isn't working as well anymore. I'm getting a tolerance for it. But it's still good enough to take me out of things.

97

But the music. Of all the songs in the world, my killer has to play that song?

Did he hear me play it? How long has he been watching me? He said the whole time. But if that's true, then he knows I haven't seen Garrett. So it must be a lie.

I hum the song and in my head I can hear him humming along with me. Or maybe that's really happening.

It's hard to tell in this dark room. The sink is not dripping. I don't even know when he left the room. All I know is that I heard the phone ring and then suddenly I was staring up at the ceiling. He had his...

Oh, God. The image of him straddling me. Taking my mouth that way. I sob. Not because I hated it, but because I loved it. I've dreamed of him and now here he is. And I despise myself for wanting him. I loathe myself for saying yes, even though I can't say no.

The music stops. A few minutes later I hear a door close. Did he leave? A little while after that I hear a snow machine.

I struggle against my bindings. They are tight, but they are also damp from the hose and I'm a small person. My hands are tiny and my wrists are narrow. It won't take much to slip through. And the ties are leather, so they give more and more as I wriggle them back and forth, desperately trying to get free. They give a little, but not enough.

Hurry, Sydney, my mind urges. *Hurry, before he comes back.*

I start to breathe hard. Panting, almost. My heart is racing with the thought of escape.

But then I stop. What will happen if he catches me?

Not anything worse than if he comes back in to find you still here!

I wriggle some more, and bit by bit, the tether around my wrists becomes large enough for me to slip my hands through. I sit up, getting dizzy from the drugs. But I push that down and reach for my legs. They are cuffed in leather with buckles, so those are much easier.

When I'm free, I stand and feel my way to the door. It's locked. I feel around the perimeter of the room, my hands scraping across the rough wood of the walls, until I come all the way back to the door he uses to enter and exit.

No windows. Not even one that is boarded up.

And I'm naked. It's winter. Freezing-ass cold outside. So what did I really think I was going to do? I scoff at my stupid plan. Escape? Naked? This thought alone is enough to make me shiver. The room is colder than it was. He must've let the fire die down. I feel my way back to the stone hearth and kneel down on the rug. It's warmer here, but not by much. I press myself up against the metal that separates me from the heat and let out a sigh.

I give up. Maybe I can lie? Or maybe he will come to accept the fact that I don't know anything? Or maybe—

A door slams on the other side and I know he's back. His

boots thud across the floorboards. There's some crackling of the fire on the other side and then a burst of heat, letting me know he's put more wood on the fire.

Just give him what he wants, Sydney.

But I don't know anything!

The floorboards creak under his weight as he nears the side of the room where the door is. The latch jiggles and I take a gulp of air. But it doesn't open.

Instead he walks away. A few minutes later I hear the guitar again. That song.

How can this killer create something so beautiful?

My eyes grow heavy as he plays it over and over. Like it's on repeat. Before I know it, I'm humming along.

TWELVE

"Of course lies play a part. That's the most beautiful part of the dance. The courtship you have with your own lies."

- Case

I play the tune over and over again, never stopping. I'm on a loop, my fingers picking the strings, sliding over the frets. Making that squeaky sound that I love.

I want to kill her. I really do. I want to make this all end and let it go. Move back to civilization. Go see my friends and their kids. Move on.

I want all those things. And killing her is the quickest and easiest way to get there.

But Garrett. I don't think he wants me to have the happily ever after. And if I kill her... well, I'll be looking over my shoulder for the rest of my life. Just wondering when he will show up.

He's not dead. Sydney has the information I need. I'm so close. I'm *so* fucking close. All I have to do is wait it out.

Tell her what I think and wait for her to crack.

And she will crack. Could even crack tonight. And then I can kill her and leave. Finish the job.

One last job.

I laugh. My fingers continue to play, but I laugh. That's what they all say. Just one last job to set things up for retirement.

Hell, I don't need the money. Everyone else's last job made sure of that. We all became richer than God with that last job. No, I don't need money. I just need peace. And peace runs directly through Sydney Channing.

I stop strumming as I accept my situation.

She's not the prisoner here. I am.

The fire has long stopped crackling and that's probably why I notice it. Humming. From the other side of the hearth.

I put the guitar down and walk over there as quietly as I can, leaning in as far as I dare with the flames.

Yes. She got herself free and she's on the other side humming along to my music.

I lie down on the rug and listen to her. Eventually it dies off, like she falls asleep with the tune still on her tongue.

I stay there. Still. Thinking. The fire is lower now, ready for more wood. But I don't feed it. Instead I stand up and press a button on the wall.

The metal partition separating us slides up and then there she is. For the first time since she got here I can see her in the light. The soft flames make shadows that dance across her face. Her eyes are closed and her mouth is open. Her hair is dark and long. She's on her side and it falls over her shoulder, shielding her bare breasts. Her skin is a milky white even though all her other features are dark. Her eyes, her hair, her mind.

She's very dark. Illegitimate daughter of a US senator. Hidden away, either to keep her safe or to keep Channing safe. Or maybe she's just always been a pawn? Isn't that why the illegitimate ones go missing? To use them later? By either side. I have to admit, I have not thought about the Company in a very long time. I know Channing was a part of that secret organization set up to run the global economy. And I know that makes Sydney a Company kid, even if Channing was never married to her mother. And I know all that shit with Sasha eight years ago was Company business too. Hell, if Sash wasn't on my side, I'd take her out as well. What she knows, what she can do—that shit is scary as fuck. But we took care of them. You can't shut down a global organization with one attack, we knew that, but we took out the highest people in the organization.

But people got away. Not everyone died that night. James had a brother who was not at all interested in leaving his prime position in the Company. They had a father too. Still alive as far as I know.

Harper had a brother as well. And I'm sure nothing

that happened to him since that day has been easy. Not in a *you're-my-prisoner-and-I-own-you* kind of way, like I have going here with Sydney. But in a *be-careful-what-you-wish-for* way that turns a perfect hostage situation into a *Die Hard* action film.

And Sasha. We killed her uncle that night, but he was inconsequential. The last of her real family died the year before. But there are others. Low-level scum existing around the frayed edges of the organization.

So no. We didn't get them all. Some of them got away. And some of them have agendas, I'm sure. But Sydney is part of something else. I can't quite put my finger on it yet. I need more time. Because I know I'm on to something. I know I'm getting close to something. But most of all, I know I'm *missing* something.

And isn't that ironic? I ask myself as I look across the flames to her perfect naked body. It glows a warm shade of gold from the low fire. Isn't it ironic that this girl and I have something in common?

Things are missing.

She lets out a long breath and turns over on her stomach, inching a little too close to the fire for my liking. I don't need her rolling over into the flames while she sleeps. And I'm too damn tired to stay awake and babysit her.

So I push the button on the wall and the metal plate slides back down. It makes a little noise as it hits the stone that it didn't make when it went up, and I wonder if that woke her.

I listen for a noise on the other side of the fireplace, but there's nothing. So I go back over to the couch and pull the bearskin rug over top of me.

Something is not right about this.

Something is very, very wrong.

Later I wake. The fire is down and it's cold in here. I get up and throw a few logs on, then go piss in the bathroom.

I bet that bitch needs to pee. Probably shit too. I zip up my fly and walk over to the door that leads to the utility room that leads to the prisoner's room. I knock.

"What?" she says from the other side of the door.

"I know you untied yourself. Move away from the door, to the far corner. Then call out once you're sitting down so I know where you're at."

I half expect an argument. Surely she must be thinking she has the upper hand right now. She got out of her bindings and there were no immediate consequences.

But that's not because I'm going soft. It's because those consequences are about to upend her world. My words will ruin her life.

And I can't wait.

"Ready," she calls.

I open the door and flick the switch on the wall since I don't have my night vision on. She throws up a hand to cover her face, blinded.

"Stand up, walk over here, and get on your knees in front of me."

"I can't see," she says.

"You'll manage."

She crawls over instead, looking down at the floor to keep the light out of her eyes. Her long hair sways across the concrete, picking up bits of dust as she goes. When she gets to my feet she kneels and sits back on her butt. But she never lifts her eyes.

Her breasts are a nice size. Not too big, but certainly not small. Somehow she has positioned her hair so that once again it drapes over her nipples, shielding herself from me. She clasps her hands in her lap and bows her head as she waits.

It's not what I expected. I expected more of a fighter, to be honest. Company kids, even the hidden ones, tend to be violent when pushed. But if what I think about her situation is true, then it might all make sense.

"Do you remember what happened last night?"

"You raped my mouth," she says back without emotion.

"No," I laugh. "That's absolutely not what happened."

"I was under duress." And now she does lift her head.

And she doesn't even squint as the light hits her eyes. They are not as dark as I thought. In fact, they are a lot like mine. She blinks as I stare at her. Mine might be more yellow than green, but hers are more green than yellow. "And I know more about you than you know about me. I know you're a genius. Recruited to computer science at Stanford at sixteen. You turned them down. MIT at seventeen for robotics. Turned them down. And at your high-school graduation in Boston, no fewer than sixteen colleges and universities from around the world showed up to offer you a spot. And you turned them all down to join the army as an enlisted man."

I smirk at her. "Someone in this room has a stalker, Sydney. But it's not me."

"Ha. Ha," she says back. "My point is, I know you're a smart man, Merric Case, AKA Merc. AKA Number... wait, what number did they give you again? Oh, yeah, you never really had one. They lied. You were only on the job so they could keep tabs on you and get you to kill off as many Company kids as—"

I slap her across the face and she goes reeling. She hits the floor so hard for a moment I think I cracked her teeth. "Get to the point, bitch."

She looks up at me again, blood coming out of her mouth. "You raped me. You know you raped me. And I'll sit here and lie to you all you want. Tell you everything you want to hear. But you raped me."

"You said yes. You said, 'Fuck me.'"

"I said, 'Fuck me then. Or kill me. I don't really care. Do whatever you want.'"

I reach down and grab her arm, then pull her up to her feet, making her stand naked before me in the light. If she's embarrassed, she doesn't show it. "Then you shouldn't have said it, wildcat. Because I take everyone at their word."

She wants to growl at me for using that word, I can tell. But she can't. And I know why she can't. Maybe she knows too, or maybe she doesn't know. No difference. I'm about to find out one way or another. "Hush," I say. She stares up at me and her scowl softens. "Do you know what that means?"

"It means shut up."

"Hush," I say again. And this time she squints her eyes in confusion. "How about now?" She puts one hand over her stomach, like she feels sick, while the other one comes up to push against her temple. I have syringes in my pocket—low-dosage sedation to keep her calm, but not put her out. More than one, just in case the dose is too low or I need more time.

"Wildcat," I say. She blinks and appears confused. I check her compliance. "Give me your arm."

She looks up at me, still fighting, but she's losing. She's lost, actually. "Hush," I say one more time, and there it is. She presents me with her arm like a gift. I grab hold of her bicep and squeeze tighter than is probably necessary. She holds still this time. But I'm not convinced this isn't all an act. I jab her with the needle and push the plunger until the drugs empty into her muscle.

It's gonna take a while. So I lead her over to the fireplace and lay her down. She does not move.

I walk back outside the room, flip open the fireplace partition, and then return, turning off the light and closing the door behind me. She's still on the rug, facing the flames. "Does it feel good?" I ask her.

She doesn't answer. I tug my shirt over my head and lie down on the rug next to her, pulling her into my arms and holding her close. She sighs.

Fucking women are so easy. So weak when it comes to men. I've always had this advantage. I've yet to have a woman turn me down for a good hard fuck.

I'm dangerous. I'm big in every way that counts. And I've got moves that will make them beg me for more while cursing my name.

I palm Sydney's breast. It's firm, but squishy. Not fake. But they are near perfect in my eyes. How she got away with never sleeping with that husband-to-be of hers is beyond me. If she was mine, I'd just take her ass. Literally and figuratively.

"Let's start at the beginning, Sydney. OK?"

She nods against my chest.

"Only this time, cowgirl, I'm gonna tell you what happened and you're going to listen. OK?"

"OK," she says back.

THIRTEEN

SYDNEY

"Compassion sends mixed signals. If it's real, it can lead to survival. Just be damn sure it's real."

- Sydney

*A*m I awake?

"Are you awake?" he asks me back. Only I didn't think I was talking.

Do you read minds?

"Do *you* read minds?"

I blink as I stare at the fire. *Am I alone?*

"You're not alone, Sydney. I'm right here. Feel me?" He takes my hand and tugs my arm at a weird angle behind my back until I feel skin. But not my skin. "I asked you a question, Sydney. Do you feel me?"

"Yes."

"Good." He leans into my neck. I'm on the floor. No. A rug. In front of a fire. I stare at the dancing flames. He's behind me and we're naked. No. He's got jeans on. "Do you know where you are?"

I do.

"Sydney. I'm not going to ask every question twice, so answer me the first time."

"Yes."

"Where are you?"

"In the hush." *Wait. What?*

"What's the hush?"

That's a good question.

His hand wraps around my throat and squeezes until I cough. "No second chances, Sydney. Pay close attention to me. Tell me what the hush is."

"The quiet place. That's where I meet him."

"Who?" His tone has changed. It's more urgent now. He squeezes my throat again, only this time he doesn't stop until my head falls forward and I'm gasping for air instead of coughing.

"Garrett," I say, taking a long draw of air. "My neck is burning." I try to reach up and massage it, but Case grabs my hand tightly and puts it back on his stomach, still at that weird angle that stretches my shoulder enough to make it painful because of the wound that hasn't healed yet.

"Your neck is burning because I choked the breath out of you. It's a way to keep you focused. How did Garrett keep you focused?"

"Fishing," I say. "And camping."

"No, Sydney. That's not how he did it."

"He made me so happy."

Case draws in a long breath behind me, blowing it out over my neck. It feels good. "I'm gonna tell you what Garrett really did, Sydney. And you're going to listen very carefully as I explain. And then you're gonna tell me if I'm right. Do you understand?"

"You killed him. You took him away from me."

"I wish." Case laughs. And that laugh scares me. My legs begin to tremble and my shoulder is on fire. "That night at the cabin when I said I owned you. Do you remember that night?"

"Yes. Garrett saved me from you." Case mumbles out some words behind me, but I don't catch them. "What?"

"He didn't save you. The helicopter did. And if my friend hadn't been in trouble I'd have finished. There was no saving you that night, let's just get that straight right now. Because this is what happened, Sydney. He drugged you. He took you somewhere far away from other people. And he brainwashed you."

I stare at the flames and think about this.

"Do you know what he did in the army, Sydney?"

"Garrett was in the army?" I try to picture Garrett as a patriot, but that just makes me laugh.

The hand is around my throat again, but I struggle against Case this time. I wiggle free of his grasp and lean my head into the rug as I catch my breath again. "Stop it," I say.

"Pay attention. And answer my question."

I nod my head, but it's very heavy. My head is spinning, but it's weird. Not the same as before. "I don't know what he did in the army."

"He was a PSYOP specialist, Sydney. Do you know what they do?"

"No." I answer quickly now. I get it. Case has got something to say and he just wants to talk. My job is to listen and answer his questions.

I can do that.

"They fuck with people's heads. They learn lots of ways to influence people into doing what they want. Some call it torture. Some call it interrogation. I did this too, Sydney. That's how I have you in this cabin right now. That's how I've managed to kill more people than I can even count. That's how I get away when others get caught."

I don't have anything to say to this, so I stay silent.

"Garrett's been working you since that day he took you from the cabin eight years ago. Maybe before that too. He drugged you. Took you away, fucked with your head, and made you into his little slave."

My mind spins again and I try to get up. But Case's arms are all the way around me now, hugging me to his chest tightly. "Hush," he says.

I do hush. I quiet right down.

"That's your trigger word. And wildcat wasn't a

nickname, was it?"

"No."

"What does it mean, Sydney? That word wildcat?"

My eyes close as I think. Wildcat.

Garrett is laughing as I kneel. He's fisting my hair, yanking me down in front of him. My eyes never leave him. I couldn't rip my gaze away even if I wanted to. And I don't want to.

Because I know what happens.

"That's not it."

"What's not it, Sydney?"

My head clears a little and I take a deep, deep breath.

"Sydney," Case says, almost whispering it in my ear. "Tell me." His hand slips away from my neck and falls to my breast. He doesn't squeeze, he caresses it. Softly. Like that feather he had. It's soft.

His lips flutter against my cheek and I realize he's kissing me. I turn into it and kiss him back. His face is scratchy. Not a beard, but not clean-shaven either. He turns my whole body until I'm facing him.

"Syd," he says.

"Don't call me that," I whisper back, lifting my eyes a little so I can see his. The fire is dancing inside them, mesmerizing me for a moment. Case furrows his brow, like I'm confusing him. "He called me that."

"Garrett?"

"No."

"Who?"

"The man in my head."

He smiles at me. And it comes so easy. "You wanna fish today, Syd?"

"Sydney," Case says, drawing me back. "Who's in your head?"

"Garrett," I whisper. "But not the mean one."

"You made that guy up, Sydney. You made him up to replace the monster."

I turn away from Case again, but he stops me and turns me back. "I'm tired."

"We're all tired. You don't get to quit because you're tired. You were brainwashed. And I know he did terrible things, so we're not gonna go there right now. But I need to know when you saw him last, Sydney. Think hard."

"The night before my wedding."

"Goddammit. No!" Case says this in an angry voice. "That was me, Sydney. I was the one you saw that night. You crashed your truck and I came and got you. Brought you here. That was not—"

"I saw Garrett too. He was at the hotel."

"What?" Case sits up behind me. "What?" He grabs my

116

chin with his hand and turns it until I have to pay attention to him.

"He was there. I saw him. He came to my door and—"

I stare at the monster in the hallway, the fear taking over. But that word he says, that stops me. It stops me. He says it again, and again. And each time, I become smaller. My world gets darker. Things shrink and I float.

"Then what happened, Sydney?"

"Come with me."
I take his hand and follow him down the hallway to a door marked for employees. We go inside and it's dark.

"What did he say, Sydney?"

"You're a good girl." It makes me sick and I lean over and throw up.

"Goddammit," Case says. He gets up and it's only then that I realize I actually did throw up. All over the rug in front of the fireplace.

He picks me up, holding me in his arms as he kicks the rug out of the way. And then he's still for a moment. Like he's thinking. He spins and so does my head. I have to close my eyes to stop my stomach from churning.

"I'm gonna be sick again," I say. And then I puke all over myself and pass out.

The next thing I know, I'm in a bathroom. The lights are so bright I have to close my eyes. I've been in the dark too long. The water is running and I'm sitting on Case's lap on the rim of the tub. He's wiping me down with a towel and when he's done with that he places me in the water.

It's hot. But it feels so damn good after all those days and nights in the cold. Every part of my body is finally warm. He positions me so I'm leaning forward, my arms resting on my knees, my head resting on my arms.

He washes me. The soapy washcloth drags up and down my back. He pours water over my head, making me gasp and struggle for air. I can't tell if this is torture or kindness.

I go with kindness. Because I've had enough torture in my life. But I know it's a lie. Just like all the other lies I've been telling myself. "My whole life is a lie."

"Welcome to the real world," Case says.

I'm not in the tub anymore. I'm wrapped up in a towel, lying on a bed. He unwraps me and scoots me under the covers. They are soft, and clean, and smell fresh. And then he slips into bed and puts his arms all the way around me again.

"We're done for now. He's got you programmed to become sick when you're questioned. So we're gonna sleep it off and try again tomorrow."

But I'm not interested in tomorrow. I'm interested in right now. I go into my head and find the dream man. The perfect one who loves me.

I turn into him and wrap my hands around his neck, pulling him close. "Fuck me."

Hands are on my ribs, one on each side. They wrap halfway around my body, that's how big they are. He's talking, but I don't hear him. I hear the river. I hear the birds singing. I hear the aspen leaves rustling above my head in the thick forest.

I reach down for his cock and find him fully erect. Hard and long. He's still talking. And then I'm talking, and I have no idea what I'm saying, but whatever it is, it makes him respond to me. He gives in to me. His hands slip down farther. One pushes between my legs and begins to stroke me in all the right ways, the way I always imagined it in the dream world.

He flips me over and fingers my asshole. "You like it like this, Sydney?"

"Hmmm," I mumble out. I do. But only from the dream

guy. "Take me," I tell him. "In the ass."

"Jesus Christ," Case says. But he whispers it. And it doesn't come out like he's frustrated. He's turned on.

Case gets out of bed, his arm wrapped around my middle, lifting me with him like I'm weightless. Like I'm a sack of nothingness that he can position any way he wants. And he does. He props me up on my hands and knees on the edge of the bed and bumps his hard cock against my ass. Teasing me. Making me moan.

He pokes the entrance to my ass a few times, then something cold dribbles on my ass and slides down, making me tremble. His saliva, I realize. His fingers play with me for a moment, working it in, making my entrance wet. "You want it, Sydney? Tell me you want it. Tell me you want it or you don't get it. We're not gonna have another misunderstanding."

"I want it," I say. "I want it so—"

He thrusts his full length inside me, the jolt of pain intense fire. A pain I've felt so many times, it barely matters. And then that sick feeling in my stomach is gone and I relax, letting him pound me from behind. Over and over again. His balls slap against the lips of my pussy. His chest falls down on my back. His breathing becomes my breathing. His moans become my moans. And then his pleasure becomes my pleasure when he shoots his hot release all over my back.

"You ready to learn to fish?"

I don't know if it's in my head or not. But my answer is yes.

"I can't always take care of you, Syd."

I know that.

Teach me how to take care of myself. Please.

Case falls over on the bed, dragging my body with him. We lie there for a few minutes, breathing hard from the sex.

I crawl away from him, seeking out my own space. And he gets up just as I find my own pillow and bury my head in it. The tears stream out as Case pulls on his jeans, his belt buckle jingling as he does this. And then he collapses in the bed next to me and pulls me close.

"Tomorrow, Sydney. We'll pick this back up tomorrow. You can sleep here for tonight."

I turn into him, wrapping my hands around this monster's body until I find his back. He responds with his own embrace.

He might be a monster, but it's dark in here. And if there's one thing I know how to do, it's live in the dark. I've met the monsters there so many times, it's familiar. And familiar is always better than new.

I drift off as he kisses my neck.

121

My eyes open a while later. It's still dark. I'm still thinking about him. Them. All of them.

I own you, Case said. And I guess he's right. He does. Because I'm here. I asked for this. My hands drop from his back and he turns a little, letting one of my hands slip down to his hips and come to a rest over a lump in his pocket.

His knife.

I swallow hard. My head is a lot clearer now, the drugs he gave me wearing off. I feel the outline of the lump in his pocket. Not a knife. I slowly slip my hand inside, one fraction at a time, until my fingertips come in contact with his secret.

Syringes. But are they empty? Or full?

There are three of them. I wrap my tiny hand around the bundle of plastic and slowly withdraw them. When I get them out I flick the caps off, one at a time. I don't know if they are empty or not and it's dark, so I have no hope of finding out.

So I do the only thing I can do. I stab him, with all three at once, and push the drugs in.

Only two depress, and I'm not even sure how much he got, because I'm thrown onto the hard wood floor before I can finish.

"You fucking cunt."

FOURTEEN

SYDNEY

"Right place, right time. Best escape advice out there."
- Sydney

I slide across the floor and hit my head on the wall. He grabs my arms, like he's got some super night vision and he knows exactly where I am in the blackness, and pulls me to my feet. He squeezes my arm so hard I cry out.

"Bitch," he laughs. "The dose was way too fucking low to drug a guy as big as me."

He throws me against the wall again. I hit it harder than the last time, the back of my head bursting with pain. My vision blurs and I start to fall to the floor.

But he's there again, holding me up. Not the way he carried me to the tub to clean me up. He slings me over his shoulder and stumbles towards the door, falling forward. Once again I hit the floor. But he loses his grip and I crawl backwards, feeling for the wall. I find it at the same time he finds me and then a hard fist crashes against the side of my head.

"You think you can play me?" He's breathing hard, his anger spewing out with each exhale. "You think you can trick me, you stupid whore?"

Even in the dark, the next blow makes the room spin. Makes my brain spin.

That's three hits. I'm not sure how many more I can take.

He lifts me up over his shoulder again and stumbles forward. This time we do not go down. I kick my legs and flail my fists against his hard body. But he's got me tight.

We go through the door and into a living room. There's a small light on in the kitchen, so I can at least see where I am. But we walk past that and towards the back of the cabin.

I need to get away. If he puts me back in there—

He throws me down on the ground. The air rushes out of my lungs, knocking the breath out of me. I gasp, trying to make my lungs work. I feel like I'm drowning. Underwater choking. But I'm not. I just can't seem to draw in enough oxygen to make up for the blow.

He fumbles with the door handle for a second, and I'm just about to start crawling away, hopeful that some of those drugs are gonna kick in, when he finally manages to pull it open and turn back to me. His eyes are filled with rage.

I don't know Merric Case that well. Hardly at all, in fact. But I know the look of evil. I know the look of a monster.

And he's definitely one of them.

He takes a step and falls.

I crab-walk backwards just as he reaches out for my ankle. He gets a hold, but I kick him in the face and he lets go. I get to my feet as he starts to crawl after me. He's so much faster than me, even drugged. Because he gets to his feet again before I can even turn.

He lunges at me, grabbing hold of my waist this time, and we go down together. He lands on top of me, and once again, I'm gasping for air.

And that's when his hands find my throat.

"I'm just gonna kill you now, Syd." He sneers the nickname he's not allowed to call me, and squeezes.

Fight, Sydney!

I turn, my knees up, pushing him off me. And even though I get some space between us, his arms are so long it does nothing for the grip on my neck. I can feel the blackness coming. But I'm not done yet. His body wobbles a little, and I throw my whole body backwards, flex my legs and find my strength, just as his is starting to wane, and deliver a two-footed kick to his chest.

He flies backward, landing hard on the floor, and I take a moment to gasp for air. It rushes in, making the stars that signal the beginning of unconsciousness fade a little. I crawl backwards until I reach the front door.

And I wait.

He tries to get up a few times. The nasty words spill out of his mouth in a slur. But he never makes it. It takes long, endless minutes for his eyes to finally close.

And even though all I want to do is sit here and cry, I get to my feet. My legs are shaking so bad they almost give. But I steady myself against the front door and give myself a moment to cope.

Cope. I do that well. Coping with violence and terror is a gift from the man in my dreams.

My lungs suck in as much air as I can. I close my eyes. I count to ten. And when I open them, I move.

I run to his bedroom, fling open a door that has to be a closet and smile when I see clothes hanging. I grab a long-sleeved flannel shirt and shove my arms inside. I don't even stop to button it up. I just grab the nearest pair of jeans. They are way too big and far too long, but fuck it. I roll them up and find a belt, and then go for the shoes. He's got one pair of boots in the closet. Boots that are like a million sizes too big. But it's the dead of winter and I can't go outside unless I have something on my feet. I grab two pairs of socks and tug them on with shaking hands, then slip my feet into his boots.

When I go back out into the living room, I half expect him to be waiting with a shotgun trained on my face. But he's not. He's on the ground still. Breathing heavy and hard. I walk past him, and he reaches out and grabs my ankle, pulling me to the ground.

"No!" I scream it in a voice I've never heard before. I kick him in the face again, and the blood spills out of his lip. One more and he lets go.

I get to my feet, ready to pass out from the adrenaline and the fear. And then I force myself to move. I bolt for the door and throw it open. It's snowing. And freezing-ass cold. There's a snow machine parked in front of the cabin. But beyond that there is nothing. Nothing but trees and darkness.

The keys, Sydney. Find his keys.

Right. I calm myself and turn back to the cabin. They have to be here somewhere.

I rifle through the kitchen drawers, then the nightstand in his bedroom. I look through the closet and check the bathroom. But even before I finish all that I know where they must be.

In his fucking pocket.

I walk back to his body, keeping more than an arm's length of distance between us. His head is tilted to the side and his eyes are open.

"*You'renotgonnagetaway,*" he says, his words slurring so bad I almost don't understand him.

"Fuck you." I walk behind him and bend down, reaching into his pocket. His hand comes up, reaching for me, but he misses. The drugs are working now. He might not be out, but he's down.

Down enough for me to shove my hand in and pull out what I need, anyway. I spit on him as I walk by. And then I grab a coat that's lying across the couch, find gloves in the pocket, open the door, and walk out.

The snow machine is covered in snow, and there are no tracks, so it's been sitting for a little while at least. But I'm a country girl. A backcountry girl. I've been riding snow machines all my life. I brush off as much snow as I can, find the ignition, and shove the key in. I turn it to the on position and then pump the primer a few times before releasing the choke.

"You're not gonna get away, bitch."

I look up and see Case standing in the doorway, holding onto it like his life depends on it. He smiles. "You cunt. There's no gas."

"Fuck you," I say, pulling on the starter cord as I do it. Nothing. "Not even you are stupid enough to ride up into the wilderness on empty."

Case takes a step forward, stumbling up to the porch railing. He's less than twenty feet away. But he's slow.

I'm slow too, but my drugs have worn off and his are just kicking in. On the fourth pull the engine roars to life. I twist the throttle a little and then put her in gear. I lurch forward, make a wide turn not ten feet away from him now, and then gun it.

There's no path in the woods. But he got up here somehow, so I find a clearing in the trees and assume that's the trail.

I give the machine some gas and take off into the dark, navigating by the single headlight. I go fast at first, but I hit a few bumps, get some air, and then calm myself. *Go slow, Sydney. If you crash, you're dead.*

I have no idea where I'm at, but trails are here for a reason. They lead places. And right now I don't care where this one leads, I'm on my way.

It twists and turns, making me go even slower. So slow sometimes, I could probably get farther by walking.

I'm freezing. I have no scarf and no hat. But I keep going. I come upon a hill of snow and gun the machine to get over it. It chokes and stalls out on the other side.

But there's something else on the other side too. A light. Just up ahead through the trees. A house!

I pull the cord to start the machine again, and that's when I hear it. The whine of another engine from behind me.

Holy fuck. He has two of them!

I get off the machine and start to run through the deep snow. My boots are way too big to run in, and I lose one when I fall into a drift that comes up to my knees.

The engine from behind is getting louder now, but I can't risk frostbite by leaving that boot. I scramble back and shove it on my foot and then plunge ahead, trying my best to make progress in the deep snow.

The light is getting brighter now, so I force myself to keep going. My foot is freezing, even through the boot, because both pairs of socks are soaked.

The engine cuts off in the distance, and I know he's found my machine in the middle of the trail. He has to come on foot now too.

I go faster. I have no idea where I find my energy, but I find it. I plow through the snow, falling and getting back up so many times I lose count. And there's a path. The snow has been cleared. A two-foot-wide area that leads up to my salvation and allows me to ask my muscles for one more burst of energy. I pump my arms and I'm almost to the house when something snags my ankle.

I fall into the snow face first and realize he's got me again.

"Scream," he says, his whole body falling on top of me. "Scream, Sydney. No one's gonna hear you."

I open my mouth—

But he's right. No one hears me because he punches me in the head so hard I have no chance. I black out from the pain.

FIFTEEN

SYDNEY

"Always know when to give in."

– Sydney

I come to hog-tied. Hands and feet bound together. Some kind of tape over my mouth. He's got me positioned in front of him on the other snow machine, and the wind and snow is whipping against my face.

I struggle enough to make him swerve and angry at the same time. He stops the machine and grabs my shoulders, pulling my face in close to his.

Breathing is difficult. For the life of me, I cannot get enough air into my lungs, but I'm trying my best. I wheeze with each intake, the tape against my mouth giving way just the slightest bit as I try to gulp oxygen. It's a trick though. Everything is always a trick. Because whatever slight bit of air getting through is just enough to suck the tape against my mouth even more when I try to inhale.

"Look," Case says in my ear. "If I don't get us home,

131

we're gonna freeze to death. You get that?" He pulls my hair, yanking my head back. "You drugged me. I'm half asleep right now so our chances are not looking good. And now I'm stopped, trying to keep your bitch ass from making me ram this four-hundred-and-fifty-pound machine into a goddamned tree. So how do you want this to go? Freeze to death? Crash first and then freeze to death? Or make it home in one piece, alive?"

I can only suck on my tape in response, but that must be all he's looking for, because he straightens out my body a little, and then we lurch forward.

He weaves in the tracks we made coming out this way, not on course at all. And this is when the panic hits home. He really could crash. Or fall asleep. And we really will freeze to death out here.

My eyes close, looking for a way to escape my terror. I hold very still as we start and stop. His coordination is getting worse by the second. And after what seems like hours, we pull up to the cabin. He stands up, hauls me up over his shoulder, then drops to his knees in the snow, spilling me face first as he does it. The snow blocks my nostrils, making me panic and wiggle. Noise is coming out of my mouth, but the screams for help are mistaken for resistance. And so he handles it. The hard whack against my head makes the whole world spin and while that is happening, he gets back on his feet and drags me by the arms, my body finally limp.

I am pulled inside and left near the kitchen table as he falls to his knees beside me.

Oh, God. If he dies, I will be left here in the middle of nowhere, tied up and helpless.

I start shivering uncontrollably. My teeth want to chatter very badly, but the damn gag stops them. My body convulses to make up for it.

Case turns his head so I can see his face. His eyes are very heavy, like he's about to pass out. But he reaches for my arm and slides me over next to him, embracing me with his body heat. I tip my chin up and find we are face to face. Very close together. He reaches up and pulls on the tape over my mouth. It takes him several tries to get a good grip, and then he rips it off.

I sob after that. It's all too much.

"Look at me, Sydney."

How he can be so commanding when he's about to fall unconscious, I have no idea. I look at him. He's my whole world right now. This cold, heartless killing machine who has no aversion to violence against women. He's all I have. So I look up at him.

He's barely there. His eyes are tiny slits, his mouth going slack from the drugs. But then he opens his lids once more and says, "If we're going down, we're going down together." And then he has another syringe in his hand. He stabs me in the arm. The needle goes through the coat and pierces my skin. I watch the burning anger in his eyes as he presses the plunger.

I just watch helplessly as his eyes close, his grip on me weakens, and his breathing becomes heavy.

I try to push him off me, but he's too big.

It's cold in here. The fire is very low. With no one to feed it, it will probably go out before he wakes up. And when he does wake up, he's gonna kill me anyway.

So I stop struggling and just enjoy the warmth from his body instead. Thankful I have clothes on. Thankful I'm not outside. Thankful he's asleep. For now.

My eyes get heavier and heavier as the minutes tick off, and just as I'm about to close them and give in, he whispers, "You know why I hate you, Syd?"

I force myself to wake a little. Make my lids open.

His eyes are open too. Just barely.

"Why?" I slur back.

"Because you love him."

I know he's talking about Garrett, but why does he care?

"And it kills me." His eyes close, flutter, and then open again. "It kills me that you fall for it. You're in the dark about everything. Why can't you fucking see it? Why can't you see *through* it?"

"Maybe I don't want to."

I wait for another response, but it never comes. He's out.

"Or maybe you're the one in the dark and not me."

"Pick and choose your battles, Syd."

134

I look up at Garrett and smile. "I always do."

"No," he laughs. "You've got a little too much fight in you."

I shake my head and cast out my fishing line. "How do you figure that?"

"You want to stay when you should go. You want to go when you should stay. You want to fight when you should yield and yield when you should fight. You've got it all backwards, Syd."

I draw in a breath of fresh mountain air. "Says you."

He chuckles with me. "When someone has the upper hand, you let them keep it."

I give him a sideways glance. "That sounds a lot like giving up."

"Nope," he says, reeling in his line. I wait for him to check the bait – gone – and then change to a lure before casting out again. He looks over at me then, his eyes gold in the sun, his body tanned and muscular. He's shirtless, because it's very warm today. "It's not giving up, Syd. It's strategy. You gotta let them think they're winning when they get the upper hand. But you never stop fighting. Even if it's only on the inside."

I wake up blind. My bindings are gone, my clothes are gone, my body is freezing. I crawl over to the fireplace but when I touch the metal, there's no warmth.

He died.

"Don't be stupid," I say out loud. He drugged me again, untied me, took off my clothes, and dumped me into this room.

Why didn't he light a fire? He must be cold.

But I can already hear water running. For half a second this makes my heart stop. *He's coming with the hose!*

But then I realize that's not what's happening. He's in the shower, I bet. Basking underneath hot water.

I tremble, cold. And I hate him. I hate that man so bad. Why is he doing this to me? Why?

"You are stupid," Case says off to my left.

I sit up and look around in the dark.

"I mean…" He laughs a little. He sounds like he's sitting down on the floor only a few feet away. "If it had worked it might've been a great plan. But I told you that machine had no gas. It's twenty below outside and snowing. And that house you thought was your salvation? Is empty."

"You're lying."

"Really? Which part of that is unbelievable?"

"I think there's people in that house. I saw lights."

"There's no light out there, Sydney. It's winter in Montana. People who own big log cabin homes like that don't come here for the winter, cowgirl. You know better. You were cold and delirious from too many drugs. There was no light on in that house. You saw the moon reflecting off the windows, that's all."

Montana. But he's right. Rich people who buy big homes out here come for the summers. For fishing, and hunting, and rafting. All things you don't generally do in January.

"I know you dream about him. So that's where this is gonna start."

A chill runs up my spine and manifests as the hair at the nape of my neck standing on end.

"Oh," Case says, getting to his feet with a shuffle. "You didn't think this was over, did you?"

He pulls me to my feet by my hair and then half drags me, half walks me, over to the door. When he opens it, the light blinds me for a moment and I have to close my eyes. He doesn't stop, just pulls me along a hallway until we get to the bathroom where warm steam rushes out in a mist. I inhale, enjoying every bit of warmth, and when I crack open my eyes, taking care not to look up into the light, I see the feet of an old white cast-iron tub.

I force myself to look up now. Right at his face.

"You smell," he says, reading my mind. "You shit yourself. Which is why I took off your clothes."

I look away, embarrassed, of all things. I shake my head a little to make that go away. Of all the things I should be ashamed of, shitting myself isn't even in the top one hundred.

"And you're covered in blood. I'm sick of looking at you like this. So wash. And be quick because you don't deserve it."

"Then why not hose me down?" I cringe as soon as the words come out. *Shut up, Syd!*

"I'm a little bit tired," he says, ignoring my sarcasm. "And holding a hose filled with freezing water isn't on my list of things to do right now. You have two minutes. And if you don't get yourself clean in that time, I *will* get the hose."

I take a deep breath and step towards the tub, then look over my shoulder to see if he will leave me alone.

"In your dreams."

I step in and lower myself down into the hot water. It stings bad, since my body is so cold. But it feels way too good to stop, so I sink all the way in and allow a sigh to escape.

I lie back and dunk my hair, closing my eyes to fully become submerged. The outside goes away for a moment, making things seem peaceful. But then his grip on my upper arm pulls me back up.

He squirts some shampoo onto my head, a thin, cold stream that makes me look up at his intentions. But all he says is, "Wash."

I do wash. I scrub my hair good. Hell, if he wants me clean, I can get on board with that. When my hair is all lathered, he reaches over to the counter for a bowl, and then scoops up water and pours it down my head to wash out the soap.

I look up again. Because I'm just not getting it. But he simply points to a white bar of soap in a dish built into the cabin wall.

I take the hint and wash my body, certain that more than two minutes have passed. But he doesn't rush me, or even speak again. He just waits until I'm all soaped up and then pours the water over me. Down one shoulder, then the other. Several times, actually. And I'm just starting to relax when he leans over and pulls the plug. The water starts rushing out with that sucking noise that tubs make when they drain. He stands before me, his arms open with a waiting towel.

When I step out, he looks my whole body up and down. I look him up and down as well. He's got a bruise on his arm where I stabbed him with the syringes.

I look down at my own arms and find the same marks. Another on my thigh. Then the other thigh.

When I look back up he cracks a smile. "I got more where that came from. But let's try to move forward. I'm not getting anywhere with the drugs, and to be quite honest, I'm on a schedule."

I furrow my eyebrows. "For killing me?" I ask in a whisper.

He ignores my words. Just wraps me up in the towel and flips the light off as he walks out.

"Follow me," he calls over his shoulder.

And what choice do I have?

So I do. I follow him down the hallway and meet him in the dark.

SIXTEEN

MERC

"I walk that line between monster and savior, and I use it against them."

- Case

She steps back into the room that has become her prison, only this time she does it of her own accord.

I need to adjust. Because so far, nothing is working on this girl and I need answers. Time is running out. When this all started I thought the whole thing would be over in two, three days, tops. But we're on day twelve now. Day twelve.

I take her hand and this must frighten her because she pulls back instinctively, but my squeeze reassures her. She's warm now. And clean. And calm. So my squeeze is a reassurance that she is still going to be all those things if she gives in. I lead her across the dark room until I get to the far wall, and then I place my hands on her shoulders and push her until she bumps into it with her back.

"What—"

I put my fingers to her lips. "Hush."

She starts breathing hard and I swear to God, I can almost hear her heartbeat. But I don't say it again. I don't want whatever it is that Garrett turned her into. I just want Syd right now.

I wrap my fingers around both her tiny wrists and bring her arms above her head. "Grab hold, Sydney." She reaches until she finds the chains hanging from the ceiling and they clink a little as she grips them.

I smooth her wet hair down. "Good girl."

She whimpers.

I lean down to her ear and say, "Shhh. Be still. I'm not going to hurt you."

"Let me go. Please."

I know she's looking up at me with those eyes and I have a sudden urge to see them. "If you can behave, I will go open the fireplace. Do you want a little heat, Sydney? A little bit of light?"

"No," she says back. "I like the dark."

Shit. That one hush was all she needed. Up until now, it's been three times to get compliance. But when I need her to resist, she gives in. Fucking figures. "We've been in the dark long enough. Let's meet up in the light."

She starts to say no again, but I interrupt her with another, "Hush."

142

Her shoulders relax a little as she continues to cling to the chains. I wonder what word Garrett uses to bring her out of it? It would be nice to have that.

"Stay here. Just like you are. I'll be right back."

I leave her there, walk out of the room, down the hall a few paces, and then stop to listen.

Nothing. She stayed.

OK, Merc. Let's figure this shit out. I go back out to the living room and throw a few logs onto the dying fire, then press the button that will lift the steel plate on the other side of the wall.

Her feet come into view first, then her legs. I can't see anything else unless I get on my knees. So I just grab the rug in front of the couch and take it back into the room and drop it down on the ground in front of the fire.

"Case?"

I turn to look at her. The shadows from the flames are dancing up her body, licking them in places I'd like to lick myself. "Yeah?" Is she back? How did she come back?

"Why did you leave me there? Was it because you thought I wasn't worth saving?"

I walk forward a few paces and stop about four feet in front of her. "What?"

"He said you'd save me. That I shouldn't worry. Because you'd save me."

"Who?"

143

"My father. He said he told you to save me and so no matter what happened, you'd get me out because I was the job. Was I not worth it? Didn't he pay you enough? You punched me in the face. I was waiting—" She starts to cry and I take a step back. "I was waiting for you. I saw you and that other guy moving in the bushes, and I was waiting. Garrett came in and then—" She lets her chin fall to her chest.

"You knew I was coming?"

She nods, but doesn't look up. "I think I know why." She does look up after this, and I wish she hadn't. She's got more hurt in that one look than any living creature I've ever seen. And I've tortured my share of people over the years. Killed too many to count. I've seen fear before.

This is not fear.

This is sadness.

"I think it's because he lied, didn't he?" She swallows hard, like she's steeling herself to admit something she'd rather not. "He lied to me. He never sent you to save me. You were always there to kill me, weren't you?" I shake my head. But she doesn't see it, or she ignores me, or whatever. "They always wanted to get rid of me."

"Who?" I take the two steps that separate us and cup her face in my hand. "Who, Sydney?" She might have the answers after all. She might give them up without having to go through with this stupid plan.

144

"Those people."

My hope dies a little. "What people?"

"Those people my father has running his PR. They found out about me two years before all this happened. I was living with my mom out in a small town, just east of Cheyenne. And they found out about me."

"Oh," I say, for lack of anything else to say to that. *Those* people. I took care of them years ago. Plus, she doesn't even have a name for them. PR people is not what I'd call them. But if you're a kid, you'd probably assume your father was on the up and up instead of a malicious child-killer. So I can't blame her for that. "No, Syd. He did tell me to come save you. He didn't lie about that."

Her face crumples a little, like I just delivered bad news. "OK."

Something is happening here, but I'm not quite sure I know what it is. But I am damn sure I need to move this shit forward. I had a spark of hope for a second there that she might tell on her own. Admit to lying, and tell me where I can find Garrett. Cop out to seeing him all these years. Cop out to being in on the plan.

But I think she's telling the truth. And that's so much worse for her than if she had been lying. Because I think she's gone. I think she's fucked up beyond all repair. FUBAR, we call it in the army. Sydney Channing has been a big surprise from beginning to end. But never in a million years did I see this coming.

"Syd," I say, getting ready to explain what's gonna happen now.

"Why do you call me that?" she interrupts. "No one calls me that. I hate it."

I think back. Is that true? Didn't Garrett call her that? Never mind. I wave a hand in front of me, trying to clear the air.

I place my hand on her head again. Smoothing her hair. It's starting to dry and it will be just as FUBAR as her once it does.

Get a grip, Merc. This bitch is over as soon as you get her to talk.

Right.

I drop my hand to her throat and flatten my palm against her throbbing artery. She's not tied—not her hands and not her feet—so I expect her to fight a little. But she doesn't, once again showing me that she is unreliable as far as reactions go. I even squeeze it a little, just to test this theory out. Again, no reaction until a few seconds pass and she begins to choke.

I ease off and press my body against hers. My chest is bare, so we are skin to skin. She is warm and so am I. Together we heat everything up. I lean into her ear and give her a kiss. She shudders, but her hands remain grasping onto the chains, just like I told her to.

146

"Did he tell you you were pretty?" I don't know why I ask that, but I feel the need to know.

"No," she says. "He told me I was expendable."

"Channing said that?" I just can't see it, to be honest. I mean, yeah, the girl was illegitimate and that's a pretty big deal in his world. But... expendable? He hired me to save her ass. So maybe he was setting all of us up? I dunno. I never pegged him as a Sydney hater. Sure, the kid was inconvenient, but why raise her up to age sixteen and then—

"Garrett," she clarifies.

"Oh." *Jesus fucking Christ, Merc. Back on track!*

I trace a finger down each side of her body, feeling her ribs. They are prominent when she's got her hands above her head like this. And she might be ticklish, because it makes her squirm. I adjust my position and then cup her breasts. It makes me feel dirty for some reason. This whole thing makes me feel dirty. I'm tired of playing with her. But I have to know.

She moans a little and this gives me what I need to continue. "Do you know what the hard fuck is, Syd?"

"I'm a virgin."

I laugh. Like hard. It startles her and she drops her hands and covers herself. It startles me too, because I actually take a step back instead of correcting her.

"Please, I'm a virgin."

"You cannot be serious." My tone has changed. It's

harsh. And this makes her reach up and grab the chains again to try to placate me. "Why are you lying? I already fucked you in the ass once. I've seen *him* fuck you dozens of times."

She doesn't react. Not to any of that. Not to the fact that I fucked her or the fact that I watched Garrett fuck her.

"That bullshit might've worked on Brett—" I stop talking and stare at her. "That's why you never let Brett fuck you?"

She lifts her head and her eyes, but only for a moment. Only to nod.

She's telling the truth. Well, no, she's lying her ass off. But she *thinks* she's telling the truth.

I step forward again and reach down to find her pussy. When I hit her clit with the tip of my thumb, she moans. I insert one finger and she thrusts her hips to force me to go deeper. "Let me ask you this question again, Sydney." I grab her hair with my other hand and yank her head back so she has to look at me. "Do you know what the hard fuck is?"

"No," she says, emotionless.

I lean into her ear and whisper, "You're about to find out." She just stares straight ahead. "Do you understand me?"

"Yes," she says, still no emotion.

"That yes is permission."

I wait to see if she will object, and in truth, a part of me wants her to. I want her to knee me in the balls. Scratch my eyes out. Spit in my face. I want her to fight.

Because if she did all those things, I might stop. It might be enough to stop me.

But again, she's compliant when I want resistance.

And then she takes it one step further. She covers the distance between us with a kiss.

My hand leaves her hair and I find her throat again. Because we're on. "Let me explain what the hard fuck is, Sydney. OK?" I growl it into her mouth, because she's still kissing me. "It means I will push you beyond all your limits. I will make you cry tears and writhe in pain and pleasure at the same time. I'm gonna make that fuck so hard you'll weep. But you will beg me to keep going. I will make your body sore, your muscles shudder, and your mind exhausted. I'm gonna take you, Sydney Channing. I'm gonna take you and once I do, I'm never gonna give you back."

"Take me," she whispers back. Her warm breath intertwines with mine, making us intimate for a moment.

But only for a moment. Because I push her to her knees, fist her hair, and drag her face towards my cock.

SEVENTEEN

MERC

"They walk that line between angel and demon, and they use it against me too."

– Case

She looks up at me, her warm breath already heating up the denim of my jeans. Her eyes are watery, like she wants to cry.

I want her to cry. I want to make her sob. I want to stuff my dick down her throat and watch the tears run down her face.

I kneel down, pushing her off balance and making her tip back a little. She reaches out, grasping the fabric of my jeans to steady herself. I grab her face and grip it firmly, squeezing her cheeks. "There's something wrong with you."

"It's your fault."

"What?" I look from one eye to the other, trying to see what's right in front of me, but failing utterly. "How do you figure that?"

"You left me there. My father hired you to—"

I push hard and she careens backwards onto the floor. She lets off a grunt and then turns over on her side, pulling her knees up to her chest. "Just do whatever you're going to do. I don't care anymore."

"Do you have any idea what's going on?" I walk across the room and then pace back, stopping with the tip of my boot so close to her lips, it might be touching. "Any idea who you are? *What* you are?"

She says nothing. Her eyes are open, but she's checked out.

"What happens when he says that word—"

"Just fuck me."

"You're a virgin," I sneer. "Remember?"

She pushes herself up with one hand, straining her neck to look me in the eye. "I am. But you don't deserve to know the story, Case. You don't deserve to know what that word does. You don't deserve to know anything. But if you want to be the first to fuck my pussy, then whatever. Take it. Take whatever you want. You're gonna anyway."

My mind whirls with the only important detail in that statement. "You really expect me to believe that he only ever fucked you in the ass?"

"You said you were watching me. You should know." She's on her feet in an instant, her fist coming at me. She connects with my cheek. Hard.

But not hard enough. I grab her arm and drag her back over to the wall. And this time, I don't ask her to hold on. I tie the bitch up. I clamp the cuffs on her wrists and tighten the chain until her arms are above her head. Her feet are still kicking and she's calling me every name in the book. I take a few blows and a knee to my chest as I grab an ankle and attach the shackle. She's still got one foot free when she stops the fight.

She seethes with hate and anger. Her breath is rushing out. Her hair is covering her face, blowing out a little with each exhale. "Do it," she growls. "Take whatever you want, you stupid coward. My father hired you to save me! And you left me there!"

"I thought that was the best thing that ever happened to you?" I clamp the second shackle on her ankle and look up at her. Caught. "I thought he was your dream guy. I thought—"

She spits on me. It lands on my forehead.

"You're gonna regret that."

"I don't think so," she says, her words low and her tone gruff, like she's exhausted. "I'm not gonna do it, Case. I'm not gonna do any of it anymore. I'm gonna piss you off so much you'll have no *choice* but to kill me."

"I can torture you, ya stupid bitch."

And then she laughs. "No, you can't." She laughs again, louder this time. Wilder. Like she's losing touch with reality.

"You can't torture me, Case. I've been through anything you can think up and more." She sneers at me. "And I have a secret. I have lots of secrets, actually. But this one takes away all your power."

I know what she's gonna say before she does and I stand up quickly, trying to cover her mouth with my hand. But it slips by me.

"Hush," she says. "All I gotta do is tell myself to hush and no one can hurt me." She looks up, through the strands of hair that are still wet from the bath and probably soaking up the sweat that is running down her face, even though this room can't be anywhere near warm, let alone hot.

"You're a sick bitch."

"Says one psycho to the next."

I grab her throat. "Let's pick up where we left off and see if we can't tip the scales in my favor."

"It's your party, Case. I'm just along for the ride." Her eyes blaze with expectations. "Fuck me. See how far it gets you. The hard fuck, you say? That's what you think will teach me a lesson? You think the hard fuck is something new for me? Ha!" She laughs again. The crazy laugh. The laugh that says, *We're done here*.

I step back. The soles of my bare feet are cold on the concrete floor as I walk away. When I get to the fire I turn my back to it, letting what little is left warm me up. "I think you've misunderstand what the hard fuck is."

"I'm gonna make you weep, Sydney," she says in a fake voice. *"I'm gonna make that fuck so hard you'll weep.* Well, I'm not sure why this is a newsflash, since you said you've been watching, but newsflash, asshole — I always weep." She spits in my direction, but I'm too far away to hit this time. "Your game is old. Your methods are tired. Your knowledge is *lacking*."

She's like a little demon chained to a wall. That's how she looks right now.

"You want me to tell you what I know?" She pauses, but I don't say anything. This is not going at all how I planned it. "I know what you're looking for. I know where Garrett is. But it's locked up in that place I keep all my secrets. The dark place. Take me there, Merc. Meet me there in the dark and I'll tell you everything you want to know."

Her use of my trade name brings me back to my senses. She's a small girl chained to a wall. I'm a six-foot-something assassin. One of the best in the world. She's proud to be able to take the violence. I'm proud about how I dish it out. But what she's saying is the rambling of someone who has lost touch. I'm not sure anything I get will be reliable. "How?"

"Drugs," she says, her voice suddenly soft.

I walk forward until I get right up next to her naked body. "Been there, done that, cowgirl. We're gonna try something different this time." I lean in and kiss her. Her teeth are there as she tries to bite me. But I calmly hold her head with both hands and force her nose to bump against mine. "I'll meet you in the dark. But we're gonna get there my way this time."

"Those other ways?" she questions back, her voice still soft. Even her breathing is soft. "Those were my ways?" That makes her turn so she has space to laugh. "I'm pretty sure you've been driving this car, Merc. I'm pretty sure I wasn't the one pushing drugs in me for the past few days."

"Weeks," I correct her. And it works, because that revelation throws her.

"You're lying. It's only been a few days."

"Versed, sweetie." I lean down and kiss her. This time she holds still for it, but she doesn't respond. "It's a drug. Versed makes it all go away. I've had you for two weeks. Your man, Brett, he never even looked for you. You've got no one who cares, Sydney. So be a good girl and tell me what you know. Then I'll drug you again. Walk out of here. And never look back. And when you wake up you'll find all the gear you need to start over. How's that for a deal?"

"You lie."

"Or we can do the hard fuck first." I smile at that. And then I dip my fingers between her legs and push one against her entrance. She's slightly wet. "You want me to relieve you of that pesky v-card? I'm pretty sure Garrett fucked your pussy. I never saw it, just the assplay. But he's not the kind of guy who saves shit for later."

"Until he is," she quips back. "He has patience you'd never understand."

"Sticking up for him again?" I smile. Because her leverage over me is gone now. "Hmmm? He's still your guy? The man in your dreams? Taking you fishing? Giving your code words to trigger your brainwashing? I bet he fucked you plenty of times while you were under. Right?"

She stares up at me, squinting. "Kill me. Just do it. Kill me and let me go."

I push my leg forward until my thigh rests against her pussy and press my chest against her breasts. "I plan on it, Syd. Just not the way you want me to. Because the hard fuck, wildcat, isn't hard because I pound the shit out of women and choke them unconscious. That's someone else's version. My version is hard because you have to beg for it."

She spits again, this time hitting me on the mouth.

I kiss her and give it back. She catches my lip this time, biting down hard, drawing blood. But I just push her off me and smile. "I like the taste of blood, Syd. Haven't you figured that out yet? You don't call yourself a killer and not like the taste of blood. It turns me on, bitch. Now beg for it."

"Fuck you."

"Oh, I'm certainly gonna fuck you. But you're gonna beg for it. And you're gonna tell me what I want to know. Because I'm gonna retrain you, Sydney. I'm gonna retrain that fucked-up mind of yours." I tap her on the head a few times to illustrate my point. "I'm gonna reprogram you. Take you down into that dark place you love so much and turn the fucking lights on."

EIGHTEEN

SYDNEY

"Sometimes it's the thing you've been running from that can help the most."

– Sydney

I close my eyes so he can't see me, but his mouth is back on mine, his tongue searching for the things I'm hiding. He knows where to find them, too. I know he does. Of all the secrets I'm keeping, that's the only one I *need* to keep. I need to do whatever it takes to keep that secret.

"I can find Garrett," I say. "I can find him. Just tell me to hush. Tell me to hush and start asking questions."

"No," Case says sternly, but in a low voice. "It's a lie, Sydney. He's pumped you up with so much misinformation you have no idea what's real. But every trigger has a release. And that's the first thing I need from you. Once I get the release, we can try this all again. You know the release, Sydney. You've heard it many times. All I need is for you to remember. And if you tell me what that word is, I'll back

159

off. I'll let you keep that dark place. Feel free to go there for an extended visit. Hell, never come back for all I care. How's that for a deal?"

My mind is whirling. I might even black out, because the next thing I know Case has me wrapped up in his arms. Holding me tight. His fingers are between my legs, gently stroking up and down. They push inside me, then draw back. He kisses me. So, so softly. His lips cover my mouth, then retreat, and enter again. My tongue reaches for him. We tangle together like that for a few moments until he pulls away, his hands cupping my face. I suck in a breath, trying to make sense of things.

"What's the word, Sydney? What's the word Garrett uses to bring you out of it?"

I open my eyes and stare up at Case's face. His fingers are back inside me, easing in and out, his thumb strumming my clit like it's an instrument. It feels so fucking good. His other hand goes to his belt. A few jingles later I'm released, his pants are open, and he's got my palm over his hard cock.

I squeeze it...

I'm in my bedroom sitting on the edge of the bed. Garrett is looking at my stuffed animals. "You're too young to be a cat lady, Syd."

I laugh a little and stretch my legs out.

"You must have two dozen of them."

"So I like cats," I quip back. "Sue me."

He stands in front of me and takes my face in his hands. I look up at him with complete trust. "I like dogs." I just blink at him. "They're loyal. They're obedient. And they don't judge me."

"I don't judge you, Garrett."

"I know, Syd. You're a dog, baby. You're a dog if there ever was one." He pets my hair. "You're good, and loyal, and soft."

My knees hit the hard concrete floor, my hands on Case's hips. The tip of his cock slips between my lips and I swallow.

He moans, his hand fisting my hair.

My tongue begins, my palms working their magic as I suck him off, twisting their way up and down his thick shaft.

"Way too many cats in here," Garrett says, pointing to the shirt I'm wearing.

"It's a football jersey," I explain, eager for his touch and focus to remain totally on me. But he's staring at the cartoon picture of a wildcat on my jersey.

"Wildcats?" He says it like a question.

Case pulls his dick out and pumps it hard a few times. I open my mouth and stick out my tongue, my eyes only on him. He shoots his come on my face, squirting me in the eye, making me blink. It's warm and maybe a little comforting as it settles on my cheek.

"No," I tell Garrett. "That's not it. Try again."

He smiles at me from above, both hands cupping my face again. "What is it, Syd?"

I smile back, a warm feeling taking over my body. And then I tell him.

"Bobcat?" Case asks, still breathing hard from his release. I look at the floor. Case puts himself back together. "That's it? Bobcat?"

I hang my head and feel the tears slip out. I am ashamed for the things I've done. I am ashamed for the things I do. I am nothing but shame.

Case walks out of the room, leaving me there on the floor. I look up at the table where he said he killed my father, and then over to the fire. Everything about me is cold. So I crawl over to the fire and lie down on the stone hearth.

I watch those flames and they remind me of my life. Rising, falling, some sparks here and there. Warm.

Not this life, though. That life. The one where this girl named Syd lives in that pretty teenage bedroom. And all the cats are dogs now.

I don't know how long I stay this way, living half in my dream and half in my nightmare. But the door remains open. Case never bothered to lock it when he left. There's lights on out there too. Some of it leaks into my cell.

I don't move. Not even a little bit. He might not even be here. He might've left already. Got whatever it was he needed and left.

I fall asleep wondering which is more real. Which one holds more promise. Which place holds my escape.

||||||||||

"Sydney?"

He calls me Sydney. This is how I know it's the nightmare and not the dream.

"Sydney? Are you hungry?"

I have never felt less hungry than right at this very moment. I reach up to scratch an itch on my face and realize it's his dried come.

I close my eyes again after that. I prefer the dream Garrett to the real-life Case.

Sometime later he comes back. Again with my name. Only this time when I don't answer, he lifts me up in his arms and takes me to the bathroom and places me on the counter.

I'm not asleep. I have doubts that any of that was sleep. So I just watch him as he wets a towel and starts cleaning my face. I don't say anything, but he talks here and there as he works.

"It's a good start," he says once. Then, "We won't need any more drugs. So you'll feel better soon."

What did he have me on? I think I remember Versed. But I've been given drugs my whole life. Whatever this is, it wipes my world. Versed doesn't wipe a world away.

"I'd like to keep taking the drugs, if you don't mind."

I think my voice startles him. He stops his washing, but he doesn't answer.

It doesn't matter. The answer is no. Whatever I want, they give me the opposite. Sydney wants a mother? They give her a father. Sydney wants a boyfriend? They give her a monster. Sydney wants to go to college? They give her a bar.

The only good thing they ever gave me was that bar. And even though I didn't want it at the time, it was a nice prize.

I like to work long hours. I hate going home. And once Garrett disappeared, there was always a fear that one night I'd go home and he'd be back.

And then Brett came. And we fit together like we were made for each other. Like two pieces to the same puzzle. His light to my dark. His easy smile to my tight scowl. His muscular upper body to my soft breasts. He was perfection.

Why did I leave the lodge that night? I could be married now. I could be living back in Cheyenne in the house he has. No more sleeping above the bar in the office because I was afraid to go home. I could be sleeping next to him right now.

I want to cry.

I want to cry so bad.

"We can try the truth instead."

I don't know how Case can read my mind like that.

"After he disappeared, how many times did Garrett meet you in the apartment you shared?"

"He never came back."

"He did, Sydney. He came back. You disappeared a few times. And those were just while I was watching. Who knows how many times he came and took you away when I wasn't watching."

I picture my life after Garrett left. I really wanted him to be dead. But a part of me always knew he wasn't. "Sometimes I'd stay at the bar so many nights in a row, when I got home I'd just crash out."

"Did you have insomnia?"

I'm on the couch now, but I don't remember getting here. Case is sitting on one end and I'm lying down, taking up too much space. My feet are in his lap and he's tracing a line up my ankle.

"Always."

I have clothes on too. A man's t-shirt. Black. And a pair of sweats. Gray. My feet are cold because I have no socks.

"So when you fell asleep, you'd just crash out? Did people at the bar miss you?"

"I have days off."

He's silent after that.

I slide my feet out of his lap and pull them up to my chest. I don't want to be touched. The flames dance along inside the fireplace. I can see through to the other side. I picture my body lying there. This is his view of me. This is my view of me now too.

I close my eyes. Because I'm ugly.

The next time I open them, I'm back in my cell. I'm on a soft rug—not covered in vomit like the last one—so that's an improvement.

The guitar music floats across the flames and soothes me. His fingers squeak along the strings. He strums and hums and I hear the lyrics in my head. It's a song about nothing. About being nothing. About wanting nothing. About having nothing.

It's a pretty good song.

"You hungry yet?" he says, his fingers never missing.

I close my eyes again. I'd like to think I'm Zen enough to want nothing. But I'm not. I want more.

"More what?" Case asks.

"Drugs."

"I stopped the drugs two days ago, Sydney."

I realize my hair is damp and I wonder how much I missed this time.

"We need to continue. I have more questions."

"I have no more answers."

"You have all the answers, Syd."

I smile at him. Standing there out on the riverbank, pole in hand. "I thought you left me." A sob escapes with the final word. "I'm so tired of being alone."

NINETEEN

MERI

"Words can be poems, or songs, or gifts. Words can also be threats, lies, and broken promises. You should learn the difference."
– Case

"Where would I go?" I ask her. She's distant, as usual. But she's talking again, so that's good.

"It's me who leaves."

She's gone. I'm not sure she's got anything left to tell, and even if she does, I'm not sure any of it will be reliable.

I was in the army for four years. Just enough time to change the course of everything. I came straight out of South Boston, a strange kid with a mind most men would covet and a body that could be molded and trained to back his shit up.

I'm the first to admit I'm sick and twisted. Kicked out of every school in the neighborhood. Truant for weeks and months at a time. A blight on the schedules of every social worker I ever encountered. And yet here I am. A player.

Did they see that one coming? Did MIT, and Harvard, and Cambridge see that one coming?

Of course they did. That's why they all wanted me.

And if people want you, your best bet is to turn and walk the other way.

The army was where my feet took me. One enlistment, one army general classification test, and one fucked-up mission later — not in the desert, no. In the US. That's where I did all my field work. Where I did all my active duty.

That is what led me to this guy I am today.

They made so many mistakes with me. Letting me in the army was the first. But when someone like me shows up for a war and can wield the weapons they know exist, but don't have enough manpower to use effectively, well, he's in.

They reclassified me six times in the first six months after basic. Creamed their fucking panties with each promotion. *Merric,* they said. *Merric Case is exactly the kind of man we require.*

Garrett McGovern was that man too. We are alike in all the ways that count to career warmongers. But we are different in the only way that matters.

I work alone. I might call on friends for help in certain missions. But I work alone. There is no team in I.

I don't think it ever occurred to them that I'd leave. Not after the success we had. Not even after the failure. What is failure to them, anyway? Just a temporary setback.

That's what my leaving was too, I guess. Nothing but a temporary setback. Because they got me on new jobs even though I was a civilian. Time after time after time.

But the last time? That time I was sent to save Sydney and saved Sasha instead? That cut all the ties that bind.

Two girls. One mission. And the absolute worst possible outcome. For them, anyway.

Sydney is collateral damage. She is nothing more than a pawn. She is weak and pathetic in all the ways that Sasha is strong and brave.

I made the right choice that day. Sasha was the right choice. Sydney is just a leftover that needs to be swept under the rug.

But that job never ended. Not when I left her that day. Not when I helped Sasha get her revenge. Not when I stole hundreds of millions of dollars straight out of their deep fucking pockets.

It's gonna end soon though. This is it. My end. Sydney's end as well.

She stirs on the bed and I know she's coming back again. This drifting she does, I have no clue what it means other than they did a good job on her. She's given up nothing of real importance. Her release word is inconsequential in the long run. It's a good first step. But is she even worth all the steps between here and victory?

171

I doubt it.

She turns over and places a hand on my leg. I'm sitting up in bed, smoking, as I let it all play out in my head. There were so many potential outcomes before she ran. But now there are only two.

I let her live. I let her die.

If I let her live and start working her for real, I get less than ideal intel. Less than reliable, I should say.

If I let her die as soon as that's over, I can take what I want right now and sift through it objectively later.

Her hand slips down my leg and grabs my cock.

I react. I like sexy Sydney a little more than I'd like to admit. I grab her hands and flip her over on her stomach. She whimpers, but not in a bad way.

"I'll take that hard fuck now, Syd."

TWENTY

"I like the sting of reality. It reminds me I have no control over any of this."

– Sydney

yd.

"Don't call me—"

His hand wraps under and around my throat, not squeezing the breath from me, but cutting off my protests. "Let's review, Sydney. I push your limits. You beg me for more. Got it?"

"Is this how you killed the other girls you were close with," I squeak past his grip. "Pushing their limits? Is this how you'll kill me? Begging you for more?"

"You can only hope." A hand slips under my hips and I automatically lift them up to allow him access. "Because hey, if it's your time to go, might as well go out screaming with pleasure instead of screaming in pain."

"Ha. I know you didn't kill those girls."

"Then why start a fight?" He plays with my clit as he says the words.

I bite my lip and hold in the moan. "Because that's what you want, right? The fight? That's what turns you on? Garrett likes submission. But that's how the two of you are different. You like the fight."

He yanks my hair so hard I cry out. I try to look up to gauge his reaction to my words, but he holds the hair close to my scalp, preventing me from seeing his face as he leans into my shoulder and whispers in my ear. "Don't compare me to him. We parted ways for a reason. We're not the same, wildcat. He kills by accident. I kill with purpose."

The words tickle my ear and I shudder. Not from his fingers, still doing that very thrilling circular motion over my sweet spot, but from the fact that he didn't deny killing the other girls even though I know he didn't. I feel a small surge of power. "So you're saying you did kill them?"

"What do you know about *them*?"

"I know they were your girlfriends. I know they went missing. And I know you didn't kill them. You sent them away."

He chuckles a little. He sounds almost normal when he does it, too, like it really is funny. "You know nothing."

"I know you didn't kill them because I was there when Garrett did."

Case goes still above me.

174

"He knew you set it up to make it look like they went missing. But he found them. Long time ago, Case. He found them and brought them up into the mountains where we were staying, and he made me watch."

"You're lying."

"He took a picture of me with a blood-covered knife to the one girl's throat."

"Liar."

"He said he was gonna send it to you if I didn't do as I was told. And then you'd come take care of me for him. And isn't that funny? That you threaten to kill Brett if I don't do what you say? You and Garrett are more alike than you think, Case. You just can't bring yourself to admit it."

There is a brief moment of silence and during these microseconds, I tell myself I didn't actually say that.

Case's fist crashes against my head, dragging me far away from that delusional wish. I see the blackness before he even starts squeezing my throat. I grab at him, buck my back and try to get him off me, cursing myself for being in such a submissive position in the first place. He flips me over, but instead of more blows, he gets up, spreads my legs and eases himself between them.

I hold my breath.

He licks me. He licks and kisses each of the poke marks he made on my upper thighs with his knife. "Did that hurt?" he asks.

"What do you think?"

"I think you liked it. I think you wanted more." He grins at me between my legs. "I think you want me to do more right now."

He does more. His mouth reaches higher, his hands gripping my legs a little bit tighter as his head moves towards my pussy.

I don't move.

He looks up as he hikes my knees up to my face and sweeps his tongue across my folds. His lips part and then he sucks my clit into his mouth. Not hard and demanding, but with just the right amount of swirling pressure to make me moan out and arch my back. No one has ever licked me there before.

He slips in a finger and teases me in two ways now. This feels so good, I have to close my eyes to block him out.

"You still wanna fight me, wildcat? You still want to have that conversation?"

But I don't. I said too much. So I bite my lip and tip my head back, enjoying it.

"You got it all wrong, Syd." I hate that he calls me that. "I already told you. The hard fuck is hard on you because I push your limits. Not because I fuck you hard."

"So push me," I whisper. "Throw me over the edge of the cliff, Case. And if you want to kill me in the process, well, I'd love for my end to be filled with so much irony."

He never responds. Or he does respond, but not with words. The time for talking is over.

He gets up and stands next to the bed. I watch the muscles in his arms move as he drops his pants and steps out of them, giving them a swift kick across the floor.

I never even try to get away. It's just not in my nature. I've been waiting for this moment. And I even take it one step further and lift both arms over my head and grab hold of the rusted iron headboard.

The crooked smile on his face says this was a good move.

We are players. We are playing.

I track his body, watching the fluid moment of what makes him so dangerous, as he walks to the foot of the bed, grabs my ankles, and pulls me so hard my shoulders cry out in pain before I have the good sense to let go of the headboard.

My body is twirled around and positioned until my head is hanging off the end of the mattress. His cock is right in front of my face, but I meet his gaze. His amber eyes are glowing from the dying firelight that leaks in from the other room.

I wait for the questions to start. He must have so many.

But he is silent as he eases his cock into my mouth. It slips to the back of my throat and my hands are instinctively there, telling him to stop.

"Shhh," he says, reminding me I have no say in the

gentlest of ways. He takes each of my hands in his and laces our fingers together, giving me a squeeze of encouragement as he pushes past my limit.

I gag, but breathe through it the way Garrett taught me. And that was my yes.

He fucks my mouth until I am choking on my own spit. But instead of withdrawing when I feel like I will drown on my own saliva, he simply turns my head to the side and lets it fall out of my mouth.

His hands never let go of mine. I never try to stop him again.

He keeps going, my head bobbing back and forth against the side of the mattress until I'm dizzy. And then he releases down my throat and holds me down with my own hands until I swallow.

Only then does he release me and back away, never taking his eyes off mine.

I hold that stare and wait for a signal like Garrett used to give.

"I'm waiting, bobcat," he says.

I cringe at the name. It's so degrading. But I'm running on instincts now. The training has taken over and I'm powerless to stop it, even if I wanted to. And I don't. So, "More, please," is my response.

"More what?"

"Take it all, Case. You told me eight years ago you owned

me. So take it. Take me. Take me the way you promised when you left me behind to die."

His hands are under my shoulders, urging me to sit up. I comply. Because that's my job here tonight. And then he grabs my hair and turns me around so my head is at the top of the bed once more. I grab the rusty rails and open my legs, inviting him in.

He slaps my tit, then my face, holding it in a tight squeeze. So hard I bite my tongue and taste blood. "Whore," he whispers.

"Your whore," I whisper back.

"Don't fucking forget it."

"It's my purpose in life, Case."

He slaps my face again, but I like the sting. I like the sting and I like the way his cock drags across my clit now that he's on top of me.

His tip pushes against my pussy and even though I'm scared out of my mind, I ache for it. He thrusts inside me and I grip the rails harder. I close my eyes, but another slap brings me back to attention. He pumps inside of me, his huge cock stretching me so wide the tears fall down my face.

But then he pauses long enough to lie down next to me and turn me on my side. His hand eases down to my clit and he begins to strum as he fucks me. He plays me like the guitar. And I play him back—like a player.

I swell with feelings. I have never felt such emotion.

JA HUSS

Such hate and love. Such pain and pleasure.

I come like that. A conflict of emotions. A paradox. Simultaneously filled up and empty at the same time.

He pulls out and comes with me, once again shooting hot semen across my back in long squirts.

He rolls over, breathing heavier than I am. I turn to watch his reaction. His revelation, if you will. And I get something I never expected. A smile. "It's not a hard fuck if it's easy, Syd."

"I'm a good little actress, Case. This is the hardest thing I've ever done." My eyes dart down to his cock, still erect, even after coming twice in the span of twenty minutes.

I look up, quick enough to catch his gaze dropping to where mine went. There's a hint of confusion on his face as he sees the proof of what I told him.

"What the fuck?" He looks up from the blood covering his dick and finds my face. "What the fuck?"

"I told you," I say in a hushed voice. The voice of trickery and lies. The voice of abuse and pain. The voice of the *hush*. "Garrett saved me for you, Case. He said to tell you to consider me a gift. For making you kill that girl." I don't want to add the rest. But I do anyway. I've practiced it enough times for it to roll off my tongue like water. "For making you kill her before you got a chance to fuck the virgin out of her."

He's quick to respond, I'll give him that. Because he's

180

got that syringe out of the bedside table faster than I can turn away. He shoots it into my arm as I gaze up into his eyes. "Don't feel bad," I say as the sting of the drugs shoots through my muscle. "It was always you, Case."

"What the fuck are you talking about?"

"My dream guy. The one who taught me how to save myself. The one who came back after you left me there to die. He was always you."

TWENTY-ONE

"It's easy to hide in the dark. But the reckoning always comes in the light."

– Sydney

I t's dark. It's cold. And I'm alone. Not alone like he's in the other room. But alone alone. Like he's gone.

And can I blame him?

My stomach cramps so bad, I force myself to sit up and throw my feet over the side. I need to get to the bathroom. But as soon as I stand up and step forward, the blackness threatens to take over.

Fuck that. I refuse to soil myself one more time. I've been drugged for so long, I have no idea how many disgusting acts my body has committed over the course of this ordeal. But it's over now. So I force myself to shuffle out the door, which is open, and into the bathroom. I don't bother flicking on the lights, just sit on the toilet and relieve myself.

When I'm done, I run a bath in the dark and then go

start a fire in the fireplace. There's a package on the couch. I rip the brown paper open and take out a pair of white snow pants and a white ski jacket. White gloves, hat, scarf, and boots. There's also a pair of jeans that is close enough to my size, a long-sleeved shirt, and a set of keys.

Under that is a wad of money and a cell phone.

There is no note.

"Best-case scenario," Garrett says, "is that we fuck up his reality so bad, he leaves you there."

I guess this is the best-case scenario. And as best-case scenarios go, it could be a lot worse.

I go back to the bathroom, flick on the lights, and lower myself into the water. There's bloodstains on my inner thighs still. A reminder of what I did. I rub my hand over them a few times and they disappear. Washed clean.

All the stuff is still here. Shampoo, conditioner—which I didn't use the last time I took a bath—even a razor. So I take my time before getting out, drying off, and walking naked out into the living room to put on my clothes.

When I'm ready I put the fire out, turn off all the lights, and lock the cabin door as I step out into the blowing snow.

In front of me is a Snowcat. Fitting, really. Since cats seem to be the trigger of change for me.

In front of that is a trail.

I get in the Snowcat and start it up, put one hand on the gas and the other on the two levers that control the treads, and ease forward out into the dark. The moon is out, and when you combine that with the fresh snow, it's not as dark as it could be. The trail is easy to follow.

I think about Case the whole time.

Does he understand what happened? Does he feel like a fool? Does he feel victorious? Does he feel vindicated? Did my v-card make up for the one he never took all those years ago, back when he and Garrett were in the army together?

Does he have regrets?

That makes me laugh. And that laugh allows me to smile as I make my way on the trail. It's almost inconceivable that I will make it out of here alive, so when I get to a fork in the path—the trail leading to the right, but the tracks of a snow machine veer off to the left—I feel a rush of relief that he's not done with me yet.

Why give me a choice to leave if he is done?

I don't want to leave. In fact, if this fork had not appeared, I'd have been very disappointed.

It's all about the devil you know. And Garrett's demons are unknowable. But Case is a mystery with a solution.

I take the path to the left and come up on that snow machine that ran out of gas about a half a mile on.

I stop the Cat and peer through the trees just to make sure I saw it right the first time.

The house. It's really there. And the third-floor window — just a crow's nest architectural detail that juts out from the roof — is lit up like a beacon in the coming night.

I take a deep breath and press the levers, slowly easing forward towards my final mission.

When I get to the house I shut off the engine and step out of the cab and walk up to the door to find a note.

Turn back, Syd. Go back where you came from. The bar is still there. Brett shut it down after I took you, but it's still there and so is he. He's waiting for you back in that life. I can handle things from here.

What a funny guy. I even laugh as I look up at the third-story lights. "Merric Case, you have no idea what's coming."

I open the door, step in, and close it behind me.

Inside it's warm. Uncomfortably so, when I'm wearing all this winter gear. I listen in the silence that takes over after the closing door. Nothing. Not even the hum of a refrigerator. I don't see a kitchen from the foyer, and it is quite a foyer, with ceilings stretching up twenty feet at least. The inside has the same cabin feel that the outside does. Well, in a more lifestyles-of-the-rich-and-famous kind of way. It's got to be five or six times as big as the cabin I just came out of. One thing I can see from the foyer is the view. Breathtaking floor-to-ceiling windows showcase tall shadows that must be a coniferous forest that covers the valley, and the outline of snow-covered mountains.

I take a deep breath as I search for lights off in the distance, some sign of civilization, but the only light is the moon and the shine of the snow.

In the time it takes me to come to the conclusion that there is no way in hell anyone would ever find me here, let alone rescue me if things get worse, I start sweating profusely. Too many drugs. Too much frigid air outside. And too much artificial heat in here.

I unwrap my scarf and pull it off. The relief is immediate, but not enough. I take off the gloves next, stuffing both of these things into my coat pocket.

The strum of a guitar makes me turn, searching for the source. It sounds far away.

I look up and see a second-story loft behind me. It's open to the downstairs, so that can't be where he is. There must be more rooms beyond. I head towards the staircase, trying to keep my eyes both above and in front of me as I navigate the unfamiliar home. There are small lights on in various places, but not enough to take this house out of the shadows of a midwinter evening.

The strumming stops just as I place my boot on the first step. I stop with it. Listening. Nothing.

Then more strumming. That song again. The one I listen to all the time. Why does he play it?

Why does he do anything, Syd?

Revenge, I think. I mean, that's the only solid answer I can come up with for why. Why take me? Why leave me, for that matter? Why tell me he'd be back? I don't understand any of this. Not the shit that happened in the past and not the shit that's happening now.

Like — why am I here? Not that I could've gotten far in that Snowcat if there are no towns around here. But that's not why I came inside. I have camped in worse conditions than this. With the right gear — and the clothes he gave me count as that — it's not so bad. And the Cat was enclosed, so no danger of mountain lions or wolves. The bears are sleeping. So even though I don't have a gun, I don't need one. Surely there is something at the end of that path he cleared for me. A truck, maybe?

Probably. I didn't see any cars outside. There was a building that might be a garage. And he had to get up here somehow. But I'm pretty sure this place is not where one spends a winter. Roads close for the winter in Montana.

This cabin has the feel of a place that closes over winter. It's probably not even his.

I take another step on the stairs and the wood creaks a little. But the strumming upstairs never stops.

He has to know I'm here. Had to see the light from the Cat as I came up to the house. Had to feel the disturbance in the inside air as I opened and closed the front door. I'd have noticed all these things with my limited skills. Merric Case's skills might be a lot of things, but limited is not one of them. I've heard stories.

I take the next twenty steps without stopping and find myself in the loft. But it's deceiving from the first floor, because there's a whole other house up here. Another staircase, in fact, not connected to this one.

It's a great open space with a few rooms scattered around. Bedrooms, I think. A bathroom. I walk past those and head towards the second staircase. The music is louder here, so that's where he is. Up in the very top. In the crow's nest thing I saw from outside.

I climb up two steps, stop, listen, then climb all the way up until I get to the top.

The room is circular, nothing but glass on all sides. The ceiling is taller than it looked outside, also glass. Merric Case is stretched out on a half-moon — bed, couch — covered in fluffy white blankets and pillows that line the windows. His feet and chest are bare, his jeans faded and ripped. His fingers never stop playing and he never looks away as I leave the stairwell and enter the room.

I'm burning up from heat in this coat.

I stop and wait for him to say something, but he doesn't. Just keeps playing that song.

I look down at my feet, a self-conscious move — a show of doubt, if I'm being honest — and see that my boots have tracked up snow. It melts into a little puddle beneath my feet. When I look back up he's staring at my boots too, frowning.

It's absurd to think he cares about the water damaging his hardwood floors, but that's the impression I get. "Should I take them off?"

He looks back up at me and the strumming stops. "Why are you here?"

I don't have anything to say to that. So I just stare at him.

"Did you at least enjoy it?"

"What?"

He resumes his playing and looks down at the fingers on his right hand as they pluck the strings. A new tune. Something simple. Just a melody.

"The sex," he says, still paying attention to his instrument.

"Oh."

"It was planned then, huh?"

His eyes burn into me as he waits. I'm preoccupied by the music and the memory of my first time. I let out a long sigh and turn away, kick off my boots and step into a puddle of water that soaks my socks. I pull them off as well, unzip my jacket and shove that down my arms.

He stares at me the whole time.

I drop the jacket on the floor next to my boots and then work on the snow pants. This takes me several minutes, and

I have to sit down on the bed once I get them over my hips. I throw those on the floor next to my coat. And then I'm in my jeans and long-sleeved shirt.

"Did I plan on letting you take my virginity?" I laugh a little and squirm in my seat. "No, Case. I don't get to plan anything. I carry out orders."

"So Garrett ordered you to sleep with me?"

"It was a message."

"Yeah?" Case asks, setting the guitar down on the couch bed next to him. He scoots forward, so he's no longer sprawled out and his feet are on the floor. "I'm not sure I speak that language, so why not enlighten me." He's pissed, I realize. For being tricked into this. I have no sympathy for that. But I can empathize. "Why not explain it, Syd. Just get it all out in the open so I can decide what to do with you."

"If that's supposed to scare me, it doesn't."

He smiles, but not in a nice way. "I'm sure." He stands up and walks over to me. He reaches out before he's close, and when he is, he cups my face and lifts my gaze up to meet his. "What. Was. The message, Syd?"

"You're even now," I say matter-of-factly. "That was the message."

"How does he figure that?"

I shrug. This makes Case drop his hands. I take a deep breath. "I don't know the story behind you two. None of it. So I have no idea."

"You're lying." He stares into me and this makes me shift my position. "Is your job done, then? You were here to what? Trick me into taking your virginity to even up a score that was never uneven, in a game I was never playing?" He laughs. "Please."

I don't even know what that means. "I'm yours anyway. So what do you care?"

"You're a gift then?"

I shrug again.

"So Brett? He's in on this how?"

"He's not."

"I don't believe you."

"I don't care."

"Get out."

"No." I stand and point at the walls made of glass. "There's nothing out there. There's nowhere to go."

"Get back in the Cat. Go back the way you came. And follow the trail I cleared for you. I've made arrangements."

"No," I say again. "I'm not leaving here. I've got questions. I've got a lot of fucking questions." My voice rises. Not much. I'm not a yeller. I don't lose control easily. "And I want answers. I want to know why you people have been fucking with my life since I was little. Why, Case? What the fuck did I ever do to you? Why take me? Why do any of this if you're just going to send me away?"

"You want answers?" He bends down so we are eye

level, placing his hands on his knees and leaning forward. "You sure about that, Sydney?"

I swallow down the fear that's rising in my chest. "Yes."

"Why would I give them to you?" He straightens up again, emphasizing the height difference between us. Like he needs this advantage.

There is no good answer for that. None at all. Why would he give them to me?

He laughs. "You don't have any idea what's going on here, do you? You're so fucking lost."

"So find me."

He turns and walks over to the stairs. Walking out, I realize. "I can't." He looks over his shoulder at me. A flash of light catches in his amber eyes and sends a chill up my spine. "It's too late for you. Too late for all of this. Everything—" He stops to take a breath. "Everything I feared would happen, well, it's happening. No, it's already done. And now I have to worry about me, Sydney Channing. And the people I actually care about, the few decent human beings on this goddamned planet I love, they are the only ones who matter now. Because if Garrett thinks this shit is over because he gave me his prize virgin, he's mistaken. Fuck you and your boyfriend. Fuck you and your gift. Fuck you and your problems, Sydney. Just fuck you. This has gone on long enough. The only girl I'm interested in now is Sasha."

And just like that, he walks away.

Again.

TWENTY-TWO

MARC

"When you find yourself alone with no options... lie."
- Sydney

I only get two steps towards the stairs when she hurls herself at my back. I lurch forward, grab the railing, and just barely stop a fall that could've broken my neck. I reach behind me, grab her upper arm, and swing her around. She hits the floor hard, her head cracking against the banister, and growls out something unintelligible.

"What the fuck are you doing?"

She's back on her feet the moment it takes for me to say those words, and I get another direct hit. This time she charges me like a bull. I stumble backwards again, lose my footing on the stairs for real this time, and we both fall over sideways. I break her fall, and a sharp pain travels down the nerve that leads to my hand. But there's no time to think about that, because she's on top of me, her fists swinging wildly for my face. She connects once, and then I snap out of it.

Girl or not, I'm gonna end this now.

I sit up and grab her hands, then give her a head butt that would knock almost anyone out. She sways backwards, stunned. Blood runs down her face where I cut her forehead open, and I swing my legs up. She is propelled forward over my head and crashes on the landing a few stairs below.

I catch my breath for a moment, sitting sideways on the stairs, to see if she will get up. I stand, jump down the stairs, and straddle her limp body. Her eyes are open though. And she's not dead.

I've been a soldier, a mercenary, and I've fought my way out of more bars in more countries than I can count.

That is a look of *enough*.

"You done?" I ask her, my chest still rising and falling, betraying how unsettled this has me. "You gonna stop? Because I can go all night, bitch."

I can. I just don't want to. I'm fucking sick of this girl.

She pulls herself up into a sitting position. Her back rests against the wall made of stacked logs. She's breathing heavy too, and she looks just as pissed off as I do. But the longer she stays silent, the clearer this all becomes.

She's mad, yeah. But she's more than that. The tears well up in her eyes and she presses her lips together, like she's trying to keep the words inside.

"Speak up," I yell. Loud enough to make her jump and angry enough to make her afraid. "Because that was it, Syd. That right there? That was my line and you just crossed it."

A trickle of blood seeps out of her mouth and I wonder, just for a split second, if she bit her tongue or if that's a sign of something more serious. But she wipes it away with the back of her hand and then spits on my goddamned floor.

I take a deep breath and ask for patience. And then I turn and walk back up the stairs. I grab her coat and snow pants and throw them down at her. The zipper on the jacket catches her lip and she yelps.

"Take the shit I gave you. Get out of my house. Get your ass back in that Cat. And take the path I spent all damn day plowing for you until you get to the end. There's two trucks there. One is yours. One is mine. Take yours. Leave mine. And never come back here. Do you understand me?" I hurl her boots next, and they hit the wall on each side of her head. Not by accident.

She stays still.

"Now!"

The tears fall down her cheeks before she can bow her head and hide them with her hair. "Just tell me why," she whispers. "That's all I want. One answer. Why?"

I hold up my hands with the urge to strangle her. "Why? What?"

"That night. Back at that cabin. The night you came to

save me—"

"I never came to save you, Sydney. Let's get that clear right now. I came to *get* you, yes. Because I got some information earlier in the day about you, Garrett, and your father. But it wasn't anything good, Syd. In fact, I've never heard such disgusting filth in all my life. I thought—" I stop and thread my fingers through my hair. "I thought you were a victim. That you needed help. That Garrett was controlling you. But you proved to me tonight that you're not. You don't need help. At least not the kind I thought. And he isn't controlling you, Sydney. You do his bidding because you want to. You're in on his plans because you like it. And let me tell you something right now. I saw you, Sydney. I saw you. I watched you and Garrett after all that shit went down. You weren't hard to find, either of you. Those two years you spent with him before he 'disappeared' should make you as sick as it makes me. And the fact that he kept you close, like a submissive dog, just made it all so much easier. I *saw* you."

She stands up, grabs her coat and snow pants, and hugs them to her chest as she looks me in the eye. "That wasn't me."

"Right." I laugh. "Let me guess. You have a twin?" I laugh again, then stop. Because hell, they all have twins, don't they? Harper has one. James has one. Why can't Sydney have one? Shit, maybe Sasha has one? I spin around and scrub my hand down my face as I consider this possibility.

"No," she snarls. "That's not what I meant."

I spin back, relieved. "Then what the fuck are you talking about?"

She grabs her boots and walks across the landing, then jumps down the stairs two at a time.

I just watch her go.

Let her go, that small bit of sanity left in my head tells me. *Just let her go.*

I do. I sit my ass down on the stairs and count the number of steps it takes her to get to the bottom. I'm still sitting there when she stops and then I listen to her pull on the snow gear. Two minutes go by, and then a rush of air through the house and the slam of the door down below tells me she took my advice.

But my curiosity is up now. I know this girl is not what she appears. I know she's had a lot of fucked-up years. Before I showed up in her life, and after. And I know that everything about her is a wildcard. She represents everything that could go wrong with my last mission. But I can't stop myself.

I follow her. I jump down to the next landing, and then take the stairs that lead to the first floor, hoping she's still outside when I get to the foyer.

I pull the door open and... she is. The way she parked

gives me a side view of her face. Her cheeks are already red under the interior dome light of the Cat, and she's cursing under her breath as she presses the ignition button.

Her head spins towards me, then she drags her attention back to starting the Cat.

I grab a coat and gloves from the mudroom off to the right of the foyer and slip my feet into a pair of boots before pulling the door closed behind me and going outside. "Let me do it." She slams the Cat's door closed before I can get there and flips me off through the ice-covered window. I pull it back open. "Locks are broken, genius."

"You want me to leave?" she growls. "Then back off and let me leave. I'm done with you. I'm done with all of this."

I pull her out of the cab and throw her down into the snow so I can take her place, and then check the choke and press the ignition.

It whines.

I look over at her and she's still lying down in the snow, her arms and legs spread wide, like she's a kid about to make a snow angel. "What'd you do to it?"

"Just go back inside, Case. I can take care of myself. You want me to leave, I'll leave."

I try the ignition again. Same shit. So I get out and slam the door. "Look, I don't know what you think is going on here, but you're crazy. Why didn't you leave? Huh? Why didn't you just follow the fucking path and go?"

"Because I need answers." She says it so softly, I almost miss it.

"I don't have any answers, Sydney." I cross the short distance between us and stand over her. "You're the one with the answers. You people—"

"I'm not one of them."

"The fuck you aren't! You're all the same. And I'll tell you something right now, I'm not falling for this act you've got going. I'm not falling for this pathetic girl thing you're pulling anymore. I told you. I *know* you. I've been watching you for years. I've seen you do so many despicable things. I've seen you at your worst."

"Well, I guess you have it all figured out then, don't you." She props herself up on her elbows so she can see me better. "You have nothing figured out, Case—"

"Quit fucking calling me Case." I can't stand that name. "No one calls me Case."

She considers this for a moment, letting me fume internally. "That's why I call you that. Because to everyone else you're Merc the killer. But ever since the day my father told me you were coming, I made you into Case the savior."

"You're sick."

"Yup," she says, getting to her feet after a few moments of struggle in the thick winter clothes. "I'm definitely that." And then she turns her back and starts walking towards the woods.

I wait it out. Wait for her to turn back so I can call her bluff. But she doesn't. She keeps walking. Right into the darkness.

And now what? I'm gonna let a girl walk out into the woods at night? Even this girl? I'm gonna let the wolves get a whiff of the blood running down her face? Let her fall in the snow and break an ankle?

An ankle, Merc?

I huff out a small laugh. I'm crazy. I've always been a little bit off, that's no secret. All the anger, and the violence, and the revenge. All the planning, and the waiting, and the watching. It's all crazy.

But this girl is far, far beyond any kind of crazy I'm used to dealing with. She's gone, man. Gone.

And yet I walk to the garage where my snow machine is. I'm gonna go get her ass. I'm gonna give this one more shot before I give up. I'm gonna suck in my pride and bring her back.

Because this is it. Eight years have passed since we took down the Company. Eight years since Harper was freed, Nick was taken into the jungle never to be seen again, and James quit being one of the hunters.

I am so filled with envy for that guy. How does he get to walk away? How does he sleep at night knowing we never figured out the final puzzle? How do I live with myself if I don't finish the job?

I can't.

I can't live with myself. Because I know it's not over. And there's only one target left.

Not me. Fuck, if this was just about me, I'd be out. Just like James.

This is all about Sasha. And they're still coming for her, I know it. She knows too much. She's seen too much. And even though her father did his best and her mother gave up her life to protect her from this shit—she didn't escape her fate.

She just postponed it.

TWENTY-THREE

MERC

"She lost her mind in the dark that night. But she carried that seed of hope like it was gold."

– Case

ven though it's been fifteen minutes tops since Sydney took off on foot, her bootprints have all but disappeared. It's not really snowing, but the wind is blowing, and that's all it takes to cover up her tracks.

Still, I have a snow machine with a headlight. So she cannot have gotten far enough away to avoid me.

I tell myself that, anyway. Because while I have my suspicions about Sydney Channing's many talents, I've really never seen them in action. Tonight on the stairs was just a sample, of that I'm sure. Garrett made her do his dirty work. I watched her approach people. Women. No, I laugh. Not women. Women are too smart. *Girls.* He needs them weak and dumb. He needs them helpless and scared to get them to participate in his sick sexual fantasies. Sydney was part of his trap. She looks innocent and sweet. She looks vulnerable and honest.

But she is none of those things.

And she knows what she's doing out here too. They spent a lot of time in the woods. But the secret to success in the snow is a shovel. A shovel can save your life out here. Dig a hole in the snow and make a shelter that hides you from predators and keeps you warmer than you ever thought possible when surrounded by ice. And she does not have one.

I go slow as I enter the woods, concentrating on what's left of her footprints. This goes on for a hundred yards or so, and that's when the doubts start creeping in. No way did she get this far on foot.

The trail is still lit up from the stars and the moon. The white snow is the perfect reflection, making it almost bright. But on either side are the woods. And they are very dark.

I turn the machine around and backtrack. I've covered up her trail, so that's no good. I cut the engine and sigh into the night. The wind is chilling and I'm not dressed for this. I just want to go home and forget this stupid girl. This stupid life. This stupid bullshit with these stupid fucking people.

God, how awful to grow up with these people.

The Company is not a corporation. It's not a business. It's a secret shadow world government with thousands of people in very high places. Think world leaders, billionaires, mega-charities, religious leaders, manufacturing, healthcare, water treatment — hell, space exploration, these days. Those are the kind of people who work for the Company. It's like the Mob, only bigger.

Or it was.

James is a former Company assassin who fell in love with the Company princess, Harper. Sasha was the Company mistake. Raised by her father, a former Company assassin trainer, to shoot straight, think clear, and listen carefully, she is the only living member of the Company who knows certain secrets.

The problem is, Sasha doesn't know she knows these things until something jogs her memory. Like we're on the road in the Mojave Desert and we stop at a restaurant-slash-seedy hotel. Sasha pops off an offhanded comment like, "Yeah, the guy who lives up in room 17, he's a Company asset. My dad and I used to come here for — " Whatever. It doesn't matter who they were, the fact that she spent her childhood rambling around in an RV with her father as he did his Company business puts her squarely into the needs-to-be-eliminated category.

Or — and this is the part that terrifies me — the needs-to-be-activated category. Because that's what these people do with the girls. They brainwash them. They use them. Just like Garrett used Sydney.

I place my hands on the front of the snow machine and

drop my head into them. I'm so tired of thinking about this shit. Why? Why do I have to spend my life chasing these assholes down? Why do I have to care? James and Harper don't seem to give a shit. Sasha doesn't give a shit anymore, either. She went to live a new life after we killed all those Company people. And since I convinced her a few years ago that things were OK, she never brings it up. Ever.

But me? No, this is all I've thought about since I met the kid eight years ago. I can't take it anymore. Why? Why do I have to be the guy who gives a shit?

Because, asshole. She's the little sister you never had. She's the only family you really got, man. She's the only one who counts.

I lift my head and sigh again. "Sydney!" I yell. "Where the fuck are you?"

I need her. I hate this so much. But I have to admit it. I need her.

I get off the machine and walk on foot, backtracking the way I came, searching the darkness of the trees on either side. I have no gun, no flashlight, and if the wolves decide to show up, I'm fucked. And so is Sydney.

So I turn around and walk back up to where I stopped the machine earlier. She's got to be here. It's a long distance to cover in the fifteen-minute headstart she got on me. But she has to be here.

I spot what's left of a footprint going off into the woods on the right of the trail, and follow it in and find more. They get clearer the deeper they go. Less wind in here. "Sydney!" I call again. I move on in the direction of the prints and I'm just about to yell again when I see her. She's sitting down on the ground, her white coat and snow pants a stark contrast to the dark bark of the massive pine tree she's leaning up against. "What the fuck are you doing? Let's go. You're not staying out here. If you want a ride up to your truck, I'll take you in the morning."

She sits still, looking down at something in her hands. I squint at them, trying to see what she has. And I have a little moment of panic thinking she has a weapon or some secret Company shit.

But she doesn't. It's an acorn. I stuffed it in the pocket of the coat she's wearing before I left the little cabin, just trying to get rid of her and everything she represents. She's twirling it in her fingers, staring at it like it's important. "You know why I keep the acorn, Case?"

I cross the distance between us and grab her by the arm, pulling her to her feet. "Good luck?" I venture, tugging her a little, to get her feet started. She gives in without a fight and walks, so I let her arm go.

"No," she says. "That's not why." And then she laughs. But she's still walking. I stop for a moment and let her pass me, so I can keep an eye on her from behind. This girl makes me nervous. She's not entirely sane. And she's dangerous in ways I'm still not sure of yet.

"Why then?" I ask, more to take my mind off how I will get this girl to give up the information I need.

She doesn't answer me, just walks.

We get back to the snow machine and she stops and waits for me to get on. I scoot back on the seat and nod my head, indicating she should climb on the front. She's tiny and I'm huge. I can reach around her and drive no problem. I don't trust her to sit behind me.

But she doesn't climb on. She stares at me. "What?" I ask.

"It's a seed." She holds up the acorn. "This little thing will grow into a huge tree if all goes well. If it has enough water and sunlight. And good soil."

"Get the fuck on the snow machine." I do not have time for existential musings right now.

"But I've had this acorn for—" She stops, looking up at something, like she's thinking. "Ten years?" And then she smiles. It catches me off guard. I've been watching this girl for eight of those ten years and not once do I ever think I've seen her smile.

I smile with her.

"I picked it up the day Garrett came into my life." Her smile drops and so does mine. "A seed." She looks at it. This is when I notice she has no glove on. Her hand is a very pale white.

"Jesus, Sydney. Your hand." There's a glove poking

out of her pocket, so I grab it and hold it open so she can slip her hand inside. She fists the acorn, never opening up her fingers, but it's good enough. The hand is definitely on its way towards frostbite and it needs to be warmed up immediately. "I gave you gloves for a reason. You know better than to take them off in this kind of weather."

She stares down at her newly gloved hand and then looks up at me for a moment. But it's like she missed everything I just said. The confused look on her face softens and then she looks away, switching gears. "I needed to feel that acorn."

That's her explanation for risking amputation?

"It has so much potential. *I* had so much potential. That's what Garrett said. And if I would just…" She smiles again. But this time there are tears in her eyes. One rolls down her face, freezing in the cold wind before it can complete its journey. "Just trust him, right? If I just gave into what he was asking, I'd become the oak tree. He was making me the oak tree, Case. But this?" She pokes herself in the chest. "I'm just dead wood, that's all I am. Dead wood."

I can't move. I'm fixated on her. Her sadness runs so deep. Her confession is more of a surrender than an admission.

"Do you know what he did to me?" she asks, slipping her hand out of the glove and dropping it on the ground so she can see the acorn.

211

I pick up the glove and tug it back over her blanched skin. "I know."

"All of it?"

"Most of it. I wasn't there ten years ago, obviously. So I missed that acorn shit. But I watched you after the cabin. For two years. On and off," I add quickly. "I wasn't there all the time. Just between jobs."

She nods and steps forward, lifting her leg to straddle the machine and take a seat in front of me. "It was always you, Case."

I'm about to start the machine, but I stop myself. "What was?"

"The person in my head who told me to keep going."

I have nothing to say to that. I talked to this girl once before I took her the night before her wedding. At that cabin eight years ago on Christmas Eve. I punched her in her sixteen-year-old face and threatened to kill her. Told her I owned her and I'd be back to finish the job. I'm not proud of this. I don't get off on hurting girls. But it was a fucked-up job. My whole life changed that night. Sasha's whole life changed that night. Hell, I can probably count two or three dozen people whose lives changed that night because of Sydney and her fucking boyfriend. And if she thinks that was me being affectionate and encouraging, she's more insane than I thought.

"I know what they did to Sasha."

I freeze as her words sink in.

"I know what they did. Because they did it to me too." And then she twists her body and gives me a glance over her shoulder. Her tears almost break me. They frost her eyelashes and freeze on her cheeks. It's started to snow in the last few minutes, only I just now notice it because her dark hair is dotted with flakes that sparkle in the moonlight. She looks like sadness. She looks like a sad, winter princess. "It's not over, Case. And if you help me, I'll help you."

TWENTY-FOUR

"Kindness is a weapon — use it like a knife, or a gun, or a lie."
                                                            – Case

I think about this offer all the way back to the house. *I know what they did, because they did it to me too.*

Did they? Did they really? I don't know. I only met Sasha a couple times before that night Garrett and his crew killed her father. But her father was a good man. She loved him. He loved her. Did they really get him to go along with brainwashing his only daughter?

And then there's the fact that her mother was dead. Didn't I hear that the mothers were the key to the future of the girls born into the Company? Sasha's mother was dead, that means she refused the deal that the Company offers each mother when she gives birth to a girl child. Sell her to them — allow the Company to use the girl as they see fit. Or give up her own life for a promise. A promise that the girl will be taken care of and married off to an appropriate partner when she comes of age.

Sasha's mother gave up her own life for the promise. And Sasha's father trained her the same way James was trained. He raised her to be as ruthless and cunning as the Company assassins. She might've only been thirteen when we took out the Company, but she held up her end of the game. Hell, there were times when she held up my end of the game too. Her father gave her skills. There is no way that Sasha and this Sydney girl are anything alike.

But. There is always a but.

How can I be sure? How do I know there is no trigger for Sasha? James had one. I'm pretty sure, after hearing Harper's tale of how that shit all went down when she escaped, that she had one too.

But James dissociated right into his own world in the end. A world where he was king and no more orders got through. And Harper? They did it all wrong with Harper. Raised her up on a megayacht. Pampered her. Spoiled her. Loved her. Even her father loved her. And she always had her twin, Nick, at her side.

No. Brainwashing on this scale doesn't grow out of love. And yet Harper killed a lot of people when she was triggered. A *lot* of people.

And Sasha is a hundred times more deadly than Harper. Sasha has real skills. Sasha is smart and worldly. Sasha has no fear. Harper was a bundle of fear and anxiety.

But Sasha. She is brave.

And that makes her the perfect sleeper assassin, doesn't it?

I need to know more about Sydney's life growing up. If her mother gave up her life for the promise and it didn't protect her, then how can I be sure it protected Sasha?

The garage light is off when I pull in, but the motion sensor triggers and it flashes on, blinding me for a moment. "Hop off," I say, when Sydney doesn't move.

She swings her leg over and I do the same. I give her a push and she starts walking. I close the garage as we leave and we trudge through the blowing snow to the house. The warm air blasts us when we get inside and I start taking off my coat.

Sydney stands there, looking at that acorn. Her glove is gone again. Dropped somewhere outside along the trail, I bet. "You know, it's pretty stupid to hurt yourself like that." I nod down to her hand when she looks up.

"Who cares?"

"Go upstairs, to the third floor. I'll throw some wood on the stove and meet you up there. It's the warmest room in the house and I do care." She squints her eyes at me. "I'm not cutting your fingers off and I'm not taking you to a hospital because you can't drive your truck out of here. So go the fuck upstairs and wait for me."

She heads towards the stairs. She responds to harshness. She's probably been conditioned that way. Threats, abuse, humiliation. It gets her moving.

I get moving as well. I stock up all three wood stoves that heat this house and then go into the kitchen and start looking for food. I grab a bag of chips and a soda, ready to head upstairs and see what I can do for her hand, when a thought comes to me.

I might catch more flies with honey.

So I put the bag of chips back and open the fridge to see what I have. Not much. I haven't had a lot of time to cook the past few weeks. But I have some elk meat thawing. And some potatoes in the cold room that are still good. I stick all that shit in a roasting pan and shove it in the oven.

A hot meal is nice. I could use one. And I've been feeding her shit for the past few weeks. It can't hurt. I make some coffee too, then take a pot and two mugs up the stairs.

She's sitting on the bed, still looking at that stupid acorn. She still has her winter gear on, and there's so much sweat running down her face, her hair is all wet.

"Sydney," I bark. She slowly raises her eyes to meet mine. "Take your fucking—" *Honey, Merc. Try honey.* I take a deep breath and beg myself to be patient. "Come on," I say, pulling her to her feet and taking that stupid acorn away. I toss it on the bed and her eyes follow it as it rolls along the white down comforter. "You need to take off your coat and snow pants."

I unzip her coat and slide it off her. Her shirt is soaked with sweat. She just stands there, so I guide her back until she bumps into the bed and she takes a seat again. I bend down and start unlacing her boots. She kicks them off when they get loose enough.

I wait, but she doesn't stand. I'm not a patient guy. I mean, I have my moments when it's necessary, but generally, I don't like to coddle people. I didn't coddle Sasha, and she was a good ten years younger than this girl here when we did that big job. I'm really not interested in coddling Sydney.

But honey, Merc.

"Take off your snow pants, Sydney."

She messes with the button and zipper, then slides them down her legs. Her pants should be dry, but they are soaked with sweat as well. She takes those off too, and then she's bare from the waist down. She looks up at me and takes off her sweat-soaked shirt. That leaves her naked, since I didn't give her underwear when I left her clothes at the cabin. I'm regretting that now. She's a cute girl. And her body…

I take the hand suffering from exposure and it's still very cold. I touch her cheek with the back of my other hand and it's warm. She leans into that like she's starving for a gentle gesture.

It makes me close my eyes for a minute. She's so needy.

It would be easy to just take care of that need.

Instead, I kick off my boots and take my shirt off, then place her hand under my armpit. She tries to pull away but I hold her still and smile. "It's a nice warm place, Syd. You have to heat up this hand. I'm pretty sure it's gonna blister no matter what, but it needs to be warmed up."

"It's gross," she says. "I can do it—"

"No," I tell her back, sitting down on the bed and pulling on her at the same time, so she can't remove it. "I'll do it."

I scoot all the way back on the half-moon-shaped bed, which takes up roughly one half of the circular room, making her crawl along with me. Her tits are nice and firm, and hang down and bounce a little in a very alluring way. I keep pulling her until she's sitting next to me, her frozen hand slipping out of place. So I put my arm around her and place her hand under my opposite arm, making her hug me a little. She stiffens when I do this and that makes me laugh a little.

"You afraid of intimacy, Sydney? Tough girl like you?"

"You're tricking me somehow, I can feel it." But even as she says this, she rests her head on my chest.

"Probably. If there's one thing you should know about me, it's that I don't give anything away for free. So now that I'm taking care of your mistake out there, let's talk about that deal. I went above and beyond. I didn't let you freeze, I came out of my nice warm house to save your ass. So the way I see it, you owe me. Start talking. What do you know about Sasha?"

"You kidnapped me."

"You came to me," I correct her.

"I left. I wasn't coming to meet you."

I let that go for now. *Time and place, Merc,* is what I say in my head. *Time and place.*

"You sprayed me with a hose. You —"

I wait for it. The ultimate accusation. But she doesn't finish. "I what? Raped you?"

She holds her words in.

"I hope you don't think that. Because you were the one filled with secrets for that little affair."

"I wasn't gonna say that." She takes a deep breath. "I was gonna say, you disappointed me."

Usually I'd laugh at that. But I'm using honey. So I don't. I think about it for a moment instead.

"You were supposed to save me, Case. You were supposed to show up that night, kill Garrett and his buddies, and take me out of there. That was the deal."

"My end of the deal was over the minute I realized your militia friends knew I was coming."

"I didn't tell them. I saw you out there and I lied to Garrett about it. I let you get close. If I had told, you'd be dead. I saved you, Case. I saved you when you were supposed to save me."

221

I say nothing. If she wants to talk, I'm gonna let her talk.

"And then you left me there. He—"

I wait for her to go on, but she doesn't. "He what?" I prod.

"Forget it. It's over. I'm not going back." She shakes her head to emphasize this. "I'll leave here, but I'm not going back. I'm not. I'll kill myself first."

I look across the room and realize I can see her in the window. It's still dark outside and will be for hours, so the glass that surrounds this room on all sides is like a mirror. "Were you supposed to go back? After the wedding?"

In her reflection, her eyes dart back and forth, like she's thinking hard about this question. "I don't think I was ever getting married that day."

"What?" I'm officially confused.

"I thought you wanted to know about Sasha?"

Interesting factoid about the marriage. But I need to keep her talking. "I want to know about you first, Syd." She notices me in the window now too. Stealth trick over. "And what you know about the hush."

That makes her tremble, and I have a moment of regret for bringing it up. "It does something to me," she whispers. "Makes me feel things."

"What things?"

"I dunno. It makes me feel out of control. It's a trigger, I think."

"So you know about the brainwashing they did?"

She stares at my reflection in the window. It puts me on edge a little. "I don't understand that word."

"Why not?"

"Because Garrett never said it."

"Then how could it affect you?"

"I said it."

She removes her hand from my armpit and looks at it for a moment. I take it in my hand and feel it. Much warmer. And the coloration is better too. I press down on her skin and the indent turns white, then a slight pink color returns after a few seconds. "That's better. But I'll need to wrap it before the blisters form. I'm one hundred percent sure it will blister. Now how did that word affect you if you never heard it?"

"Why are you being nice all of a sudden?"

I laugh. "Don't get ahead of yourself, wildcat. This is just a debrief."

"I hate that name."

"Why?"

"Because that's the word that Garrett used. And then I'd say *hush* in my head to make it stop."

"Make what stop, Sydney?"

"The urges."

"So you knew? You were aware of the trigger and that it was implanted in you?"

"I've been conditioned since I was three years old, Case. I'm twenty-four. I lied before. I know what you did in the army. Garrett reminded me all the time. You were PSYOPS too. You brainwashed people. You tortured them and got information. You turned them into sleepers by making them dissociate from reality. You caused them to go crazy and then you triggered them and made them do your bidding."

"Like you?"

"Like Sasha," she counters.

I let out a long breath. I'm not sure I'm ready for that shit. I'm really not. "You seem to know a lot about this for someone who claims to be brainwashed."

"Claims?" she snaps. "Fuck you. You didn't live my life. You didn't grow up with me. You didn't have to endure all that *conditioning*. That's the innocent word you use for it, right? For the things that have to be done to people to make them into walking weapons? Walking zombies? You take away their freedom, only they never know it. You take away their free will. I know what I went through. I know what they did. I broke my conditioning six times since I was fourteen, and each time they put me back into compliance. That's a nice innocuous word too. Do you talk about conditioning and compliance in your meetings, Case? Or do you call it what it is? Or maybe you have a nice fun slang word for it? Like—"

"That's enough," I growl, cutting her off.

224

"Why?" She turns all the way around, breaking the skin-on-skin contact we have, so she can look me in the eyes. "You don't want to be associated with them? You want to pretend you have some justification for doing that shit? How many little girls did you steal away? How many little girls did you ruin?"

"Let's just get this out of the way right now. I know the techniques." She makes a disgusted face at the term, but I let it go. "I've used the techniques. But not on little girls and not for the reasons you think."

"Justification," she says, crossing her arms over her chest. Maybe to cover herself or maybe just to demonstrate her disgust. "I put all my faith in you, Case. The last words you told me, I kept them in my head. It got me through so much. But now…"

"But now you know," I say softly.

She takes a deep breath and then holds it.

"I'm not gonna say I'm innocent. I'm not. I've done a lot of terrible things, Sydney. But I promise you" — I try to turn her so she has to look at me again, but her body is stiff now — "I promise that I have never hurt a child on purpose."

"On purpose?" she snorts. "You think that's an excuse? And Sasha was a child."

"I didn't brainwash Sasha. Please."

"You used her. You used her for all kinds of things."

"She was trained for that job, Syd. She wanted to do it.

She wanted her revenge. And she came through just fine."

"So you say."

I stop for a moment. "She *is* fine. She's better than fine, in fact. She's very successful. She's brilliant and social. She's put it all behind her. And maybe we can sort this out for you, Sydney. Maybe we can sort this out and you can live a normal life too."

"She's not fine. She's sleeping."

TWENTY-FIVE

"What you deserve and what you get are almost always two very different things."

– Sydney

I know I'm pushing his buttons, but he's pushing mine too. Turnabout is fair play. And since he suddenly wants to talk, I'm gonna go for it. "You know what I nicknamed Garrett? I mean, if he can make me into his wildcat and have me bobbing on his cock whenever he felt like turning me on—and not in the way I'd prefer to be turned on—then I can have a name for him too. Maybe I couldn't control him with it, but it made me feel better." I scoot away from Case. I want clothes. It's hot up here—getting hotter in fact, since he added wood to the stove—and he had me in his night vision for God only knows how long, but he doesn't deserve to see me.

His look softens as I pull away and I know it's a trick. Men like him don't do anything without a motive. He needs information about Sasha from me. And now he's being nice to get what he needs.

"What did you call him, Syd?"

"Don't call me *Syd*."

Case puts his hands up, a little give-up gesture. "Fine, Syd-ney. What was his name?"

I lift my chin to gather my nerve. "Soul splitter. Because that's what he did to me. He split me in half. He took my soul—the one thing everyone has ownership over—and he gave half of it to someone else. Someone *inside me* that I had no control over. And you do that too. You split people in two and steal their souls. I hope one day you get split in half, Case. I do. I really do."

Case rubs his hand down his face. "I'm making food. Let's go eat and then we'll get some sleep."

"I don't believe this act. Just so you know. I don't believe you're being nice to me for any reason other than you need to use me. Do you know why they do these things, Case? Do you have any idea?" I pause here. I want an answer.

He shrugs. "Power? Obviously."

I scoff out a laugh. "Really? That's all you have? Power?"

"I'm hungry," he says, standing up, giving me a cue to stand up as well. I stay sitting. I'm done following the cues. "Let's eat, sleep, and talk again in the morning."

"Helplessness," I say, just as he turns his back to me. "They want me to feel helpless. So they can control me.

And they did a really good job, right? You came in and I sat there begging for you to save me because I was helpless. And then I let you leave me behind and I let Garrett take me again, because I was helpless. I asked you for help out on that mountain road because I was in an accident you probably devised, and so I felt helpless."

He walks to the stairs.

"I'm done, Case. If you walk away, I'm done. Kill me. Please. Put me down like a dog and end my misery right now."

He shakes his head but doesn't turn around. "What can I do to make you feel in control, then?" He looks over his shoulder at me. A snide, sidelong glance. "Tell me how to change this and I'll do my best."

"Save me."

"That makes no sense. You want control? You save yourself."

I stay silent. My speech is over. His ball now. I can't wait to see what he does.

"I think you're lying about Sasha. I think you need something from me and this is all a ploy. I think you know exactly what you're doing."

"Then I guess we're even then, right?"

"I feel sorry for you. I really do."

That cuts me deep. I'm not after pity.

"But I'm not the guy who made you into this person,

Sydney. I'm the guy who can turn you back."

And then he walks down the stairs and leaves me there. Alone, naked, and completely helpless.

I have no idea what to do, but my hand, which started out numb when I came inside, then started to tingle, is now burning.

There is nothing else to do now. I need Case on my side to take the next step. And he's got his own agenda. That Sasha girl is his only priority. Must be nice to have people who care.

I get up and turn the lights out, ready to be done with this day, and then go back to the half-moon bed and get under the comforter. It's soft and warm. Down, probably. I gather a pillow under my head and gaze up the windows in the ceiling. Perfect for stargazing.

I lose myself in that, dozing off. But the creak of the steps jolts me awake some time later. Case is back with a bottle of water and a tray of something that smells too good to ignore. My stomach rumbles. He smiles. I don't smile back.

"Sit up and eat." He walks into the room and sets the tray down on a small side table that holds the lamp. He doesn't turn the lights on.

I'm sitting up before I realize I just followed a command. That pisses me off. When I look up at Case again, he sighs.

"I'm not trying to order you around. I'm not trying to make you feel helpless. I'm just trying to take care of you. Is that off limits too?"

His rough voice, his shirtless chest, his good looks, it's the perfect package. When a man comes up in your time of need and says things like that, you want to melt. I want to melt.

But I know he's lying.

It makes me so sad that the only offer I get is a lie.

He bunches up the comforter around my legs, being careful not to pull it down to expose my breasts — not that he hasn't seen them a million times — and then gets the tray and places it on the mound of blankets.

I inhale the aroma.

"Roast," he says, reading my mind. "And potatoes. It's game, elk. But I know you like elk." He pulls out a wad of gauze, some cotton balls, and medical tape from his jeans pocket and sits down next to me. "You eat with the good hand. I'll wrap up the bad one."

I'm still as he takes my burning hand and even though it hurts when he touches it, I don't pull back.

I like the touch. I can't help it.

"Eat," he says, noticing my stillness. "It's hot. I ate downstairs, if you're wondering. But if you think I drugged it, I'll eat half with you." He smiles then. "You can feed me. Will that make you feel in control?"

I melt a little more. I might even blush. But I come to my senses and scoop up a forkful of meat and deliver it to his

231

lips. He takes a bite, wincing, like it burns his tongue, and then he chews.

"See," he says. That melty smile is back. "It's not drugged. One for me, now one for you. Eat."

I take a bite for myself and have to tuck down the moan at how good it is. I feed him another bite, and he says nothing as he wraps my hand in white gauze. He puts a cotton ball between my fingers to keep them from touching. I take more forkfuls of meat and potatoes, mostly forgetting to feed him. And when he's finally done with my hand, I'm done with the food.

"Did that hurt?" he asks.

I nod. It hurt like fuck.

"Then why didn't you say something?"

"What's the point?"

"I'd know to be more careful."

"You were careful." He was, too. I've seen this done before. You don't live up here and not know what to do with a minor case of frostbite.

"It's a signal, Sydney. So I can tell what's going on inside your head."

"You really do not want to know what's going on in my head, Case."

He takes my tray away and puts it back on the table, then hands me the bottle of water and sits down next to me. "I really do."

"You want to use me."

"I just want to know you."

"God." I laugh, then take a drink. "Such a player." I cap the water and lie back, pulling the blankets up to my neck.

He studies me, like I'm some sort of specimen, then stands up and unbuttons his jeans, letting them drop to the floor. He's not hard, from the quick look I get at his junk before he slips into bed next to me. He wraps his arms around my waist and pulls me close to him. "Are you tired?"

"So tired," I say, meaning it in more ways than one.

"I'm just the wrong guy, Sydney. That's all I can say. I'm the wrong guy."

"Wrong for me, you mean, right? Because you were the right guy for Sasha. You were the shining knight for her. I'm just not Sasha and that's all you have to say."

"You're not Sasha. But that's not why I'm the wrong guy. I'm just..." He drops off for a few seconds. "I'm pretty much everything you said. All of it is true. And I'd hate for you to count on me and then it just fucks you up more when I don't come through."

"Well, I've got nothing for that." I close my eyes, the issue settled in my mind. Merric Case is not in my corner.

His hand travels up to my breasts and he fondles them for a few seconds, maybe gauging how I will react. "I had no idea you were a virgin," he whispers. "That fucked with my head pretty bad."

"Why?"

"Garrett and I were in the army together. We did… shit. Military shit, obviously. And none of it was good." He stops here. Like that admission was a huge step for him. "Did Garrett tell you what we did?"

I shake my head. He did tell me some things, but I don't want Case to stop talking. This is quickly turning more personal. And I like it. I don't want him to go silent again. Or walk away. Or give up on me. Even if he is just using me to save his friend. I guess I have to take what I can get. "Garrett made me memorize that little speech to give you. After… you know. That's it."

"You didn't deserve any of this shit, you know that, right?"

"I know that," I whisper.

"I don't think you do." Case places his hand on my shoulder and turns me around. I don't really want to face this new Case. I don't know what he's doing or what he wants, but I seriously can't take any more lies. I'll just die if this is a ploy. "It's not your fault you were born to that Company asshole. It's not your fault your mom died when you were born and you never had that—"

"She didn't," I interrupt. "Die when I was born, I mean. She died when I was fourteen. I watched it happen, actually. She was very allergic to peanuts and she was on a school field trip with me. Some kid in my class had a peanut butter

234

sandwich. And the smell of it was strong enough to trigger her allergy. She had one of those Epipens, you know? For emergencies? But her throat swelled so fast, it didn't work."

He's silent for a few moments, like he's thinking. "Still," he finally says. "It's too young to be motherless. And that sucks about your mom."

I nod. "It messed me up. I know that's what allowed them to control me more. I just stopped fighting. It was the second worst day of my life."

"Second? Jesus, what was the first?"

"That night you left me, Case. That was the worst day of my life. Ever. I just slipped away after that. Being here with you now, it's made me think clearer than any other time in my life. And I just know—even though you hated me then, and still do now—I know that if you had taken me with you, I'd have turned out different. Better, maybe."

Case sighs as I turn away from him again. I can't bear to see his face after that pathetic admission.

"I can't take it back, even if I wanted to. I did the right thing for me that night. The right thing for Sasha."

I think about this for a moment. A few moments, actually. He relaxes behind me and his breathing is deeper. Like he's about to fall asleep. I wait a little longer, until I'm sure he is. And then I speak the words I want to say, but I'm afraid for him to hear. "You can take it back. Just say it and I'll believe you."

Silence.

He's asleep.

I'm relieved and heartbroken in the same instant. So I just close my eyes and chalk it up to another pathetic Sydney failure.

"I can try to make up for it, Syd," he says after a little while. "But I can't take it back." He whispers it, leaning in to kiss my head. I don't move. I don't want him to know I'm still awake. Because it makes me want to cry.

TWENTY-SIX

"When you know you're not a man's first choice the worst thing you can do is settle for second pick."

– Sydney

When I wake up I'm alone in the crow's nest. But I can smell food wafting up from below. The meat was good last night, but I've missed too many meals in the past couple weeks to be satisfied. I swing my feet out of the bed, put my clothes on, and wander down the stairs.

Case is talking to someone. On the phone. I guess that means he gets service up here.

I could call someone. Brett, maybe. But do I want to bring him into this? Do I want to leave this game we're playing before it even gets started?

I get to the bottom of the stairs and spy Case in the open kitchen, cooking and talking at the same time.

He smiles, and continues his conversation. Like he

237

didn't kidnap me and hold me prisoner. Like we didn't beat the shit out of each other last night. Like I didn't trick him into this in the first place.

Well, I have to give him a pass on that one. He has a clue, but he's still in the dark.

He waves me over and then says goodbye to whoever it was on the other end of the line. "Hungry?" he asks, flipping pancakes on a griddle.

I walk over to the kitchen and take in the place now that I can see it all properly. A huge, huge cabin. I know what these things cost, and I know the value of the land he's got here, since it backs up against what I think is the Yellowstone River. Millions of dollars.

But his style is not pretentious. It's not that fake log-cabiny feel that you see rich city people decorate in. People who aren't really a part of this world, but want to feel like they are when they vacation in their million-dollar homes with their bazillion-dollar views.

It's country-ish. Homey. The couches aren't even leather, like you might expect from a man. My fingertips drag along the back of one as I step closer to the kitchen. Cotton. Soft. With throw pillows that look like he uses them to sleep, because they are all crumpled.

"Sydney?" he says, his tone a little more commanding. "Are you hungry?"

I look up at him as I make my way past the furniture.

He has a nice dining table too. Rustic, but looking like it was made by hand by someone very skilled. I drag my fingertips over that as I walk as well. Polished and smooth. "Yeah," I answer, taking a seat at the quartz-topped bar that also serves as a counter. He's got butter and syrup out and there are two place settings with silverware.

He fills a plate with pancakes and slides it down the stone. It comes to a rest directly in front of me. "You'd make a great bartender with that slide," I say with a smile.

"I've seen your slide, Syd. It's dead on. Like getting that mug directly in front of a customer is winning a gold medal for you." And then he turns to let me think about that.

He's been watching me for years. So how much does he really know?

He slides a glass of orange juice next and I catch it in my hand when he overshoots. I get a shrug out of him for that.

I study his back as he flips some more pancakes. He's hot. I didn't want to tell him that the last time I thought about it. But there's no denying. Merric Case gets what he wants because a) he doesn't take no for an answer, b) he's got the skills to back up his 'requests,' and c) he's handsome.

He fills his plate, walks around the counter, and takes the barstool next to me. "Eat," he says, pointing to my plate with a fork. A second later he's stuffing his face.

I take a bite, then a few more before gulping some juice and coming up for air. "Mmmm. It's good."

"I know," he says smugly. "I have two real talents, Sydney Channing. Killing and cooking."

I nod and stare at my food. Right.

"So do you want me to take you to the truck?"

I take a bite of pancakes to think about this.

"Or do you want to hang out?"

"Pfft." I look up with a laugh. "You kidnapped me."

He shakes his head. "You came to me. I just kept you longer than you expected."

"You drugged me. Hit me. Fucked me."

He shrugs. "I did."

"So now you want me to believe you want to hang out with me?"

He stabs at his breakfast. "You can if you want, that's all I'm saying."

"So now I get to do what I want?"

He shrugs again, but doesn't look at me. Just chews and stares out the window at his bazillion-dollar view. "I guess I'll take you back, then."

"Back where? Where do I go from here? Back to Brett? The bar? How? What the hell will I tell them?"

"Most people who've been kidnapped, drugged, hit, and fucked by someone they hate would go right to the police." And then he drags that heated gaze over to meet my confused one. "You can go to the police, if you want."

"Because you're untouchable? Because you have so

many people on your debts and favors list they can't get you? Because they're afraid of you?"

"Come on, Syd. I'm one fucking guy."

"One fucking guy." I shake my head. "One dangerous, insane, out-of-control guy is more like it."

He drops his fork on his plate with a sharp clang. "If you want to turn me in, then fucking do it. I've decided not to kill you, so—"

"Oh!" I laugh at that.

"—do whatever you want."

I pour some syrup on my pancakes and we eat in silence after that. He finishes before me and leaves me sitting there as he cleans up his mess in the kitchen. "But if you stay," he says, his muscled back moving as he wipes the griddle down, "I'll cook you lunch too."

He's trying to fix the mood we have going. I give him a point for that and volley back. "What's for lunch?"

"Well," he says, clicking his tongue, "I don't have much, sorry. I really didn't expect to have you here at the house, let alone cook you actual meals. I have elk. Lots of elk. So we can have roasts or stew. But we've eaten that a lot lately. I have some turkey. And some frozen salmon I caught last spring when I took Sash fishing in Alaska."

"Hmmm. I bet that was a nice trip."

"It was. We go every year."

"I'll take the salmon." But it makes me long for the

dream guy in my head. He took me fishing too.

"Do you like to fish, Sydney?"

I nod. "Yeah. I do."

"Maybe you can come with us this year?"

God, that hurts. Because now I know he's just making this up. He doesn't like me at all. He's using me, just like I suspected. He's trying a new approach. Violence, drugs, and insults didn't work. Let's try food and fishing.

"Something wrong?" he asks, turning back to me now that the griddle is clean.

I shake my head and it ends with a sigh. "I'd like to fish with you. That would be nice."

"Then why do you look like I just killed your dog?"

I take a mouthful of pancakes, but they are cold now. The juice helps me wash it down and then I push my plate away. "Maybe I should just go. I really can't take it."

"Take what? Me being nice? You take the insults and the violence just fine, but normal? You don't do normal, do you?"

"Not that you would know." I fold my hands in my lap and wish I had my acorn.

He crosses his arms across his chest, flexing his muscles when he does it. I look up into his eyes to figure this out.

Do I believe this is genuine? I could fool myself into believing it, that's for sure. It would be easy enough to just enjoy him for a little while.

But when he turns on me, that might break me up even worse.

"What are you thinking about?" he asks.

What am I thinking about? "This is a nice place. It feels like a home. You're surrounded by nature. You seem to have some semblance of a normal relationship with Sasha. You—" I stop, trying to put my sadness into words. "You have so much more than me."

"I'm just rich, that's all. I bought the land the first year we got the windfall money. Then spent the next six years building this place."

I huff out a laugh at that. "You built this place?"

He shrugs. "I hired people, you know. I did some of it. I helped. But no, I didn't build it myself."

"I really figured you were squatting here. Living in some billionaire's summer home for the winter."

"And I only have Sasha because of you, if you think about it. I would never have that girl in my life if that night at the cabin never happened."

"Well," I sigh. "You got a lot more out of that night than I did. I think I should go." I push back from the bar and stand up. He's right there next to me before I can take a step away.

"Look," he says, placing his hands on my shoulders. I still have a bit of pain from where he shot me with—what was it, anyway? A tranquilizer dart, I guess—so that makes me wince internally. But I'm not about to show this man any more of my inner feelings, so I tuck it away. "I get it. This is weird."

"Weird?" That hardly covers it.

"But you don't have to go."

"I don't have a reason to stay."

"Stay for me. Talk to me. Tell me what's going on."

"That's all you want from me, isn't it?"

"What do you want from me?"

I take a deep breath and just decide to say it. I'm leaving anyway. With any luck I can be driving away in an hour. "I want you to save me." I look up at him, the tears I want to stop so badly welling up out of my control. "I realize that is a very sad and pathetic thing to say. To you of all people. But I wasn't lying when I said that, Case. When I said you were the one who kept me alive all these years? In my head, telling me to go on? That you would be back? That was all I had. And now that I know you never meant it the way I tricked myself into believing, I just don't think I can stand to be here. I'm stupid. I'm so, so stupid."

"I don't know what you want me to say. I can't say anything right. If I tell you to go so you can figure shit out, I'm abandoning you. If I tell you to stay and help me, I'm using you. So this is up to you, Sydney. You have to decide to trust me or not."

"I want to trust you. But I don't. Everyone I have ever

trusted has lied to me. Everyone I have ever believed in has used me and let me down. Everyone, Case. I mean, really, fishing in Alaska?"

"Why not? If you like it? Sasha's not gonna come this year. I know it. She got into grad school—"

"Jesus Christ. She went to college? Grad school? After all that fucked-upness, she's getting some PhD so she can live out her dream? And what did I get? That stupid bar?"

"I thought you liked the bar."

"I wanted to go to college too. And no one ever swooped into my teenage life and saved me from my fucked-up life. No one ever came and bailed me out of shit and sent me to school. No one ever took me fishing in Alaska every spring. No one *ever* did this shit for me. It pisses me off."

"So you're jealous?"

"Fuck, yes, I'm jealous! Holy shit. You didn't know that? Well, congratulations, Einstein. You've figured me out."

TWENTY-SEVEN

"In difficult cases I win them over with recognition. I let them see themselves in me."

– Case

She walks over towards the three-story-tall windows. The jeans I got for her are too long and they scuff on the polished hardwood floors with each step. Her arms cross, a defensive position, trying to ward away this conversation. But this all needs to be said and it needs to be said right now. I'm sure this is very uncomfortable for her, not being in her own house. Not having a place of her own to retreat to.

"Just take me to the truck."

I walk up behind her and grab her left forearm, bringing her bandaged fingers up so I can look at her hand. "How's it feel?"

I expect a snarky remark. Maybe something along the lines of, *Like you care*. Or, *None of your business*. But she just shrugs. "I have a high tolerance for pain. And I can't do anything about it. It will heal."

"I can try to make up for it, Syd. But I can't take it back." I repeat what I said last night in her sleep, but it makes me feel like I'm going too far. I don't want to get attached to this girl. I don't want to make all this shit more compacted than it already is. "All I can do is try to help you now."

"I don't believe you," she says in a sad, soft whisper. "You never wanted to save me. You wanted to make money that night. I was nothing but a job. And now I'm just some kind of solution you have to tolerate."

"I don't need money, Sydney. I haven't needed money in a very long time. Not that night, not that year, not that decade. I made so much money over the course of my adult life, it's meaningless."

"That makes it even worse." She turns to me, her mouth drawn into a straight line. No hint of what she's feeling. Does she feel? Can she feel? I'm not really sure of that. She's been mindfucked for so long, she might not have much of her real self left. "Take me to the truck or just get it over with."

I shake my head at her. "I'm not taking you back to the truck yet. And I'm not sure what you think I'm doing here."

"Killing me, right? You brought me out here to kill me."

I stare at her, wondering how much I should say right now. That is the reason I brought her here. And the last time

I checked, it was still my goal. But it's not going the way I planned.

"Will I die like him?"

"Who?"

"My father. You killed him back in that room? On that table?"

"He deserved it."

"And I do too?"

It's a loaded question. In so many ways. One I can't answer right now. So I change the subject. "Did you love him? Your father?"

She takes a deep breath and turns back to the window. I see her crack a small smile in the reflection as she gazes out over the river. "This is the Yellowstone River?"

"Yup."

"I did love him. He used to bring me to this river when I was very small."

"How old were you?"

"Small. Before I ever went to school. He showed me how to hold a fishing pole once." The hint of a smile disappears. "He's the one who taught me how to hunt. Ducks, back then. I never shot any with him. I was too little. But he told me what to do. Explained it to me."

Hunt. In my world it has so many meanings. But what does it mean to her?

"Who taught you how to hunt, Case?"

"The television."

This makes her chuckle, and I get a little satisfaction from my off-the-cuff remark. "How did the TV teach you to hunt?"

"Survival Channel. Don't leave home without it. I started watching that shit when I was a kid. It fascinated me. I grew up in Boston, one hundred percent city boy. But I never belonged there and as soon as I turned eighteen I moved west."

"I thought you joined the army when you turned eighteen?"

"I did. But I didn't want to be known as the guy from Boston. So I moved to Wyoming, set up camp in Cheyenne, got a month-to-month lease and an address. And once I settled in, I enlisted."

"Why bother?" She turns to me, genuinely interested in my story. "What difference does it make? You still grew up in Boston."

I tap a finger on her head. "It makes all the difference in the world in here, Sydney. It changed everything. Inner-city kids from a broken Boston home are a dime a dozen. I didn't want to be that guy anymore. So I made myself into someone else." She squints her eyes at this, like she's thinking. That's good. I want her to think about this stuff. I want her to think about all of it. "And it's that easy, ya know? New town. New clothes. New music. New truck.

New address. And bam, just like that I went from being Merric Case to Merc."

She blinks up at me a few times.

"You can do it too, ya know. Just walk away. Stop being Sydney Channing and be someone else."

"Who?"

"You."

She shakes her head at that, not quite ready to put all the pieces together. So I turn away and walk over to the coffee table and pick up the remote. Her arms are crossed over her chest and she's hunched into herself a little, like she's frightened about what I might do.

I flick the TV on and punch in the number for the Survival Channel. There's a guy talking about hunting snowshoe hares. He's middle-age, weathered, and looks like he can kill anything that comes at him with his bare hands.

Sydney wrings her hands as she watches from across the room. "I know how to hunt rabbits, thanks."

"It's a metaphor, Sydney. If you don't want to live in Boston anymore, all you gotta do is teach yourself how to survive. And then just walk away."

TWENTY-EIGHT

"See yourself as someone who survives."

– Sydney

I feel like we're talking in code. "It's not even remotely similar."

Case takes a seat on his white cotton couch and kicks his feet up on the coffee table. He watches the big screen that hangs over a large stone fireplace. I tip my gaze up as well. The guy on the Survival Channel is digging a pit trap. "What kind of skills do I need?"

Case looks up at me. "You could try…" He stops to think. Because he knows I'm right. It's not the same. Leaving civilization and coming to the west is easy. But leaving the wild and becoming civilized is not as clear-cut.

"And I already *was* living in the city. I had a boyfriend, a bar, an apartment. I don't even know what you're talking about."

"Going to school." He shrugs. "Taking some college classes in… whatever."

I huff out a small breath at that notion. "History of Western Civilization and English Lit is gonna erase my life and make a new one?"

"Do you think I became Merc by watching one guy catch rabbits on TV? I joined the army."

"You did terrible things."

"That was my plan. Become Merc. The army was a way to do that. But before I left for the army, those little steps made it real. I lost the accent. I lost the tough-guy attitude. I mean, almost everyone out here can survive. They might not be geniuses, but they know how to survive. So I became the guy out here. It's just a first step."

My gaze wanders back to the man on the TV. He's tying a snare made out of thin copper wire.

"Look at me, Sydney." Garrett's eyes are blazing with anger as he fists my hair and makes me look up at him. But as soon as he lets go, my head rolls back to its original position. An electric current in my collar shocks me awake again. But only just. "You need to pay attention."

"You have to understand who you are and then decide what you want."

I look over at Case, oblivious to what I am.

The man on the screen says, "There, all ready to go," and then walks away from the trap he set.

"We're on a tight timeline here. You need to do your job and I need to do mine. I won't always be here to help you."

"Help me," I whisper as my whole body begins to tremble.

"What?" Case sits up, his feet hitting the floor. I look back up at the screen and now there's a rabbit hopping down a bunny trail. "Sydney?"

Garrett has the rabbit in the live trap. Not a snare. He likes them alive. He told me before we came out here in the woods. He likes them alive for training purposes. I'm gonna learn how to skin a rabbit today. He walks out towards the wire cage and picks it up by the handle. Like he's carrying luggage at the airport and not bringing some small animal to its death.

Case shakes me by the shoulders. "Syd," he says, his face right down into mine. "What's happening?"

"Have you ever heard a rabbit scream, Sydney?"

I look up at the rabbit on the screen again. It's getting closer and closer to the snare. A little hop this way or that way, and it might go around it. But its nose is pointed in the direction of the bait.

"Have you ever heard a rabbit scream, Sydney?" Garrett laughs as he sets the cage down on the wooden table he has set up for butchering in the back of the cabin. "You're about to." He hands me a knife.

The bunny has no chance once it moves into the snare. The loop of wire slides along its thick, white fur. One more hop and he's caught. The wire tightens…

"What am I supposed to do with that?" The knife is long. And sharp. "That's not how you kill a rabbit."

"You're a fucking genius, I guess, huh?" The electrical shock stuns me silent as it jolts the skin on my neck. It's so tender from all the training, I double over and push my head into the ground.

Garrett hands me the knife and I take it. I have no choice but to take it. And then he pulls me up by my hair until I'm standing.

"You have thirty seconds, Sydney. And then we're gonna call this test a failure."

The snare tightens around the rabbit's neck on the screen.

I reach into the rabbit's cage.

I scream, just like the rabbit on the TV.

I grab the rabbit by the fur, roughly, so it can't slip away. I look up at Garrett, and he's smiling, pleased that I'm finally doing as I'm told. And then I pull the rabbit out of the cage and fling it across the yard. It hits the snow with a thump, and then it's off, those large feet acting like snowshoes as it makes its escape.

Be the rabbit, Sydney.

But I am not the rabbit. I am not getting away. My neck is burning with electrical shocks as Garrett pulls me back into the cabin by my feet.

TWENTY-NINE

"Answers come to those who seek them."

– Sydney

I think this is it for me.

"What?" Case is next to me. I'm in bed with him. I can feel his bare chest up against my feverish back. His arms tighten around me as he repositions. I want to open my eyes and see if we're in the crow's nest room or some other room, but I can't quite do that yet.

"Sydney?"

I hope we're in the crow's nest. And it's daylight still, so maybe I only lost a few hours? I really like it up here. It feels good to be tall, looking down on things, instead of small, always looking up. It feels like a watchtower. A place where you can see the bad shit coming from a distance and prepare.

"Syd," he says, a little softer now. "I didn't want to drug you again, but you were hysterical. It was the only way I

259

could calm you down. I won't do it again, but I need you to help me out here. OK? Can you do that?"

Help him out. I bet. I tuck my head into the soft pillow and will myself not to cry. "Just be someone else, you say?" I croak out the words. My mouth feels like it's filled with cotton. How many times have I been drugged since he's had me? "But all I've ever done is be someone else. I don't even live in the real world anymore. I can't imagine any more versions of myself, Case. I have tried so many times. I have lived in my head for days on end. I have refused to see the truth in hopes those memories would just fade away. I have been the good girl, the bad girl, the defiant girl, the sexy girl, the compliant girl. And it gets me nowhere."

I turn my body so I can see his face when I open my eyes. We are in the crow's nest, and that just makes me sad. Because no matter how nice this place is, he's still the guy who left me to die. And I don't know what he's doing right now. Or why he's being nice. Or why I'm even still alive.

But I know none of that is because he *sees* me. He doesn't see me. He says I need to change into someone else. And that's all they've ever told me. Change into someone else. Split me in half, that's what they've done. But maybe it's not just half. Maybe I've been quartered, like an elk when we hunt it down and kill it and then have to carry it back to camp in pieces.

"I am not the rabbit."

He swipes a finger down my cheek and I realize he's wiping away tears. I look up into his eyes. How many times have I wished I could be this close to those eyes? They are bright, like the room. Not brown, not green, not blue. Hazel. With specks of yellow in them that make them that amber color when he's standing in just the right haze between dark and light.

I take a deep breath and let it out.

"I don't know what that means, Sydney. The rabbit thing. It was a trigger for you? You saw the rabbit on the TV and it triggered something?"

"Yeah," I say softly, wishing I could just curl up and die. But what's the point of fighting him anymore? What is the point? Who do I want to protect here? I run the list of names in my head and only come up with one.

But it's not fair. It's so not fair that I will be fucked when this is all over. So I opt for answers before I give in. Maybe I can die peacefully if I at least get some answers. "Did you turn that show on to trigger me?"

"No," he says. No hesitation. "I do not know Garrett's triggers, Sydney. If I did, this would be a whole lot easier. I could help you. If I did. I could try to set this shit right. Do you know the triggers?"

"Bobcat."

"I don't think that's it." Case lets me go, pulling his arms away, and stands up. "I don't think that's it. If bobcat or wildcat were triggers and releases, we'd be making progress. Climbing out of that dark hole. But we're not climbing out. You're still falling in, cowgirl."

"Jesus Christ," I mumble into the pillow. "How much farther can I possibly fall?"

He sits down on the edge of the half-moon bed, leaning his elbows on his knees and then his face in his hands. I guess he has no clue. And neither do I. "More drugs," I say. "Just give me more. Give me so much I never wake up."

He doesn't even answer me. Just walks away. I listen to each step as it creaks on his way downstairs. And then I listen to noises that have no meaning to me. Finally, after about twenty minutes of this, the door slams.

He walked out.

Isn't that what he does? He says he'll save me, but then he walks out.

I close my eyes and go back to sleep. This room is too bright. I need the dark.

When I wake, it's twilight, which isn't quite as good as dark, but I can't make myself go back to sleep. So I sit up and look outside. It's snowing again. But there's a trail from a snow machine still a little bit visible.

I kick the covers off and then make my way to the edge

of the bed and swing my feet over. I'm not dizzy. Whatever he gave me, it was a small dose. Just enough to calm me down, like he said.

I am hungry and thirsty. So I make my way down to the second floor and stop off at the first bathroom I see, relieve myself, and then gulp water from the faucet.

I pull back, wiping my mouth, and look at myself in the mirror. My hair is long and dark and it hangs down my front in tousled waves. It's messy, but cute. That makes me smile for a second. That I can be here, looking at my hair at a time like this. My face is marred with scratches, a bruise that is one of the remnants of the many head punches Case delivered. And my eyes are tired, but bright.

I wouldn't say I *feel* bright. But I do feel better than I have in days. Weeks, I guess. Since he took me weeks ago now.

I touch the bruise and wince. But the hatred I feel for Garrett each time he made one of these appear doesn't manifest for Case like it should.

I should hate him. But I don't.

I should want to plot revenge. But I don't.

And it's not some sick Stockholm syndrome thing, either. I tried to love Garrett. I tried out that Stockholm shit on him. Thought it might make it easier if the man who was beating me was sexy and liked to fuck me.

But it never worked with Garrett. So I think I'm immune

to Stockholm syndrome.

Besides, I have loved Case for years in my head. Long before this. He was my savior. So fuck it. I'm allowed to love him now too. He has no idea what's happening. He's just doing his best to figure it out. And if I wanted to make him stop hurting me, I could just tell him.

But I'm not some magnanimous do-gooder. Like it or not, I'm just as ruthless as him. And I want what I want.

I want him to like me. I want him to say, *I'm so sorry for leaving you behind. I fucked up.* I want him to want me the way I want him. I want him to love me. I want to be loved so badly.

I flick the light out and see a large bedroom through a pair of open double doors. I step forward into the room. I know he's gone. And I'll hear the snow machine if he comes back.

Oh, God. What if he doesn't come back? What if I go downstairs and there's a pile of clothes and a note telling me to get lost? He's moved on and so should I?

Instead of dwelling on that, I start looking around the room. He's got a connecting bathroom in here. All his shaving stuff is out on the counter. A cup to hold soap. I pick up the cup and smell it — sandalwood. And a nice brush to lather up his face. I swipe my fingers along the soft bristles and picture what it would be like to watch him do that.

Nope. No Stockholm syndrome for me.

I flip the lights off and go back to the bedroom, taking a seat on the edge of his bed. There are nightstands on either side made out of a highly polished wood that is so dark it almost looks black. His house is not decorated like you might expect a huge luxury log cabin to be. Most of the elements are contemporary and new.

I open the drawer in the nightstand and find guns.

Of course you do, Syd. He's an assassin. I pick each one up and handle it, checking the weight, the chambers — they are all loaded — and then put them back and close the drawer.

I never want to use a gun again. Ever.

The second nightstand on the other side of the bed has a closed black case and a first aid kit with a selection of drugs. None of them are the cocktail he's giving me, because they are all antibiotics, heart-rate things, antagonists, and epinephrine. A crash kit. To save a life.

Nice to know the man whom I am lusting over, not for Stockholm-related reasons, is prepared to save me from too much anesthetic, should I ever require it.

I pick up the black case, spy a lock, and therefore expect it to be locked when I trigger the mechanism.

But it isn't. He must not get many visitors up here.

That makes me let out an involuntary cackle. I think I might be losing my mind for real. Like, irretrievably for real.

The two guns inside are... magnificent. Black matte FN Five-SeveNs with custom grips and an aftermarket laser.

There's writing on the grips, so I pick one up and turn it sideways to read it.

The only gun you'll ever need. Happy birthday, Merc.
~ XXOO♥♥✳ - Smurf

I have no idea who Smurf is, so I just put it back inside the case and look at the three cartridges, which are also lined up, like this was made for a display. They have writing on them too, so I take one out to get a better look. *With love, Sasha*, it says three times over.

I guess she is the Smurf. Figures. That kid has had his heart since the night he left me out at that cabin. It makes me so furious to think that she got a cute nickname and her fairytale ending and I got…

I don't want to think about what I got. It brings up bad things. Things better left buried.

I put the cartridge back and close the case and then the drawer. I don't want to shoot Case. So I'm not even remotely interested in nabbing one of his guns.

The sound of a snow machine draws me out of my introspection, and I get up and make my way downstairs so I can meet him at the door.

God, I'm so pathetic.

THIRTY

"Eventually... you have to trust someone."

— *Sydney*

I settle for the couch instead of greeting him at the door so I don't look like I've been waiting for him. Or like I'm happy he came back.

The couch faces the living room window, so I peek over the back of it. He comes through the door, stomping his snow-covered boots on the mat, and then hangs his hat and takes off his gloves.

He sees me just as he unzips his jacket. "You're awake. I wasn't sure how long you'd sleep. I didn't give you much, I swear." I can see his muscles through his long-sleeved thermal shirt as he hangs up his coat and kicks off his boots. "I had to go out and do some things," he explains. Like I'm his wife, wanting to know where he's been.

I do want to know, but not because I think he's out hooking up with some chick. We are in the middle of

267

nowhere. And Merric Case doesn't strike me as a guy who fucks around a lot. Either on the side, or otherwise.

He walks into the living room in his socks. There's sweat on his brow from the warm clothes and the heat of the wood stoves. "I just didn't know what to do. Sorry." He looks down as he walks to the kitchen and starts pulling out some food.

I want to say something, anything to break the silence, or change his mood, because he seems worried. And I don't want that worry to be because of me. I'd like him to save me, yes. But I don't want him to pity me. I'd rather die.

But I'm not a social girl, having grown up in the wilderness. Cheyenne doesn't really count as a city, even if I told him it did a few hours ago. It's a small place filled with small-place people. So I don't know how to start this. I tuck my feet underneath me and stare at them instead of trying.

"You feel better?" he asks, unwrapping some meat from white butcher paper and throwing it in a pan. "Hungry?" He throws in some potatoes and then drops in baby carrots too. He puts it all into the oven and closes the door. I guess we are having a roast. He opens the fridge back up and pulls out two beers, pops the tops off with a bottle opener, and walks out into the living room.

I take the one he offers me and he plops down on the couch. Close. Very close. Like we're together and we always have beers on the couch in the evening. Not like he kidnapped me a few weeks ago and washed me down with a fire hose. That should piss me off, because it fucking hurt. But it doesn't. I'm not mad about any of it and I wonder if there are more drugs in me. Calming drugs. Anti-anxiety drugs. Things to keep me on an even keel.

I hold the beer up and he looks at me. "Should I be drinking this? Will it interact with the drugs?"

He takes a swig of his own bottle, but for a second there, I think I see a wince of shame. "I think you're OK, Syd. I gave them to you this morning. I think they're out of your system by now."

He seems genuine, so no. Drugs are not the reason why I don't give a shit about all the stuff he did. And since we're clear that this is not Stockholm shit, I have no other ideas about why this might be.

"You wanna tell me about the rabbit?"

I close my eyes tightly, to keep the images from popping into my head. That noise, though. That scream the rabbit gave when I picked it up. It's burned into my memory.

Case puts a hand on my leg and gives it a squeeze. "You don't have to," he says. "I think I get it."

I give my head a small shake. "No, I think you have the wrong idea about pretty much everything, Case. Be the rabbit." I look up and he's listening, but confused. "Be the rabbit is what I used to tell myself when things got bad. It gave me hope and calmed me down. I was supposed to kill a rabbit that Garrett caught. And I know how to kill a rabbit in a live trap, OK?" I search Case's eyes. "I know how to do it right. But what Garrett wanted me to do was cruel. So I let it go."

"It got away?" Case asks hopefully.

One more small shake from me. "No, the dogs got it. They ripped it to pieces."

Have you ever heard a rabbit scream?

"I have seen many things in the woods. Nature." I look up at Case. "You know? The rules of nature play out every moment of every day, and we hardly give it a thought. But I lived with that for a very long time." I look down at my beer and realize I haven't taken a drink yet, so I raise it to my lips and have a good long gulp. It goes down cool and soothing, so I take another. "Garrett treated the dogs better than me. At least they never got shocked with a collar."

When I look back up to Case, he's frowning. "Look," he says, almost a whisper. "I am sorry I didn't take you that night—"

"Stop," I say. "Just don't, OK? I saved myself, so forget about it. When things got bad, I just imagined I was living a different life. It got me through." I gaze out the window, into the darkness hiding the beautiful view beyond. "It got me through. I'm still here."

I can feel him nod, but I don't see it. Because I can't look him in the eye.

He guzzles his beer, gets up and walks into the kitchen, and then tosses it into the garbage with a clink that tells me he's been drinking a lot while I've been drugged. The top comes off another and then he walks over to the stairs. "I'm gonna get a shower before dinner. Make yourself at home."

I watch him walk up the stairs. He climbs slow, and maybe I'm imagining it, but it seems a little bit somber. But beer and bad news will do that to a person. He disappears and a few minutes later I can hear the shower running.

I finish my beer too and grab another from the fridge. It's a local brewery out of Jackson. I stock it in the bar. God, the bar. What's even happening to my bar?

And that's when I spy his cell phone on the counter. I walk over and pick it up, glance up at the stairs to see if he's watching, and then swipe my finger to see if I can unlock it.

It's not even locked. I open up the keypad and punch in the number for the bar, but just as I'm about to hit send, I stop. "What the fuck will I tell them?"

I set the phone back down and go back to the couch. It's not Stockholm. It's not. I just have no good reason to want to go home. There is nothing good there for me. Nothing. I know this. I love that bar, I really do. I'd give anything to be able to wipe away all the things keeping me from it and go home. Because that place — filled with drunk cowboys, shitty country karaoke, and ninety-nine-cent microbrew nights—was the only place I felt *real*.

Cowgirl, Case calls me sometimes. I am a cowgirl. I like that girl. Maybe I can be that girl instead of this one?

But I can't go back. Not until I know what's happening to me. Not until I figure it out. And I know my only hope of figuring out what I'm feeling right now is to let Case in on things.

I want him. But I don't trust him. And just as that thought consumes me until I feel like I will explode—I hear the music coming from the third floor.

THIRTY-ONE

MERC

"Moments are permanent. You can't take them back or change them. You can only make new ones.

– Case

The music has always saved me. But it reminds me so much of Sydney. That song—my fingers pluck it out, just from habit. I learned to play it years ago, back when it first came out and it was on the radio in Sydney's car every single day. I know that not because I was in the car with her, but because I have been stalking this girl for eight years.

I was relentless the first two years. I had Garrett in my sights so many times. I could've killed him a thousand times over if I had acted then. But Sasha needed me. My friends needed me. I saw all that shit through with them, and Sydney was an afterthought while we pieced together the final mystery.

Only we never solved it. We got the money we stole. But that final piece of the puzzle never materialized. And now Syd is here, a place where I've imagined her a million times—but this is definitely not how I imagined it going down.

In my head it was quick. Some torture. Some questions. Some answers. Mental persuasion was always an option, but I never, ever saw things turning out like this.

Like what? I have to ask myself that. Because I'm getting tangled up in her past. I'm letting her get to me. I'm allowing her sadness to take over all my plans. And I'm not quite sure what to do about it.

That scream. Now that I know she was imitating the rabbit, it makes sense. But it was blood-curdling. It was evil. It was fright on a level I've never experienced before.

I have killed a lot of people. Even some women. I don't discriminate in that department. If they deserve it, if the money is right, I finish the job. But I have never heard a noise come out of a person's mouth like that scream today. Drugs were my only option. She was hysterical. Just gone.

The stairs creak and then she appears in the shadows. I have one lamp on. And I guess it sets my mood. Low. That's how I feel. On the bottom of something.

It's not a good place to be in the middle of a job. And the feelings, I'm not used to the feelings. I care about people— not many, but I do care about them.

I should not care about this girl.

"Hey," she says, flashing her bandaged hand in a wave.

"How's that feeling?" I ask, still strumming out the tune I can't seem to get out of my mind.

She looks down at her hand. "It's better."

"We'll take the bandages off tomorrow and have a look at the blisters."

She nods and takes a seat on the bed. Not far from me, but not close. I'm on the floor, one knee up, skin showing through a hole in my jeans, with the guitar in my lap. No shirt on. Not to make her look, even though she looks. But just because it gets so damn hot up here with the wood stoves burning downstairs.

"You must really like that song."

I flash her a small smile. "I got it from you."

"I realize. So…" She crosses her legs and I glance at her bare feet. She has a tattoo on the top of her left one. A rabbit. I've seen it before, but figured it was some girly thing. It's running, its long hind legs crossing its front legs, and looking over its shoulder. Like it's in the middle of a mad dash for its life.

"So, yeah," I finish for her. "I've been watching you for a very long time."

"I've been thinking about that." She wrings her hands a little and then looks me in the eye. "If you want to kill Garrett so bad, why not do it a long time ago?"

"So you believe that he's alive now?" I stop playing, letting her know that this is not a casual question. It's an important conversation, if she allows me to continue it. Maybe the most important in her whole life.

She shrugs. "I really don't know what's real and what's not."

I look away and start playing again. Because that was my answer. She's not ready. Even though I know she knows Garrett is alive, and she admitted to talking to him the night before her wedding—the very night she ran like a rabbit—she's not gonna talk about it tonight.

"You know why I like that song?" She nods to my guitar.

I look down, letting my still-wet hair fall over my face, and hide a small smile. It's not about Garrett, but it's the next best thing. Her. "Why?"

"Because it's got a good message. *Nothing At All*. The title says everything I feel. And the words, they just… it's like they're talking about me."

"I guess that's the secret of all good songs, right? Words that are personal to the writer can speak to millions."

"I want everything and nothing."

"Me too." I strum it a little harder and pick the strings a little more carefully.

"Because you never know what you really want. It changes every day. And you get things, and then they're not what you want."

I nod as I play the ending, letting the music get louder and louder, mimicking the building crescendo. In the real song, it sounds chaotic, like life is taking over and nothing makes sense. But if you listen carefully, it all fits together perfectly until the final bit of guitar that evens it all out and makes it OK.

"That's life, right?" I say in the ensuing silence. "You bust your ass to get to the place you want to be, and then you realize it's not what you expected."

"It's a letdown."

"Makes you want to stop wanting things." I look up and smile. She laughs a little and bows her head. I've seen her in so many situations, but I've never seen her confident. I've only ever seen her afraid. Or shy. Or helpless. I bet she's never seen herself as confident, either.

I reach for her leg and give her a squeeze through her jeans. "When I'm not thinking of you, this is the song I usually play." I take a breath and then say, "One, two, three..." and then I start strumming. She lets off a little laugh. "So you know it?" I ask.

"I love Shinedown."

"Shit," I say. "Bitch, this is Skynyrd. Fuck that cover shit." I look up to see how she reacts to my joke. But she's got a nice grin on her, so I continue to strum. I've never seen her happy either. I'd like to see that just once. So maybe I can make that happen tonight?

"Are you a *Simple Man*, Case?"

"I try." I bow my head a little as I play the bridge. "But

I'm not so sure I've been successful."

"Did you have a mother to give you simple advice on how to get on in life?"

I shake my head and keep my eyes closed, seeing the music in my head. "No. She died from a fire when I was eight." I look up at her. "So we never got to the good parts."

"What are the good parts?" Sydney scoots down, dropping her ass to the floor like mine and stretching out her legs. She's close to me, almost shoulder to shoulder, and I wish I could ask her to sit across from me so I could get a better look at her.

"You know, the part where I make her proud." I stop strumming and take a deep breath. "My old man was an asshole, but compared to the torture that Company kids endure, he was perfect. I mean, he drank and shit. Was an alcoholic, actually. But after thinking about him for the past fifteen years… I've come to the conclusion that he was just heartbroken. He loved her, Syd. And how can I be mad at a guy who can't pull himself out of the fact that he was the one who started the fire that killed the love of his life?"

"Yeah, I get it."

I start playing again. Mostly to change the subject without having to say anything.

"Well, I had a mother for a little longer than that. But I don't think she'd have had anything to say even if we did get to the good parts."

"What would be the good parts for you?"

Sydney stays silent. Thinking maybe. "My wedding day, I guess. A real one. Not the one I agreed to just to make my life have meaning."

"So you don't love Brett?"

She shakes her head and her hair covers her face.

I stop playing and reach over, dragging her hair behind her ear. She looks up at me, startled, and I give her a nice smile to ease her down. "I like looking at you."

"Why? I'm covered in bruises."

"Ouch," I say. "That stings me a little."

"Did you really want to kill me?" Her eyes fill with tears and I know I'm pushing her tonight. It's not a good plan, but I can't seem to help myself. I've never had a real conversation with the girl. And she's pretty. And I fucked her all wrong the other night. All wrong.

"I would not have had sex with you that night if I'd known you were a virgin." It's not the answer she wants, but it's one that makes her think. Maybe see me in a different light. Not many people get that opportunity, and I wonder if she'll bite.

"Why?"

She does. And it's not a challenge—not the way she says it, anyway—but I feel challenged for some reason. I have a good answer though, so I let that feeling drop. "Because every major moment in your life was stolen from you. And you had that one moment left. By luck, or planning, or whatever, you still had it. And then I was the one who stole it from you."

She drops her head back on the edge of the bed and looks up at the ceiling. "It doesn't matter anyway. Who cares? It's just a moment, ya know?"

"But that's all life is. Just one moment after another. Stacked on top of each other. A good friend explained it to me that way once. Stackable moments lead to things. Sometimes things you planned. But sometimes they lead to new things. Things you didn't plan." I stand up and put the guitar on the stand. And then I reach for her hand. And wait.

Her face is puzzled. She looks at my hand and then her eyes find the cut muscles of my waist and travel up my chest until they meet my eyes.

"Take it," I say.

She does. But she swallows hard when her skin touches mine.

I pull her to her feet and wrap my hands around her waist, pulling her close. Inhaling her scent. Feeling her warmth. I lean down and kiss her neck. I can feel the prickles of hair rise up on her nape and the chill that runs through her body when I whisper in her ear. "Have you ever had the soft fuck, Sydney?"

Another hard swallow as she tilts her head up. Her

throat is exposed, like an offering. "I don't know," she breathes. "I don't think so."

"Cowgirl, if you did, you'd know it." And then I slip my hand under her shirt and caress my way up her ribs and kiss her mouth at the same time. She's stiff at first, her lips tight against mine. "Want me to give you a sample?" I ask, pulling back.

"Why?" she asks softly. She's not looking to say no. She's looking for a reason to say yes. "Because you feel sorry for me?"

"Nah," I say, still trying to get her to respond to my kiss. I bite her lip, not hard, just enough to make her pay attention to what I'm doing. "Because the way I took you, Syd, that was not my best performance. And I think I can do better."

"Why do you want to?" She pulls away from me a little, unsure of my intentions. Hell, I'm not even sure of my intentions.

"I just want you." I let her pull back a little more, but only so I can see her face. She's scared. Out-of-her-mind scared. Her eyes are wide and her mouth is open now, even though I couldn't get it to open with the soft touch of my tongue not two seconds ago. "It's not always rough, Sydney. Sometimes people fuck and they actually like each other."

"Do you like me?" It's such a soft whisper, I barely hear it.

"I'm not gonna kill you, if that's what you're asking."

"I need to know why, though." Her face scrunches up a little, like she's having a hard time pulling herself together. I know I have her. I know if I just push a little more—squeeze her nipple in just the right way, press my hard cock against her stomach—she will give in. But if I'm gonna make up for the way I took her the other night, that's not how this is gonna go.

I take my hand from under her shirt and pull her hair back away from her eyes again. She's struggling right now. In all the ways I've seen her over the years, struggling with kindness has never been one of them. But that's because she never had the opportunity. I tip her chin up and press my thumb into her bottom lip.

She whimpers and that little noise makes me even harder.

"You're pretty. Garrett never told you that?"

She shakes her head.

"Well, he's a dick. Your face is like an angel's. And your hair, fuck." I laugh a little and she takes a deep breath. "I've pictured you on top of me and that long, dark hair of yours dragging across my chest as you fuck me from the top so many times."

"No, you didn't."

"I swear to God, I did. You've got a hot fucking body too." I place my palm on her ribs again, only this time I let it slide down, tracing the line of her waist and then the curve

282

of her hip.

My hands go to her jeans and they are unbuttoned before she has a chance to protest. And then I lift her shirt up by the edges of the hem. Slowly. Looking down at her breasts as I do it. When the fabric releases her nipples I feel a little anticipation.

"I'd like to show you my best work, Sydney Channing. And make you forget your first time. Replace that night with this one. Nothing can be taken back. But you can replace the bad stuff with something else." I shrug. "That's all I got, sorry."

She says nothing. So I lift her shirt over her head and drop it on the floor. "Take off your pants." She bites her lip and I'm about to yank them down her legs at the sight of it. I control myself though and let her do it her way. She wiggles a few times, her hips moving back and forth, and we are so close this makes her rub against me in all the right ways. They finally drop to the floor and I take her hand as she steps out of them.

"You're more than pretty, Syd. Your body is so much more than hot." And it is. In this low golden light, with the backdrop of the windows on all sides, she is perfection. "I've always known it. I've always seen you in a sexual way. I've always wanted you."

She looks like she might cry, so I put my finger to her lips and murmur, "Shhh. Just close your eyes and let yourself feel happy for a little bit. Forget the past. Forget tomorrow. Forget everything except right now."

And then I push her, just a little bit, until she takes a step back and her knees hit the bed. She bends without me even asking and sits down. I straddle her knees, still standing, and guide her body back until she finally accepts what I'm offering and settles into the blankets and pillows.

"What are you gonna do?" she asks, her eyes closed.

"Make you come. Make you come so you'll never want to run away from me again."

I part her legs, exposing her pussy. It's wet with anticipation. And even though we haven't even started, her thighs tremble. I lean in, my breath as hot as my desire for this girl, and circle her opening with my tongue. She stiffens again, but when I flick it across her clit, she forgets everything and moans. Her hand reaches for me, finds my hair, and she pulls.

She pulls me closer. She pulls me inside her.

I add a finger, then two. She's so tight, she bucks her back from the stretching. But I go slow. Like she deserves. I doubt this girl has ever had a slow fuck in her life and it thrills me to be her first. I already ruined her the other night. I can't take that back. Nothing can be taken back. But things can be made up for.

I make it up to her.

I lick and suck, and she begins to relax. Her mind, which

must race with confusion every second of every day, slows down as my tongue takes its time giving her pleasure.

I can feel her muscles clenching, almost ready, and that's when I stand up and unbutton my jeans. She's breathing heavy as she looks at me, her eyes half-mast, her breasts taut and firm, ready for the moment I've promised.

"Please," she says. "Don't stop."

"I have no intention of stopping." I let my jeans fall to the floor, my cock hard and long, ready for her in an entirely different way than last time.

I lean over her and scoot her up to the top of the half-moon bed. My knees press down into the soft white comforter on either side of her hips and my mouth finds the soft skin of her stomach. I nip her with my teeth. Just a small nip. She gasps in some air as I drag my tongue up her body, stop to take another nip at her bunched up nipple, and then find her mouth. Her breath is warm and her lips are tender as I kiss her.

"Look at me, Sydney." She obeys, but only for a moment. Her mouth tightens, like she might cry. "Shhh," I whisper. "Don't do that. Don't feel sad right now. Please. Just forget everything and only think about how I make you feel."

And then I ease down on top of her, my forearms on either side of her head.

I kiss her forehead and she lets out a sob. "I don't know what to do," she admits with shaky words. "I don't know what you want or why you want it. I'm lost."

"You're not lost. You're here with me, where you belong. And I want you to do whatever you want, Sydney. But don't do it to please me. Do it because you want to please yourself. Do it because you enjoy it."

I kiss her again and she opens her mouth this time, our tongues twist together, reaching for each other in a way only tongues can. It's slow, and sensual, and erotic.

Perfect.

My tip bumps up against her opening and she almost bites my lip with surprise. "Shhh," I say again. "We're gonna go slow this time."

I ease into her, just a little bit. She gasps with pain, so I hold still for a moment, letting her get used to my size. When she relaxes I push in a little farther, and this time she accepts it. She opens her legs wider. Her hands stop clawing my shoulders and drag down my biceps. I'm the one who moans now.

This girl, man. She can make me moan with a touch. I push inside her farther and she presses against me, urging me to begin.

But I don't. This is the slow fuck. This is the sweet fuck. So I don't pound her hard. I love her deep. I kiss her mouth and slip one hand under her ass, cupping her cheek in my palm. The other hand plays with her hair.

Our hips move in unison. Slowly and with one purpose

in mind. To feel each other. She comes first, a slow wave of contractions that clench against my cock, and it takes every ounce of self-control not to come inside her as she does.

When she stills, I push deeper, making her arch her back. I reach up and palm her throat, gently so it doesn't scare her. I don't want her thinking of anything but me. And when her eyes finally open and meet mine, I pull out and explode on her stomach.

We lie there in each other's arms for a long time, until the smell of the roasting meat from down below wafts into my mind and wakes me out of my half-sleep. I empty a pillow out of a case and wipe down her stomach, wondering if I can get her in the shower later. And then I toss it aside.

"I don't know what to say," she says, when I finish. "Maybe, thank you."

I pull her up off the bed and she watches me dress. I lean over and grab her shirt, then tug it over her head. She sighs as her body is once again covered. But I don't think it's with relief. I think it's with regret. Not for letting me fuck her like that. But because we have to stop.

I smile as I hold open her jeans and she grabs my shoulder for support as she steps into them. And then I button her pants up and take her hand.

"Let's not say anything right now. Let's just eat."

THIRTY-TWO

"Never forget that you are vulnerable—even when you feel invincible."

– Sydney

We walk downstairs hand in hand. I have no idea what's happening, but I don't care at the moment. What he just did... what he just made me feel... I had no idea sex could be like that. I have never felt the tender touch he used on me tonight. I have only had it angry and hard. No soft words telling me I'm pretty. No slow movement, no thoughts about me at all. Garrett took me. That's about how I'd describe what we did in the dark. He never asked. He never even made me come. Never even asked me if I did.

But Case... how can this man be so soft with me?

It's confusing. And all kinds of doubts creep in.

He's using you, Syd.

I'm not even sure whose voice that is. Is it me? Is it Garrett? Is it the imaginary man in my head? I'd go with

289

option three if it weren't for one thing. That man was always Case.

And I'm not crazy. They think I am, but I'm not. I've just been in the dark too long. Lied to too much. Betrayed over and over again.

Even Brett. I don't know what that relationship was. Business? I'm not sure. He was always interested in the bar. But he was… friendly. Not like Case. Brett never offered me a soft fuck. I said I was a virgin and he assumed I wanted to wait until our wedding night. I've been dating him for over a year and not once did he ever push me.

How does a man control himself for that long? If he wanted me, wouldn't those urges get to him? Wouldn't he at least start a conversation?

He did other things—with his fingers. He did make me come. Not always. And I made him come. I gave him oral sex.

I'm so confused.

When we get to the kitchen I take a seat at the bar and even that feels weird. I always served Garrett. Even Brett liked me to wait on him.

But Case, he doesn't seem to mind cooking for me. Or cleaning up.

That's because he's using you, Syd. He wants the answers he knows you have.

I do have some. I've lied about a few things since he

took me. But I was his captive. Why should I be expected to tell him the truth?

"What are you thinking about?" Case asks as he puts a plate of meat and vegetables in front of me.

I let out a long breath and decide to be honest as he sits down in the stool next to me. "I need to know what you want." I look down at my bowl of food, my hair falling forward.

And he does that thing again where he pulls my hair aside to see my face. I look up a little, just enough to catch a grin when he pulls away. "I want you to eat. And then I'd like to take you to the shower and wash you up. And put you to sleep in my bed wearing my clothes." He shrugs when I scrunch up my face. "I don't have any more clothes for you. So…"

I clear my throat to give me the courage to continue. "But what will you want tomorrow?"

"I left today, you might've noticed." I nod. "And I have something to show you tomorrow. Hopefully, anyway. We'll have to wait and see."

"What is it?" I can't help my curiosity.

"A surprise." And then he starts eating.

And I do too. I let it all drop away for now. I'm OK. I'm not drugged. I'm not in any danger, I don't think. He's being nice. He's handsome in so many ways. I mean, I've dreamed about this man since he left me out there in the wild. I've felt every emotion for him over the course of time.

I've cursed him for leaving. I've begged him silently to come back. I've loved him, hated him, wanted him, and forgiven him so many, many times over. I feel like I've lived a lifetime with this man. And yet I had no idea he could be so…

"Sydney?"

I look at him.

"You done?"

I look down at my plate and see that it's empty.

"You want more?"

I nod and he makes to get up. But I catch his arm, making him stop. "Not food, Case. I want more… of…"

"Me?" he asks, grinning like a man who knows he's desirable.

"Yeah," I manage to squeak out. "More of that."

"So what's the problem?"

"I'm afraid," I whisper. "It's not real. I don't think it's real. How can life be so… easy?"

He leans over and cups my face in one hand. His lips touch mine. "You know what makes it easy, Syd?" He waits for me to shake out a no. "Doing the right thing for yourself makes it easy. When you're fighting with yourself, that's when things get hard. When you have to talk yourself into being someone else to survive, that's hard. But when you can let all that go and just relax, just act honestly—that's how you make life easy."

"How do you know that? How did you get so smart?"

"I'm a genius. And I'm ten years older than you. I've seen more. Lived more. Done more. You pick this shit up by experiencing it."

"But you're a…"

"Killer."

He says it so easily. Like it's his true self and he owns it. And that's part of my problem. He's dangerous in so many ways. He wanted to kill me last week. He tied me up, drugged me, hit me. "Does it bother you? Being a killer?"

"No. It's just what I do."

I lean forward and put my head in my hands. The bandaged one is warm, but the other one is cool and it feels good on my face.

"But you know what else I do?"

I shake my head no, not sure I want to hear it.

"I'm a decent kisser." I huff out a breath and make my hair fly up in my face. "I can love you soft or hard. I can give you advice. I can be a good friend. Hell, I can even be a good father. I'm not Sasha's father, but it's good practice."

I look up at him now.

"To learn how to take care of people. I take care of her. She doesn't need money, she has more than enough. She doesn't need a best friend. She has those, too, I'm sure. But she calls me, Sydney. When she has something to talk about. I'm the guy she tells her problems to. I'm the guy she calls when she needs advice. So yeah. I kill people. But I am so much more than a killer. It's complicated. I get that. But what I do is not complicated. What I do is simple. I survive and I make sure everyone I care for survives too."

"Do you care for me?"

He puts his fingertips to my lips. "Not tonight. We're not gonna have that conversation tonight."

"I think I need to go."

"Tomorrow, Sydney. After I show you what I did today, tomorrow you can go. But right now we're gonna go upstairs, take a shower, and go to bed."

I take a moment. And in truth I need so much more than a moment to gather all this shit up in my head and make sense of it. But I don't have more time. And I don't have any answers, either. I have nothing.

Nothing but this man.

So that's what we do.

He leads me by the hand again. We retrace our steps up to the second floor and take a shower together in the master bath. He shampoos my hair and talks about his life. His first hit was a gangster in Boston when he was seventeen. He tells me how he had an appointment with MIT the next weekend and met his best friend. He talks about lots of other jobs too. Girls even. The two girls Garrett killed. Case explains that he dated them, had regrets for getting them involved in his life and set them up in Mexico to try and forget about what that might mean. The fact that Garrett killed them bothers him, but not much. He talks and talks and talks. Most of the stuff is nothing I want to know. But he tells me anyway.

He is a killer.

But then he dresses me in a white t-shirt that smells like him, and a pair of boxers that are way too big, and tucks me into his bed.

His arms wrap around me. His body heat gets tangled up in my own. He kisses me on the lips and says goodnight.

He is a killer.

But he is this man too.

"How?" I ask, when we are settled into bed. "How can life be so complicated and easy at the same time?"

"It's a joke, Sydney. And the joke's on us. Sanity, morals, right and wrong. They are all illusions. And sometimes we can see them clearly, and sometimes we can't. But you always know when you're OK. You always get that feeling that nothing can touch you. And tonight nothing can touch you. So close your eyes and let it go."

I stare up at the ceiling after his breathing evens out and wonder if I'd be doing the world a favor by grabbing a gun out of his nightstand and shooting him in the head.

Probably. That's the conclusion I come to. I have no idea what all that means. I have no idea if I believe him or not. I have no idea if he's wondering right now if he should just pull a gun out of his nightstand and do the world a favor by killing me too.

I'm just glad he doesn't. I'm OK with this. Because even though he is that killer, he is this man too. The one who feeds me and fucks me softly. The one who knows who I am and what I do. And he, of all the people who have floated in and out of my life, is the one who's *here*.

You can say many things about Merric Case, but you can't call him a hypocrite or a liar. Because he was one hundred percent honest with me tonight. He basically stood up on a mountain top and screamed, *Here I am, take it or leave it.*

I decide I don't want to leave it.

He's morally questionable. He's violent and possibly even sick. But I am all those things too.

My eyes grow heavy and finally close. And I drift off knowing that I was right about him for all these years.

He is the man who shows up when no others will. He is the man who looks death in the eye and laughs. He is the man who will pull that trigger when the whole world stands there in shock, unable to move.

He is the only man who can save me from myself.

THIRTY-THREE

"When your whole world is made up of lies it's OK to be irrational. But when the time comes, you must be prepared to let it go."

– Sydney

I wake up first and go downstairs. I look out the floor-to-ceiling windows and wonder how two fucked-up people can be immersed in such beauty. The mountains, the snow, the frozen river running through this perfect valley.

And I come to the conclusion we are wild. And that's why we belong here.

He comes down a few minutes later with the first-aid kit in his hand. The smell of coffee brewing permeates the house and calls out like a morning wake-up.

"Morning," he says, reaching for a cup in the cupboard. He pours a cup, takes it black—the way a man like him should—and kisses me absently on the head as he walks by.

I almost drop my own coffee cup.

"We can eat later or now."

297

"Are we in a hurry?" I ask, composing myself before he takes a seat at the bar and gives me his full attention.

"I don't think so. You've been here for weeks and no one came looking."

God, that stings.

"But I gotta get on the trail and I need you to come."

"OK," I say, finishing my coffee and walking over to the sink.

"Come sit so I can take a look at your hand before we go."

I do as he asks, letting him unwrap the bandages and look the blisters over. He dabs the ointment on the blisters that have popped, and then wraps it back up. "You need some pain pills for this?"

"No, thank you. The last thing I need is more drugs."

He gives me a strained smile and then another absent-minded kiss on the head, his hand lingering in my hair just long enough to make me feel... loved.

And how crazy is that? How, after one perfect day, can things have turned so completely around?

Because you're needy, Syd. You want affection, and even the affection of this killer who did all those terrible things to you is better than none.

Stockholm syndrome comes to mind again. How did I get here? The music, the soft fuck, caring for my hand... I add it all up in my head.

Things look so different in the light of day. I guess that's why I prefer the dark.

We dress in our snow gear and then I follow him out to the garage. He backs the snow machine out and points to the seat in front of him as I watch. "Let's go."

He's businesslike today. Like he's on a job and not like he wants to make love to me. But that would be normal, right?

He's gonna take you out into the woods and kill you, Syd.

He could do that. But why? I'm here. No one lives anywhere near this house. He could kill me in the driveway and leave my body there until spring. Let the wolves eat me. No one would come looking. No one would ever know.

I get on and his chest presses up against my back. We ride along for a while. The recent snow has covered up all tracks from the last time we were out here. It's just a blanket of white so blinding I wish I had his sunglasses.

When we finally stop, I'm ready to panic. He's been silent the whole time. And I realize that a snow machine and conversation do not go together, but some sort of communication would make me feel a whole lot better about letting him get me into such a vulnerable spot. How appropriate would it be for him to talk me up with all that shit last night, only to dump me into the wilderness to be hunted by wolves? Or freeze to death?

He cuts the engine and we sit in the silence for a moment.

"Ready?"

I have to swallow hard. "Should I be?"

He swings his leg over and then reaches for me, pulling me off the seat. "Depends, Syd."

That's all I get out of him. He puts his hand on my shoulder and I feel like a prisoner being led to the firing squad. We trudge through the deep snow that has drifted up between the trees and finally come to a halt about a hundred feet from the frozen Yellowstone River.

"What are we doing, Merc?"

He does not miss the fact that I called him by his trade name, and he shoots me a look. "We're gonna check a trap."

My heart starts to beat wildly and my feet are frozen in the snowdrift I'm standing in. "I don't want to check traps."

"I know," he says in that voice that tells me he's all business. "But you're gonna anyway."

He walks a little further on, almost dragging me now, and then we both slide down an embankment—sending a small avalanche ahead of us.

"Are you gonna cut a hole in the ice and drop me in?" I laugh a little, but the frown he sends over his shoulder makes me shut up.

"Don't get crazy on me yet." He reaches out and pulls a long pine branch, making the snow fall off as he gets it free.

My heart skips when I see what's inside. "What are you—"

"Shhh," he says. "Don't freak out on me now. OK?" I look him in the eyes for that, because this is most definitely the killer voice.

The rabbit inside the cage is paralyzed with fear.

I know the feeling.

Merc picks up the cage and shakes it a little to get it free from the twigs that he used for camouflage. The rabbit goes berserk inside, bouncing off the wire walls. "Follow me, Syd."

He walks a little further down the embankment right to the edge of the river. The Yellowstone freezes, but it's not always safe to walk on. "I don't like the ice!" I call out, several yards behind him now. My feet feel heavy. My body is reacting to what we might be out here doing. If he makes me kill this rabbit—

He sets the cage down on the bank, squatting down with it. He's wearing white camo winter gear, like me. We match and we blend. This thought gives me the courage to follow.

What is he doing?

He looks up at me, pushes his sunglasses up to the top of his head, and then smiles. "What did you tell me yesterday about the rabbit? Have I ever heard a rabbit scream?"

"Did I say that out loud?"

"Uh—yes." He gives me a stern look, his amber eyes catching the sunlight out of the east.

"I don't think I did," I reply, already out of breath from

that one brief mention. "I don't think I've ever said those words out loud before."

"I drugged you, Sydney. Remember? You were hysterical, going on and on about a rabbit. That show triggered a memory. You talked about it a little. You told me—"

"No!" I scream it so loud the rabbit begins to squeak, and I swear to God, if it screams—

"Sydney, sit down. Now. Right here," he says, patting the ground in front of the trap.

"I don't want to," I whisper. "I really, really don't want to be near the rabbit."

"Do you realize it's irrational to refuse?"

I nod. I do realize that.

"Do you understand that this will help you get past it?"

"No. It won't. It will just make everything worse. This is why you want me out here! This is why you've been so nice. You wanted to trick me into telling you things!"

"Do you have things to tell me, Syd?" He asks that question so calmly. His reaction is such a stark difference between us.

"I don't want to talk about the rabbit. I don't want to talk about the rabbit!"

"Sit," he commands.

I close my eyes. I know this is wrong. Everything about this is wrong. But when he gets up and takes my hand, I feel helpless again. Just like all those years I spent with Garrett. I follow him over to the cage where the white snowshoe hare is in shock with fright.

I know that feeling.

"Open the cage, Sydney."

Dear God, please, please don't make me kill this rabbit.

"Open it."

I get up and walk to the cage, and then bend down and unhook the latch on the door. I look over my shoulder at Merc and he nods, so I lift up the wire and fling it back. It clangs against the top, but the rabbit is too frightened to move.

"Now step back here with me."

I walk back and squat down next to him, unsure of what's happening. "Now what?" I whisper.

"Now," he says, turning to me with a smile, "we wait."

"For what?"

"For the shock to wear off and for the rabbit to leave." I frown at him. "We're setting it free, Syd. We're setting you free too."

THIRTY-FOUR

MERC

"All I can do is open the door. I can't make you walk out."
– Case

She has the most confused look on her face. How can it be so hard for this girl to get it? "He brainwashed you, Sydney. It took years and years and years to do that. Do you understand? I was a PSYOPS in the army. With Garrett. We did it together, like a team."

She sits her butt on the ground. Not to get comfortable, I don't think, but because she doesn't have the strength to squat anymore.

She's in shock. Just like that rabbit.

"We were in charge of people. Company people, Syd. Do you understand what I mean by that?"

She nods. "People like me."

"Yes, unfortunately. People just like you. Mothers and daughters. You know what it means to be born a Company kid. You know they own you if you're a girl. You know that

305

they ask the parents when a girl is born if they agree to the mother-daughter promise or not. And what happens to the mothers when they don't agree?"

"They kill them." She says it like a robot. She's caught up in her memories.

"That's right. They kill them. So if a Company girl grows up with a mother, even if that mother dies when she is small, what does that mean, Sydney?"

She looks me in the face for this and I know, of all the terrible things I've done for the wrong reasons, this terrible thing is for the right one. "The mothers agreed to sell those daughters and allow them to be... used."

"That's right. Your mother agreed. At least at first. I don't know what happened with your mother. Or your father. I only know that part is true. She did this to you. They both did this to you."

"Was I your assignment? In the army?"

"No. I saw you for the first time out there at that cabin. But I had other assignments. Garrett and I had them together. I didn't understand what the Company was back then. I didn't understand that they were a shadow government that exists right here in the US, right alongside real people and regular governments. But I got an order once — Garrett and I got an order once. Probably the same kind of order that the Company man who killed your mother got."

She licks her lips and the cold wind dries them

immediately. Her face is flushed and I know that if I were to check her heart rate right now, it would be off the charts. But she's holding it together, so I continue.

"And we were ordered to take care of this Company mother-daughter pair."

"Did you do it?" She has hope in her eyes that I didn't, and it kills me to admit that I did.

"Yes. I did it. I did it because Garrett had already raped the mother and he was going for the little girl next. She was twelve. The same age Sasha was when they tried to take her. Her mother never gave her up. They killed her before Sasha ever left the hospital when she was born. But her father did things that were against the rules. It was a father-daughter kill that night I was sent to save you. And I chose to save her instead."

"You left me there."

"I know."

"Because I wasn't worth saving?" She's crying now. Silent frozen tears.

I lean in and grab her face, holding it in both my hands as I look her in the eyes. "That's not why," I whisper. "I just figured you would be OK. You were sixteen. Sasha was only twelve. I made a choice and I'd like to say I regret it, but I don't. I love Sasha very much. She is the only good thing that has ever happened to me."

"But I wasn't OK."

"I know that now. But I really thought you would be. I really thought you would be, Syd."

A noise off to our left drags our attention away from each other and back to the cage. The rabbit hops forward once, then twice. It sits there at the edge of freedom and hesitates.

"Be the rabbit, Sydney."

"The rabbit gets eaten by dogs."

"No, watch."

She does watch. She strains so hard she might be giving herself a headache. But the look on her face when that rabbit finally figures out it can run — it's amazing.

She gasps as the small animal zigzags across the frozen river and disappears in the thick woods of the opposite bank.

"Be the rabbit, Sydney. Get away from him. Garrett filled your mind with lies. He filled you up with instructions and triggers. He's been using you to do his dirty work. And even though I never saw him again after he disappeared, I know he was taking you. Wasn't he?"

If she knows, she holds it in. And I let her.

Because I just set her free. And now we're ready for the final step.

THIRTY-FIVE

SYDNEY

"You can hope for truth, but always be prepared for betrayal."
– Sydney

We check the rest of the trap line and if there's a rabbit in there, I set it free. It's amazing how something so simple can mean so much. My mind clears as the morning moves on. Memories come back and others recede. I'm feeling pretty good, and when we get back to the cabin, Case—or is he really Merc?—starts making something for us to eat as I watch from the barstool, nursing a beer.

His phone rings and he looks at the caller ID and smiles. "Sash," he says. "Sash?" He looks at the phone and then I can just barely make out the three hang-up beeps from the speaker.

My head begins to pound.

"Huh," he says. "She called me yesterday with news of a boyfriend." He shoots me a smile. "I do background

309

checks on them. And she had a date and needed one pronto. But I had things to do." He smiles at me. "You needed me more yesterday." And then he chuckles as he dials again. When there's no answer, he shrugs. "Probably in a remote area and lost signal."

I close my eyes as my mind starts to swirl.

"You OK?" Case asks.

I open my eyes again and shake my head. "I feel funny." He looks worried. "Dizzy, almost." *And confused,* I don't add. "All that rabbit stuff, maybe."

"Maybe you're just hungry?" He pushes a plate of salmon and a glass of water in front of me.

I drink the water and push the plate away. "I'm really not feeling well."

"You want to go lie down?"

"Not really," I say, squinting my eyes from the sudden headache. "But I probably should."

"It was too much, maybe?" He picks me up and carries me towards the stairs, climbing them easily. He takes me into the bedroom and sets me down on the bed. "I'll stay with you if you want."

I nod and close my eyes as soon as my head rests on the soft pillow. "I feel a little better already."

He pulls his thermal shirt over his head and throws it on the floor, then kicks off his boots and goes to work on mine. They drop with a thud. I study him as he stands at the end of the bed. He's hard to ignore. Perfect, really. His muscles are cut into his body like a statue's, hard as stone.

Which is how I'd have described his personality as well, a few days ago. But now I'm not sure what to make of that mind of his. The killer part of him I can accept. And this tender part, the part that wants to fuck me softly — I'd like to accept that too.

But right now something feels *wrong*.

He crawls up the bed, his hands and knees on either side of me. And for a moment, when I look into those blazing amber eyes, I see him as the predator he is. My whole body trembles.

Then his hand is on my stomach, underneath my shirt that belongs to him. And the coldness I've imagined is not there. He is warm. And he smiles at me. I take a deep breath, not sure I want to do this stuff in the light. The darkness hides me. I like it. But the sun is streaming through the large windows that have the same view as the crow's nest and it makes me self-conscious.

"Want me to stop?" he asks.

"No," I whisper. I want to keep him forever. But even though he's been nice and I don't think he wants to hurt me, he's flashing a red danger sign right now.

"Relax," he says, lifting my shirt up so he can kiss my stomach. "And tell me what you want."

"I want to be sure."

"Of what?"

"That you're real, and this isn't a trick."

"Why would I trick you?"

"Because you need information."

"You said you don't have it."

"I know, but—"

He stares at me. "But what?"

"But you don't believe me." And then I take a deep breath and gather my nerve. "Do you believe me?"

He goes back to kissing me. He makes me feel like I'm being tortured with pleasure as he licks a small circle around my nipple, gently squeezing the other one at the same time, until they are both erect and tingling. He scoots up a little and takes his kisses to my neck. "Do you think I'll hurt you, Syd?" His hot breath makes the words skim across my skin. I feel like I'm floating.

"Not physically. Not anymore." I say. My head is spinning again, not the same way it was downstairs."But—"

His mouth steals my words and even though I have this pressing need to know if he's genuine, I give up. I just give up and kiss him back.

It's a long, slow kiss that makes my heart ache. It's a sad kiss. One that has so much meaning, I can barely breathe. I want him to be real so bad. "You were always in my head, Case. You came to me in a dream and told me how to survive. You taught me to fish and hunt. But it wasn't about

312

fishing and hunting. It was you, splitting my mind into yet another piece. Not the way Garrett did it, with fear and threats, but with smiles and sunshine. It was you I dreamed about when he made me do things."

"He brainwashed you, Syd. We've been over this. He told you a lot of things." Case unbuttons my jeans and then sits up and drags them down my legs, tossing them onto the floor with my boots. And then his warm chest covers my cold one and never have I ever wanted to hug a man like I do this man right now. I wrap my arms around him and pull him close. "He gave you triggers, Sydney. Little things that only you know about. Words like bobcat."

"And hush," I say.

"No, cowgirl. Not hush. But there are more things I need to know. More words and symbols that hold his secrets. Do you remember any of them?"

"I feel like I'm floating."

"Shhh, Sydney. Try to answer my question. Do you know of any more words or symbols that he planted in your head to make you do things? He might want you to hurt me, for instance. Did he give you a word that would make you hurt me?"

I'm flying. I'm high up in the clouds. I can barely open my eyes.

Case is on top of me and we are naked. "I want you," I say. It comes out like an echo in my head. I'm not even sure if I said it out loud. "I want that soft fuck again, so bad."

He spreads my legs and hikes one knee up to my chest, the tip of his cock pressing against my clit. It feels so fucking good. "You need me to fuck you, Syd? To remember what he said?"

I can't answer that. "My stomach hurts."

"He planted a trigger that makes you sick, Sydney. If you talk about it."

"I feel so weird."

"Concentrate now, OK? Did he tell you where he was? He came to you, remember? All those years you thought he was missing, he came to you."

"I don't think he did."

"You told me he did, Sydney. You told me a lot of things when I had you under the drugs the last time. So you don't need to pretend anymore. Just tell me where he is."

"He's gone."

Case lets out a long breath and then slips his dick inside me. It's painful, he goes too fast. But when I cry out, he stops and lets me settle. After a few seconds, he begins again. Slower this time. Softer than anything I've ever felt. I grab his shoulders and try to squeeze, but I have no strength. I open my mouth to ask why I'm so weak, but Case is there with his lips again, his tongue twisting up my thoughts and making me confused.

He flips me around, spooning me from behind, and

then his cock fills me up again. He reaches around my waist and his fingers find my clit, strumming me like the song he played last night. The music plays in my head and my excitement builds with each stroke of his fingers and thrust of his hips.

"Where is Garrett, Syd?"

"He's gone."

"Where did he go?"

I'm about to answer, but the climax I've been driving towards is building. I hold my breath and press back against his body, into his cock, wanting him to take me deeper. The moment I find my release, he pulls out and spills his hot come all over my back.

"Did it feel good, Syd?"

"Mmmmm."

"Now concentrate," he says, wrapping his arms around me and pushing his mouth into my neck. "Where did Garrett go? Where can I find him?"

"You don't need to find him," I say back, feeling so, so sleepy. "I heard the trigger. He's on his way here."

Case throws me aside and is off the bed in an instant. But the time I gather enough sense to open my eyes, he's already dressed at the end of the bed.

"Where are you going?" I slur out. "I need to go with you."

"You're staying here," he says.

"No!" My heart begins to beat wildly as I try to sit up. I don't even come close to sitting before I am slumped over, my face in the pillow. "You drugged me. You drugged me again, and you promised you wouldn't."

Case leans down and whispers in my ear, pulling my hair so I'm forced to look up at him. "I'll take care of you when I get back." And then he releases my hair and my head drops back to the bed.

"But you were nice to me. You said you weren't going to kill me. You promised not to drug me!" I try to swing my legs out of the bed but he shoves me back.

"I lied, Sydney. But if you stay real still and go back to sleep, you'll never have to think about it again."

THIRTY-SIX

"Always have an ace in the hole."

– Case

I turn away from her and hastily get dressed, wondering where Garrett is. How far he's gotten, what his endgame is. How he'll play this out.

"Sasha," Sydney says from the bed.

I whirl around and look at her. Her eyes are drooping pretty bad from the drugs I put in her water. Her head is slick with sweat and she's lying sideways across the sheets, like she's been trying to get up while I was lost in thought.

"What?"

"He's got Sasha."

My stomach rolls as her words sink in.

"He's got her and you do not want to know what he's gonna do with her."

I reach for Sydney's hair, fisting it hard and pulling her face towards me. "Where the fuck is he?"

317

"He's waiting for you, Case." Sydney tries a smirk on for size, but it comes off as a grimace. "At the end of the trail."

I let go of her hair and get up, pulling a thermal shirt on as I jump down the stairs.

Motherfucker. The call. The call Sasha made earlier. That was Garrett. That was the trigger Sydney was talking about—it has to be. She was in on this from the beginning. My ringtone must be a trigger for her. Which means that asshole has been close enough to me to hear it.

I clench my fists as the anger runs through me. But the anticipation is there too. I will end him today. Nothing else matters. Garrett is a dead man.

THIRTY-SEVEN

SYDNEY

"In the end it all comes down to what you're capable of. Rescue means debt. Save yourself and you owe no one."

– Sydney

I don't wait for Case to leave. The drugs are taking over and if he comes back to find me rifling through his medications and puts a stop to it, well, that's the chance I have to take. Because I have about two minutes before I pass out for good and either way I'm dead.

I roll across the bed one more time and reach for the drawer in the nightstand. My hand misses it a few times, but finally I hook a fingertip through the pull and it slides open.

Downstairs a door closes with a slam.

My hand waves around inside the drawer for the first-aid kit and I'm just about to get frustrated when it hits me.

He took it downstairs to bandage my hand.

Fuck. Sixty-seven thousand fucks are running through

my head right now. Do I not deserve to catch one break? One?

I roll over again and fall to the floor. I don't know if I can make it downstairs —

"Syd," beautiful Garrett says.

Is he Garrett or Case? Who is the man in my head?

"Grab the guns," he says, the beautiful mountain landscape behind him shimmering. Aspen leaves, yellow, like it's fall. No, golden. Everything about this dream man is golden.

"Grab his guns, Syd. The ones in the case. Then go downstairs and find the kit. You know what to do. They told you about overdosing in your training."

I don't care who that guy is at this point, I'm taking his advice. I grab the gun case and pull myself up. There's furniture I can lean on to make my way to the door. But as I stand at the top of the hardwood stairs, I have serious doubts I will be able to get down them without breaking my neck.

Sit on your ass and scoot, that guy says, whoever he is.

I plop down and fall forward, my head hitting the banister with a crack. There's no pain. I'm far too numb from the drugs to even know how badly I'm hurt. I grab hold of the banister and pull myself up again, then scoot down one step at a time. When I finally get to the bottom step I let out an ironic laugh. I got all this way—I can see the kit on the kitchen counter—and I'm gonna die here on the steps. Or maybe reaching for the kit, my hand outstretched—

Shut the fuck up and get over there!

That guy in my head is the one who needs to shut the fuck up, that's what I think. In fact—I force my legs to stand. My eyes are almost closed, that's how sleepy I am—I think I'm gonna kill that guy in my head with these guns...

Shit. The guns are up on the steps where I fell over.

I shake my head to try to snap out of the growing lethargy and drop to my hands and knees so I can crawl. My hair drags on the polished wood floor and I have a moment of relief that Case is so neat. No dust bunnies on his floor to soil my hair.

A laugh bursts out at that thought. I'm really fucking losing it.

I make to the bar and stand up. If I open that kit and there's no antagonist in there to stop this drug, I will die laughing.

It's in there, a little vial of clear liquid in a tightly sealed container. I rip the metal tab with my teeth, twisting the bottle, peeling it off. And then I rip open a sealed sterile syringe and push the needle into the rubber cap.

Poison training? I took that, right? Garrett told me how much of the drug to use for my body weight when we went over poisoning. I know he did.

But I have no clue. My arms are so heavy. My fingers barely work. So I draw in enough liquid to fill the syringe, pull it out of the rubber top, and stab myself in the upper arm.

I don't feel a thing. Not the stab, not when I push the drug into the muscle, not when I fall over and barely avoid cracking my head on the floor as I hit the ground palms first. But I do know I'm still in the game if this works, because a snow machine roars past the house outside. He just left.

||||||||||||

I come to screaming as I sit up straight. My lungs inhale a huge breath, a gasp that echoes up into the cathedral ceiling of the house. I am instantly alert and the past few hours come rushing back.

Case. That motherfucker.

Sasha.

Garrett.

I run up the stairs and get the gun case, opening it up there on the landing where it fell.

Three bullets. What fucking good are three fucking bullets? I run back in the bedroom and open the other nightstand drawer. But of course the other guns are gone. He took those and left these collector's items behind with three stupid bullets.

I smile. I guess that just means there's one for each of those assholes, and none left over to spare.

I load one bullet into the chamber of the first gun, and two into the magazine of the other. I dress in my snow gear and stuff the guns in my pockets as I head out into the cold. I reconnect the wires that I pulled out on the Snowcat to buy myself some time the other night when Case told me to leave, and follow his tracks down the trail.

THIRTY-EIGHT

MERC

"Even a man with nothing to lose can lose things."

– Case

I cut the engine on the machine at the fork in the trail and haul my sniper rifle over my shoulder as I trudge through the snow. It's a decision that will cost me some time—the snow is deep and I have to wind my way between drifts to make any progress at all. But this party only starts when I get there.

I'm the guest of honor.

The garage where I keep the trucks in the winter comes into view sooner than I'm ready for it. My heart—fuck, my heart has never been filled with such dread before in my life. I should've known it was Sasha he was after. I should've seen that coming.

But she's been well-hidden over the years. Living out a quiet life in private schools and summers overseas with her adopted family. Good grades and dreams of the future driving her instead of looking over her shoulder. She's had some trouble, but none of it was Company trouble.

Hell, even I stopped looking over my shoulder. It's my own damn fault I've been up here preoccupied with his bait while he was planning how to get the only person I ever loved.

I walk slowly and carefully up to the back of the garage, my eyes darting up to the trees in case he came with a sniper.

But that's not Garrett's style. He works alone now and he uses women to do his dirty work. He's always been like that.

He's starting to remind me a little too much of myself.

I press my back against the garage and then peek around the corner, my rifle in the ready position, my eye looking down the sight.

A big, black truck idles in the center of the cul-de-sac. It's pointing away from me, like it's getting ready to leave. Black smoke puffs out of the tailpipe, clashing with the pristine white snow that surrounds it. It's angled in a way that gives me a clear view of the passenger side, but not the driver's.

Sasha is in the front seat. I know her profile. Her dark blonde hair is recognizable to me anywhere. I could pick her out of a crowd of hundreds of people.

It hits me then. He has my Sasha. He's gonna kill her. Right here. Right now. And he's gonna make me watch.

A sound disrupts my thoughts and then her door swings open.

I look through my scope to find him. *Where are you, motherfucker?*

Sasha is pushed through the door and falls out of the truck like a dead body. Her hands are tied behind her back, her feet are tied together, and there's tape over her mouth.

My heart stops. And then she starts kicking her legs and trying to scream. And it starts again.

She's alive.

"If you hurt her I will rip your goddamn throat out!" I roar it so the whole forest echoes with my threat.

Silence. And then the creak of the other door. He ducks getting out or I'd have his head already. But he knows me. I have skills he does not. Fucking punk.

"Did you hurt my Sydney, Case? Or don't *my* girls matter?"

"Fuck you." I duck back behind the garage and stalk the length of it, peeking out around the corner again and then making my way to the opposite side. Now I can see the truck a little better. More front on, but still, no Garrett in my sight.

"How about we play a game, Case? You tell me what you did to Sydney and I'll tell you if I did the same thing to Sasha."

All the things I put Sydney through flash into my mind.

"Drugs? Oh, that one's a given. Sasha here might be a good shot, but she's not been subjected to very many drugs, has she. It didn't go well."

My whole body heats up with rage.

"Torture?" he calls again. "Sydney is quite good at withstanding torture. But again, this one—not so much."

"What do you want?"

"I want my girl back."

"She's at the house. Go get her."

"Not that girl, Case." He laughs. "You know how we have that whole *I owe you, you owe me, and then we're even* thing going in the Company? Well, you owe me, Case. And today we're gonna make it even."

THIRTY-NINE

"There will be a day of reckoning. I call it a reality check"
– Sydney

The snow machine in the middle of the trail has me hyperventilating for a second before I figure out he ditched it to get the element of surprise on Garrett.

I ditch the Cat as well and make a run for it, following in Case's footsteps. A half an hour ago I'd have bet a billion dollars that I could not make a run for my life through deep snow. But that was before the antagonist cleared out all the drugs in my system and made me into a new woman.

I feel like I can run forever. But I know it will wear off, probably soon, so I use up all the extra adrenaline while I still have it. A building peeks out from between the thick cover of pine trees, and the trail winds around a little more. I cut through the woods to save time.

Case's booming voice stops me dead in my tracks.

They're out there. Both of them. And Sasha.

JA HUSS

I really don't know what's going on. A few bits and pieces have come back to me since I left the cabin. But nothing makes much sense. Garrett sent me here, I realize that now. But the gaps are still too wide and the images firing off in my head are blurry one moment, clear the next.

And Case. I don't want to believe it's true. I've held him up on some imaginary pedestal for so long, his final words undo me. He lied. I get it. He drugged me and used sex and longing to get what he needed from me.

But it felt so real. That's what hurts the most. The shame I feel because I fell for it. How he must be laughing at me now. I have to stop in my tracks and clutch the trunk of a tree as I bend over. The sick feeling in my stomach is back, but what it means, I just don't know.

Garrett's black truck comes into view just as he calls out, "You owe me, Case. And today we're gonna make it even."

I pan the area. It's like a cul-de-sac with the garage at the head. No other houses are out here so it must be on a private road. Garrett's truck is in the middle, slanted at an angle, giving me a good view of the passenger side. But I don't see him.

"What do you want to make it even?" Case yells back.

My attention snaps to my right. Case is not far from me. Maybe twenty or thirty feet.

"Oh, we are not to negotiations yet, friend." Garrett laughs. I know he's crouching down on the other side of the truck, out of view of Case's sniper scope. Garrett's told me stories of the Company assassins. Ruthless men. Inhuman. And extremely bent on finishing the job once they start.

What is Case's job here?

Jesus, Sydney. You really are dumb.

I pull myself together and take my attention back to Garrett. He's still hiding behind the truck, playing it safe. "Don't you want to know how poor Sasha has fared since her captivity?" he yells. "Let's compare prisoners, shall we Case? You fucked Sydney, right? I mean, that was in the plan, so I know for sure you did."

And there it is. I am nothing but Case's job and Garrett's plan.

"If you raped Sasha," Case growls, "I will string you up from a tree and let the wolves eat you alive."

"Semantics, Case. I gave you Sydney to play with. You've had her for weeks. I've only had Sasha a day." Garrett laughs. "She can fill you in later if you save her. We'll see how that goes. So don't get on your high horse about what I did to Sasha. Sydney didn't exactly want to let you take her v-card. But in the end, she gave in. Because if there's one thing that Sydney is that Sasha is not, it's malleable. She bends. This one here, not very bendy. She's a fighter, huh, Case? Did you teach her that? Or her father? Did you know I planned that whole night? Hell, did you know I've been planning your demise since the day you shot my girl?"

"She wasn't *your* girl."

"Oh, yeah, that's right. You wanted her too. But instead of accepting the fact that she was mine, you decided to kill her."

Silence from Case. I have never heard this story. Even though my head is every sort of fucked up from all the lies and manipulation, I know I've never heard this story.

Case steps out into the open, his rifle in front of him, like an offering.

Garrett peeks up over the top of the truck and he smiles as he walks around the front end.

Sasha is lying on the ground in a tied-up heap. She has no coat on and it's freezing out here. No gloves. Her face looks half frozen already, since it's planted firmly in the snow. Her eyes are wild when she sees Case, and she starts kicking her feet.

"Let her go, Garrett. She has nothing to do with any of that." Case's voice is steady but low. Like he's raging inside and one wrong move will set him off.

"Oh," Garrett laughs. He's dressed in top-to-bottom white snow gear, just like me. I feel like we're a team just looking at us. It makes me sick. "You killed my girl, Case." He removes a gun from his pants and points it at Sasha's head. Case readies his rifle again. "We were soldiers. We follow orders."

"She was twelve fucking years old!"

"Just like Sasha. Is that why you really saved her that night, Case? Sydney told me under the drugs what you said to her that night. You'd be back? That's what you told her?" Garrett laughs. "You set this whole thing up. It was the perfect opening. A path to revenge."

"I undid Sydney," Case says.

"You sure did," Garrett snarls. "You did it just right, Case. Fucked her up even more than I could ever hope, I'm sure. You're the best, huh? I always knew you'd come through."

Listening to these two men talk about me like I'm a thing is the most degrading moment of my life. Worse than Case fucking the virgin out of me. Worse than being drugged and manipulated by Garrett to do his bidding. I'm not even a person in their eyes.

"Our orders, Case, were to kill the mother and take the daughter to make an example of them. I did my part—"

"You raped that woman. Tied her up in a shed and kept her for days before you killed her."

"—your part was to hand the daughter over to me."

"I asked her whether she wanted to go with you or die. She chose death, Garrett. She would rather die than be with you. That's why I killed her."

Garrett shakes his head slowly and with a disgusting smile on his face. "I think you really believe you did the right thing back then. I really do, Case. So let's see if you can do the right thing again today. Your choice back then was to let me have her or kill her. So your choice today is…" He stops to huff out a laugh and a shiver runs down my spine. Because I already know what he's gonna say. "Kill her"—he nods to Sasha—"or let me take her away. Alive."

"Or," Case says, his voice still that low rumble that's just on the verge of wild, "I kill you and she leaves with me. Alive."

"That will never happen, Merc." Garrett uses his trade name like they are friends, and it makes Case stiffen, as I'm sure it was intended.

"How do you figure?"

And then Garrett looks straight at me and stretches out his arm. He points to me, beckoning.

Case backs up, his rifle still trained on Garrett, and realizes I'm still in the game.

"Because the acorn never falls far from the tree."

FORTY

"Sometimes all you can do is fire that gun and pray your aim is true."

- Sydney

My whole world spins as those words echo through my head.

The acorn never falls far from the tree.

My two guns are in my hand before I even realize I've pulled them out. My feet carry me out towards Garrett and Case. But only one man is being targeted.

Case.

The other gun is aimed at Sasha.

We had my trigger word wrong the whole time. Case never undid me, it was a trap. The whole thing was set up by Garrett to be a trap.

"Sydney," Case says off to my right. "Sydney, listen to me. Remember when we talked about what he did, Sydney? He brainwashed you. He just triggered you."

I know this. I know with every fiber of my being that

335

I'm on autopilot. But I can't stop. I'm not even sure I *want* to stop. Case ruined my life. I was sixteen years old. The brainwashing had worn off again. It was an opening, a crucial moment in time where things could go either way. Salvation or damnation.

Case chose damnation. He damned me to hell that night. All to save that girl out there in the snow. I was a job and he never finished it. I wasn't worth it to him. I was nothing to him then and I'm nothing to him now. *I lied, Sydney. But if you stay real still and go back to sleep, you'll never have to think about it again.*

"Sydney," Garrett says, and glances at me for just the splittest of seconds. "If he makes one move towards me—"

Case takes the opportunity and gets off one shot, right through Garrett's gun hand. Garrett spins as flesh and weapon go flying, drops to the ground, holding his injury as blood spurts out where fingers used to be. He lowers his eyes for a moment and catches his breath. And then he looks up. And the evil in those eyes makes me want to piss myself. "You're gonna regret that." His voice is even and steady as ever. "Shoot him, Sydney."

Case takes a step towards Sasha, his gun aimed at Garrett, but my itchy trigger finger stops him. Sasha yelps as snow and ice splatter across her face from the shot that misses her by inches. And the bullet from the other gun flies past Case, because when I look over, he's still alive.

What the fuck am I doing? Oh my God, I almost killed them.

"Finish her," Garrett says, "and then shoot Case."

My head floods with chaos. Memories. Violence. And more. So, so much more. Humiliation and servitude. My life is a living nightmare.

I have to blink my eyes to stop the spinning.

"Sydney," Case says. The world is in slow motion as I turn my head. His rifle is trained on me. "Sydney," he says again. It comes out in slow motion too. *Syyyyyddd-neeeee.* I find his face, just in time to watch his mouth move. "Hush," he says. "*Huuuuuuuush.*"

I am still. The spinning stops for a moment.

"Sydney," Garrett says, in that low growl he reserves for punishment. "You are my *acorn*. And you *will* shoot him."

I take a step forward.

"Hush," Case repeats once more. "Take a deep breath and keep still, Sydney."

My lungs obey him, even though I have no idea what's happening.

"Shoot. Him," Garrett orders. "Shoot him or you will hear that rabbit scream for the rest of your life."

I raise my gun and aim it at Case. I can see down the barrel of his rifle. He shakes his head at me. "I'll kill you first, cowgirl. My trigger finger is faster. Just hush and stand aside. Let me finish him off. Let me make this right for you. Let me set you free, like the rabbits we set free this morning."

A long breath rushes out of me and Case starts to relax. Garrett starts screaming his threats.

I have no clue what to do. But everything suddenly makes perfect sense. The acorn. The hush. Two men with one thing on their minds. Revenge. And two girls caught in the middle.

I walk towards Sasha. "Give me your gun, Case." I aim mine at Sasha. "Give me your gun or I'll kill her."

"Don't do his dirty work anymore, Syd. I'm here now. I'll take you away from all this. You will be saved today if you just put that gun down and let me finish him off like I should've eight years ago."

I look down the sight of the FN Five-SeveN that Sasha gave him as a gift. It's almost more irony than I can take.

"Don't make me kill you, Sydney."

"Please," I say, never taking my eye off Sasha. "Kill me."

Case drops his rifle in the snow.

"Kick it away," I demand. He does, and it comes sliding towards me. I'm not stupid enough to pick it up. I keep my eyes on Sasha.

But I have so much to say.

"You too, huh?" I look over at him, aiming the other FN Five-SeveN at Case's stoic face. No emotion at all. And what did I expect? He's a cold-blooded killer. He's got an agenda and nothing else matters. He hates me. The only reason I'm alive right now is because I saved myself and got away. "You brainwashed me too. With that word hush."

He's shaking his head as I talk. "It's not like that, Sydney. You don't know the whole story."

"I agree. I don't know much at all, do I? I'll probably never know what really happened here. Or in the past. But I do know one thing. You're not here for me. You're here for her." I shake the gun that's pointing at Sasha. Not a move or a whimper out of her at all.

"He used you, Sydney," Garrett says.

I change my aim to Garrett and shoot him between the eyes. His head splatters all over Sasha and the front end of the truck. Bits of bone go flying and Sasha's calm is gone. She wriggles in her bindings, trying to inch away like a worm.

Case comes towards me even though the other gun is still trained on him. "You only had three bullets, cowgirl. Show's over now."

"I know," I say, looking him in the eyes. "And that's the only reason you're alive right now."

I drop the guns and rush him, delivering a two-handed push to his chest. He rocks back, but does not retaliate. I punch him in the face so hard my knuckles split open along with his lip. Blood spurts out and my hand begins to throb.

Nothing from him. I'm not even worth a fight.

The anger, and hate, and feelings of betrayal that I have

towards him are seeping out of me like sweat. His cheek turns red where I hit him, but he just stands there.

"I *hate* you." And then I spit in his face. "I hate you so fucking much." The tears start to spill out, running down my cheeks in a way I've never experienced before. "This was a game to you. You knew he was coming. You knew I was programmed to do this shit. And you used me. You planted that word in my head. When was it? Huh? Before I woke up in that torture cabin? That place you took me to die?"

Case just stares at me. Guilty. "I thought you were unsalvageable," he says softly. And that kills me. It fucking kills me that he's so good at that soft stuff. He uses it like a weapon. And because I need that tenderness so much, I actually hesitate. "I figured it was too risky for you to stay alive. But I had an idea. I wanted to help you—"

"Liar! You're such a fucking liar! You wanted to kill Garrett, fuck me over again, and save your precious princess here. You used that word to make me *love you*. That's why nothing you did back there bothered me, isn't it?" He stays silent as I put that piece of the puzzle together. "I hate you. And if I ever see your face again, I will blow it right off your head."

I turn on my heel and walk away, picking up my guns as I go. Wishing he'd shoot me in the back. Take me out of my misery. But he doesn't.

So I just step over Garrett's dead body, get into his truck, slam the door, and drive off.

Be the rabbit, Sydney. Be the rabbit.

Oh, I will, I assure that inner psycho in my head. *Because running is all I have left.*

FORTY-ONE

"It's a haunting feeling to look back and know you fucked it all up."

– *Case*

I watch the truck drive away with more sadness than I've ever felt in my life. And then some muffled whimpers make me realize Sasha is still on the ground. She's just picking a knife out of Garrett's pocket, trying to get herself free, when I walk up to her and take it out of her hand.

"One sec, Sash, sorry." I rip the tape off her mouth and even though that must've hurt like a bitch, my Sash stays quiet. I cut her hands free, then her feet, and help her up.

She hugs me. No tears. She stopped crying a long time ago over this shit. But the squeeze tells me everything I need to know.

"You OK?" I ask her.

She nods into my coat. "I'm sorry."

"Me too, kid." And then I give her a little push and we

start walking back to the snow machine I left on the trail.

"What about him?" Sasha asks, gesturing behind us once we get into the trees.

"Wolves will take care of him. It's better than he deserves."

The silence overtakes us as we make our way back to the house and when Sasha gets off the snow machine behind me, I can't seem to make myself move.

"I'll be inside," she says.

"Sure," I say back, propping my hands on the front of the machine, then dropping my head into them.

I have no idea how long I stay out there, running the day back to the beginning, wishing I could do things different.

Hell, I know I did the right thing when I killed that girl all those years ago. She would've ended up just like Sydney. She knew. Her mother told her everything and they were caught trying to escape the compound where they were held. Death or sexual servitude. They both wanted death.

The daughter got off easy, because at least she didn't end her life being raped by that monster. Garrett would've never let her go.

Still, I killed her.

How many people have I killed over the years? Way more than I can remember, that's for sure.

I think back on my conversations with Sydney. Not the ones out in the cabin, but the ones here at my home.

Are you a Simple Man, *Case?*

Yeah, sure. I'm fucking simple, all right. Kill or be killed. That's the rule I live by.

My mother would be so proud.

It's well past dark when Sasha appears in the garage doorway. The lights have been off for hours. I've been sitting out here in the cold. The wolves started howling a little while ago and I know, if I were to ride back down the trail, they'd be having a feast.

I momentarily think of joining Garrett out on the dinner table. It would be better than I deserve, and that's the only thing that stops me.

"Are you gonna come in?"

I look up at Sash and shake my head. "I don't think I can." I huff out a long, sad breath. "I know I can't, Sash. I can't face what happened in there today. I did it all wrong, man. But I panicked when she said he had you. I just fucking panicked. I thought I was gonna lose you and you know what?"

Sash bites her lip and shakes her head. The worry is plastered all over her face. Has she ever seen me like this? Has anyone ever seen me like this? I don't think so. I left this guy behind in Boston. The kid who used violence to shut out his fear. Who wanted to be an emotionless mercenary to make the feelings he didn't understand go away.

No one but my dad has ever seen me like this.

"Tell me. Merc. Because I'm scared right now." She is too. I can feel the fear all around her. Not *of* me. I'd never hurt her and she knows that. But I've always been a very self-destructive man. She's worried *for* me.

And I do not deserve it.

"I saved you that night because I killed that little girl." I nod at her, but she says nothing. "And I thought I could wipe that sin away, ya know? But all I did was make it worse for someone else. Sydney was caught in my guilt and she suffered. I can't even comprehend what she's thinking right now. The level of betrayal she must feel."

Sasha walks over and places a hand on my shoulder, giving it a little squeeze of support. "You know what?"

I take a deep breath and ask, "What?"

"I think you made a mistake when you chose me."

"Fuck that."

"Because I've never needed saving, Merc. Never. I was always gonna get away that night. I knew they were coming for me and I was ready. Maybe I was only twelve, but my father spent every minute of our time together training me to take care of myself. I never needed you that night and she did. And she still needs you, Merc. So I think you just need to admit you should've done it different and forgive yourself for it."

I don't know what to say back to her. How can I admit that choosing her was wrong? "That decision seemed so

346

easy at the time, Sash. How did I manage to fuck it all up? Would letting Garrett take that first little girl have made Sydney's life better or worse? There's just no way to know. And I guess that's what the hard choices really are. Leaps of faith that you're doing the right thing. Leaps of faith that you're doing enough."

When I look up at her she's frowning. "You did your best, Merc. No one is judging you for that choice but you."

"And Sydney."

"No," Sasha says. "She's mad, she feels betrayed. But she's not judging you. How can she say her life is worth more than mine? I'm certainly not saying my life is worth more than hers. But she can't judge you, Merc. Because she knows that given a choice like that, she couldn't be trusted to make the right one either. She can't even make the right choices for herself, let alone three other people."

It stings that Sasha includes that first little girl in this equation. Maybe killing her wasn't the answer after all. Maybe my whole life is a lie I've been telling myself.

"No one knows. You just do what you can and hope you did enough," she continues.

"I didn't do enough. I know that now. I could've gone back for her. I had opportunities. And I didn't. I let my lust for revenge take over my life. And so here I am. The noble choice I thought I made is just another sin in my long, long list of unforgivable acts.

Sasha sighs. "Sometimes, Merc, things are just unwinnable. You have to accept it like the rest of us little people."

I shoot her a look.

"Or," she smiles. "You suck in your pride and take it back." She squeezes my shoulder one more time. "And then make up for it."

I look up at her and wonder how to admit I made the wrong choice? Because all her stackable moments add up to this smart, strong, beautiful woman. And if I had left her to fend for herself that night, where would she be now? "It's unwinnable, I guess."

"Hey, Merc?"

I stare at her. "What?"

"If you don't think you did your best you still have time, you know. You're a genius. Go do something genuine." And then she walks away and leaves me there.

FORTY-TWO

"When you've done all you can, you've done your best. No one has a right to ask for more."

-Sydney

Brett is sleeping when I let myself into his house and make my way to his room. It's a nice house, for Cheyenne, anyway. He's got about fifty acres, which sits idle. Just blah grassland surrounding his home. Not many trees, but there's a big pond on the property, and that gives it some much-needed character.

It's too big for one guy, too. Four bedrooms, full walk-out basement, plus a finished attic. But if you have a large family, it's perfect.

I wish I could say that's why I was here. To get back to my old life and have that wedding I missed. But I can't.

I press the FN Five-SeveN into his temple and whisper, "Move, asshole. Give me a reason to blow it off." I really want him to give me a reason. I really want to picture Case's

349

face as I do it.

Brett opens his eyes, startled enough to try to sit up before he realizes what's happening. "Sydney?" He really does look confused.

But I know better now. It was a long drive home. I can't even count how many times I had to stop on the side of some desolate dirt road just to scream the demons out of my fucked-up mind. Took me two days to get here because of it.

"Why all girls, Brett?"

"What?" He laughs a little so I press the gun against his temple a little harder. "Sydney, what are you doing?"

"Those nieces of yours. Why all girls?"

"I don't know—"

I slam the butt of the gun down on his face so hard his teeth crack. He sits up, reaching for my weapon, but I shoot him in the shoulder. The suppressor on the end of my barrel lets off a soft supersonic crack that sounds more like a harmless firecracker than a gun.

But it does the job and blood splatter is everywhere. Brett rolls with the force of the high-velocity cartridge and he ends up face down on the bed.

I wish I had time for a lengthy conversation—I'd like to get some answers. Maybe an apology. Or even a pathetic justification. *We're saving the world, Sydney.* I wish I had time for that, because maybe I'd feel better about the evil people do in the name of the Company.

But I don't have time for that. I feel sick and I just want to leave. Plus the back of his head is too much of an invitation to let it pass.

Assassination-style is how Brett enters the darkness.

My heart doesn't even beat fast over this kill. Not one bit. Because he deserves it.

The many stops on the side of the road came with memories. More proof that my life is just one long lie.

The sisters up at the lodge? Not sisters. Wives.

Those adorable tow-headed baby girls? Future collateral damage.

My wedding to Brett? A promise made years ago by my father.

Garrett knew, which was why he bowed out of the 'relationship' we had and disappeared. Oh, the brainwashing continued. I was too volatile to leave to my own devices. But over time, I stopped resisting with the help of drugs. Brett made sure I kept those up while we were officially together.

When all this hit me on the way home, I thought there was no way I could change any of it. I was still reeling from the lies and betrayal. Still filled with self-loathing and shame. And maybe this doesn't change anything? Maybe those wives of his really are on board with what they're doing? I have no way of knowing.

But taking this man's life has to change things in some

way. Even if it's a small way. Maybe it makes those little girls' lives better. Maybe not. But knowing Brett met his end gives me peace. At least I tried. I can't kill their mothers and live with myself. I'm not Case. So I settle with erasing Brett's influence over them.

It'll have to do, because it's all I've got.

I did my best.

FORTY-THREE

SYDNEY

"Revenge is never sweet if it's justified."

– Sydney

The drive home fills me with more dread than I expected. Everything about it is lies. I just… I just can't face it.

But I've been missing for weeks. On the road for days. And I need to stop running right now. I need to face facts. I need to pick myself up and figure out a plan. I need to figure out how the person I thought I was and the person I really am can come to terms.

My escape fantasy life is gone. I didn't even mean for it to happen. I guess reality has consequences. But it's hard. I feel so alone.

I drive down the quiet Cheyenne street in Old Town. When I get to my building, I park in the alley behind the bar, planning on sleeping in the truck before I try to figure out what to do. But if I'm going to leave and find my own

353

way in this world, I'd like to take one more look at the only thing that ever gave me pleasure.

I get out and remember that I have no keys. The building is a hundred and twenty years old though. Not all the windows lock properly. I don't need keys.

I climb the fire escape up to the second floor and shimmy through the office window. The sun is just coming up, so a little light seeps in when I push the curtains aside.

Looks the same as ever. My desk is a mess of bills and delivery receipts. The walls are decorated with pictures of various ribbon-winning 4-H livestock that I've purchased at the state fair auction over the years. Boxes of unopened liquor bottles are stacked in one corner. My coats are hanging on wall hooks near the door. There's a nice layer of dust covering everything too. I think I love that the most. It makes me feel better that Brett didn't come in here after I was gone. It makes me feel like he never cared about this place like I did, like it really did belong to me and only me.

That's something, I guess. Not much, but something.

I make my way downstairs and head over to the cash register. I know it's empty, but a girl can hope. I don't dare take any money out of my bank account. I did, after all, just kill Brett Setton. Some precautions are in order. It makes me feel like I'm making an effort to live through this and not give up.

There's not many windows in the bar. And the ones

it does have are all high up and small. Like basement windows. But there's enough light to see. The bar is clean and the chairs are stacked on top of the tables. Like it would look any morning. Like all that shit never happened and this is just another day.

But it's not. It's my last day as Sydney Channing. I don't want to be her anymore.

I press the buttons on the cash register to make the drawer pop open and then stare down at it for a few seconds before I can come to terms with what I'm seeing.

Stacks upon stacks of twenty-dollar bills. All neatly tied together with one of those paper ribbons the bank puts on them.

"I figured you could use it."

I turn to a dark corner where the quiet voice came from. Merc is sitting in the shadows, his face hidden until he leans forward and a beam of dim sunshine decides to give him up. He hasn't shaved. There's a weathered cowboy hat on the table, his arms are stretched around it, and his hands are folded out in front. He looks as tired and sad as I feel.

"I don't need you," I say.

"I know that."

"Then why are you here?"

"Because I need you."

I back away from him, even though he hasn't moved and he's all the way across the room, until I bump up against the liquor cabinet. "Get out."

"I will," he says, standing up but not taking a step forward. "But I deserve a chance to tell the story my way. If you want me to leave, leave knowing why I really did all those things. Not because you've conjured up some story in your head."

"Oh my God." I laugh a little. "I might not know everything, but there are a few indisputable facts that can't be ignored about you, Merc."

He squints his amber eyes at the name. "Don't call me that."

"Why not? That's who you are, remember? The man you made yourself into. Own it, Merc. You're a killer. You're a liar. And you use girls to do your dirty work. Just like Garrett did. So stop with your holier-than-thou attitude and just own it."

He shrugs, but looks away for a moment. Doubts, that's what that look says. "I deserve that. But if you've got me on a timer, I'd like to have my say before you verbally punch me in the face and tell me to get out."

His hands are folded in front of him now. He's standing still and tall as he waits for my answer.

I throw my hands up. "Talk then."

He clears his throat and lifts his chin up. Steadying himself for something.

It makes me more nervous than I'd like to admit. What

will this monster tell me next? What bad news does he have to deliver now?

"I take it back, Sydney. Leaving you behind like that. I made a mistake—"

"Fuck. You." I feel the tears well up in my eyes. "After all that shit you talked to me? You think I'm going to let you walk into my fucking bar and fill me up with more of your lies? Fuck you."

He stands silent.

"You fucked up."

"I know."

"You never chose me, Merc. You never put me first. You only helped me to help yourself. When I said I hated you, I meant it. My verbal fist just punched your time clock. Get the fuck out."

He lets off a huff of air and nods. "OK." And then he grabs his hat and walks around the table towards me. I have a moment of panic that he will both come towards me and leave for good. But he doesn't do either. He stops about fifteen feet from me, in the middle of the room, pretty much.

"That word, though, Syd? Hush? I gave you that word the summer after I left you. I'd already started watching you. I saw some things that Garrett was doing. I didn't know about the brainwashing. I swear I didn't know. Not until I got you out to the cabin. That's when I figured it out, and the whole hush thing, it was just…" He hesitates. "Fate,

I think. I mean, I felt a lot of guilt about leaving you, believe it or not. But my decision to save Sasha had nothing to do with you being unworthy. I need you to know that." He shakes his head. "You were never unworthy, I was. I never should've left you there. I fucked it up, Sydney. I fucked your whole life up. And I take it back. I'd do it different if I could."

I am speechless. But I'm not sure why.

"I gave you that hush word when I saw you crying once. You weren't even seventeen yet. Garrett left you in an apartment you shared out on Bowling Street—"

I picture that place in my head. He was there?

"—and so I felt like it might make things better for you. You know, if you could talk yourself out of being afraid—"

"It *was* you in my head."

He shrugs with his hands, his knuckles white from clutching his hat. "I don't think so, Sydney. I mean, maybe it started that way because I was messing with your mind with the hush. But I think that in your head was all you. It wasn't me getting you through the hard times or teaching you how to survive. You knew what to do, and you came up with a coping mechanism to get you through. I didn't try and make you love me using that word. I only wanted to ease your pain. The pain I caused by leaving you behind."

I mull this over. But I'm still too confused. I'm so far away from figuring that shit out.

He clears his throat again. "And I don't know what you think I was doing that last time I drugged you, but I wasn't trying to kill you. I knew you were about to give up the answer I needed and I just didn't want you involved when I faced Garrett. I didn't plan on you coming out there…"

"Obviously," I snort. "You counted on me being helpless."

"… I just wanted you to be far away from that final moment. And I failed at that too. I didn't save you when you were sixteen and I didn't save you the other day. I made you save yourself both times. I'm sorry for not being there. I'm sorry I fucked it all up. So I'll leave, but I left more than just cash in that drawer. If you ever want to see me again, you have a way."

And then he puts his hat on and walks towards the back room. He stops just before he passes through into the dark hallway, but he doesn't turn. "Can I ask you one thing? And you can tell me the truth, no matter what."

I swallow down so many things I want to say right now. I want to stop him from leaving. I want to scream at him for leaving me when I was counting on him to save me. I want to run away and run into his arms at the same time.

"Are you looking for the hard truth or the soft truth?"

I mean it as a joke, but he looks over his shoulder at me and I can tell I just cut him deep. But he recovers and turns his body a little to answer me. "Both. If you have time."

"Shoot."

"Would you still have wanted me if I did save you?"

"What?"

"You know. If you hadn't made me out to be some hero and lived for the day that I came back to kill you. If I never gave you the hush. If none of this ever happened and we didn't spend those weeks together the way we did. Would you still have wanted me?"

I think about this for a moment, and I have the hard truth on the tip of my tongue. But he came here and put himself out there. Took it back. And I made him a promise of sorts, back at his house in the mountains. I told him all he had to do was say it and I'd believe him. He could've said it then and he didn't. But people can change.

I give him the soft truth instead. Because I can change too. It's my only hope and I'm gonna hold on to it. So I walk over to him and take his hand. And then I lean up on my tiptoes and plant a kiss on his cheek. "No," I whisper softly.

He drops my hand and walks out.

FORTY-FOUR

SYDNEY

"Judge a man by how he treats his children."
— Sydney

For some reason my little act of revenge doesn't feel as sweet as I thought it would, and the emptiness he leaves behind — both in the bar and in my heart — is overwhelming. Maybe I really did love him? Maybe he does have feelings for me? But how in the hell am I supposed to sort that out now?

It's unwinnable. I cannot win. If I trust his word right now and I'm wrong? Then what? How many pieces will I break into then?

But if I let him walk away and he really is sorry. If he is the man I truly love and I don't at least try to find my way through these feelings of betrayal... how many years of regret and sadness will come from making the wrong decision because I'm scared?

I sit in the chair at the table where he waited for me

to come back. I have no idea how long he waited here. It could've been days for all I know. It took me long enough to get home.

And after I wallow in sadness I brought on myself for what seems like hours, I remember that he said he left me something besides money in the cash register. So I get my ass up and walk back behind the bar. I take out all the stacks of twenties and count it up in my head as I go. Twenty-five thousand dollars.

He didn't really leave me money. He left me another chance. Maybe to make up for the one he took away from me that night eight years ago. Maybe just to ease his guilt a little. But it's more than nothing when I add in the way he delivered it.

Humble.

Apologetic.

Sincere.

There's a phone in the drawer too. Maybe the one he gave me back at the cabin when he wanted me to take the Snowcat and leave. I had in my coat pocket, but when I remembered it when I was on the road in Garrett's truck, it was gone. Must've fallen out when I was running through the woods.

I flick my fingers across the screen and it comes to life.

It's just a generic background picture with all the standard icons on it. But the green messages icon has a little number one up in the corner.

He had something more to say. Something he didn't want to say in person.

It scares me a little, if I'm being honest. There's a very good chance it's bad news.

But there's no way I can't read it. My finger tabs the icon and the message appears.

It's a video of Merc.

I press play and he gives me a weak smile. "I know the hush made you think you loved me when you didn't. I can't change that. I can say I didn't mean for it to happen, but I'd be lying. Because I love you so much right now and I wish you still felt the same. And I lied about something we talked about back at my house too," he says, looking down so his dark hair covers his eyes. "No surprise there, I guess." He looks up again and all I see is pain. "I can do more than kill and cook, Sydney. So I'm gonna show you something genuine. And no matter what you choose to do from here on out. This is real."

He reaches out of the view of the camera and pulls a guitar in his lap. "I'm a pretty good player." He smiles and I smile with him. "And I can sing. So I'm gonna sing you this song, and then, just so there's no misinterpretation of what it means from me to you, I'm gonna tell you."

He clears his throat, something I now realize he does when he's nervous, and begins to strum the guitar. His voice is… well, it's hard to believe that that hard man can sing so soft.

The song is *Daughters* by John Mayer.

I start crying in the first verse and by the time he's done, I'm a sobbing mess. He sets the guitar down and folds his hands in his lap. Another gesture of nerves. And then he looks straight into the camera. "Those Company people, Sydney. They did this to you. They took away your right to a childhood. Your right to a father. I don't have any daughters, Syd. But if we had daughters, I'd be good to them." He stops for a moment, just enough time for my chin to start trembling as I try to pull myself together. "I'd be good to you too. I'd make everything up to you by breaking this cycle. And your daughters would never, ever have to have a conversation with a brutal killer like this. I would lay my life down for them." He shrugs apologetically. "It's all I've got to offer so I'll understand if it's not enough."

He reaches out and turns off the recording.

And I have never felt so misled in my entire life. Have I been wrong about him all this time?

Another message makes the phone vibrate in my hand. He must have seen the delivery notice when I opened the video.

It says:

I swear to God, I'd be good to you.

FORTY-FIVE

MAC

"A real man knows how to treat a woman softly."

– Case

I watch the message screen for several minutes, just hoping she will write something back. I hope, but I don't expect it. Because nothing can make up for what I did.

And I'm just about to put the truck in gear and give her the space she needs when the back door of the bar opens. She peeks out and I know immediately that she's crying.

She takes a step outside and sees me, waiting in my truck down the alley. I get out and walk towards her.

"Syd," I say, stopping when she's a few feet away. "I can't prove myself unless you give me a chance to be the man I know I am. And you can't know if you love me until I give you a chance to experience it." I hold out my hand to her. "I don't have a guarantee and I know I don't deserve another chance. But I want one, Sydney. I fucked up and

365

I'm sorry. I take it back."

She walks forward and takes my hand and I pull her into a hug. I lift her up off the ground and let her wrap her arms and legs around me like an octopus.

"I'll be good to you, I promise. I'll do whatever it takes to set it right. I think you're amazing. You're the bravest person I've ever met because you did it all alone. You pulled yourself up with no help at all. You fucking astonish me with your strength. And you're so beautiful. I don't understand how they never loved you. I really don't. Hurting you is the last thing I want. I want to make you happy, make you smile. See the confidence I know you have. When you drove away out there in Montana, you split me in half, Sydney. You said you hoped I felt that pain one day, and I did. I felt it. You ripped my heart out when you drove off and I knew I fucked it all up. My father never recovered after he caused my mom's death and I came here to beg for you. Fight for you. Because I don't think I can recover if you never forgive me. Even if you walk away right now, as long as you know I'm sorry—"

She leans back from my embrace and stops me with two fingers over my mouth. "*Hush.*"

I let myself crack a small smile as I squeeze her. "It doesn't work on me, cowgirl. It doesn't need to though. Because I already love you."

She kisses me on the neck and leans into my ear

whispering, "It doesn't work on me either. It never did, Case. I saw the man you *could be* back when I was sixteen. I just saw him eight years before you did. I put my trust in you for a reason. And maybe we didn't fall into love the way most people do. And maybe it took us a lot longer than most to find our true selves. But I'm OK with that. We're here. We made it. *Together.* I have always loved you and no word could fill me up the way you do right now."

"I owe you a happy ending."

"This might qualify."

"So I guess we're even."

"I guess we are."

I set her down and we walk back into the bar to close it up. Maybe not for good. But for now. All the mistakes we made need to stay where they belong. In the past. Because the only thing worth living for is the future.

We slip out of the darkness like that. We get in the truck and back on the road so I can take her somewhere bright.

We never look back.

We only look forward, our eyes fixed on the sun.

EPILOGUE

"You can live in the heat of hell and still be happy. As long as that hell is your home."

-Case

"You know why we like the desert, Syd?"

She's looking at my safehouse on the outskirts of Palm Springs with utter disgust as I try to find the right key for the front door. I don't blame her. I have a four-million-dollar log home up in Montana and this is... well, I think the whole thing cost me seventy-five grand after renovations.

"Who's we?" she asks, simultaneously shaking off a spider that is trying its best to crawl up her flip-flop and wiping the sweat off her brow. It's ninety-seven degrees today. And it's only late March. We've been traveling for weeks, just enjoying each other. And the freedom we have to be ourselves. But I'm ready to settle down, so I brought her here. My favorite place in the whole fucking world.

Plus, it's nothing but sunshine for as far as the eye can

see.

"Uhh…" Fuck. I'm not an assassin anymore, and I'm not here to dry out, either. But I already started to tell her that us assassins like to come to the desert to dry out after the kill. So I have to say something. "Me and you," I answer back, recovering.

"It's hot here."

"It's supposed to be hot. It's the desert."

"And this place, Case… I've lived in the woods for weeks on end at times. But" — she fans herself now as I try another key in the lock — "it's *hot* here. Is this house even up to code?"

The door swings open and a rush of cool air hits her in the face. She remembers I was talking and looks up at me with a smile. I love that smile. "Why do we like it here?"

I pull her inside and watch her face as she takes it in. She walks down the stairs to the sunken living room and with each step, the temperature drops. Three-feet-thick adobe mud walls will do that for a desert house. Especially one that is mostly underground.

She takes in the comfy couches and the cool tile floor. There's artwork on the whitewashed walls and a guitar over by the Spanish-tiled fireplace, which I use on cold winter nights. And then she wanders over to the archway that leads into the kitchen. A chef's kitchen with industrial appliances, white cabinets, and a nice stone countertop. I follow her in there, enjoying her reaction.

"We like it here," I say, pulling her attention and her body back to me, "because I'm gonna make love to you in every room here. And get you pregnant here. And we're gonna raise kids here and build an oasis in the backyard with a pool and a water slide. We can do anything we want here. Be ourselves forever here. We're gonna start our new life here, Syd. And that's why we like it here. We like it here… because it's home."

Jana Aston, my seriously talented personal assistant and BFF, just messaged me on Facebook and asked if I was raised by killers. I shit you not. Well, first she asked me, all innocent like, "Dude. When u write shit do u worry people will think u r fucked in the head or r u past that?"

I laughed. (I am past that, if you're wondering. I am not this book. I am not these characters. I am merely their voice.)

But I started asking myself where the hell this book came from about halfway through writing it. This mind control stuff freaked me the fuck out. I had to do research, so I Googled it, and six hours later I was convinced Al Roker and Tila Tequila were under the influence of Illuminati MKUltra mind control. I slept with my gun that night, I swear to God. I even loaded an extra magazine I had sitting empty in a drawer for five years, and put it within easy reach. (Jana: "But the illuminati can mind fuck around your gun.") #ThanksForYourSupportJana

I did not like the research at all, and even though the mind control stuff in this story is pretty intense, it's nothing like the shit I saw and read online. I tamed it down by huge orders of magnitude because it really bothered me.

I don't know where I get these ideas, they just pop into my head. But I will tell you a little bit about this process as it relates to Merc, because he is really the only character where I had so many background constraints that came out of so many completely different scenarios.

Merc first appears in *Slack: A Day in the Life of Ford Aston* which released in December 2013. And in that book Ford picks him up at the airport and delivers him to Cheyenne where Ford first encounters Sasha as a twelve-year-old girl. *Slack* took place on the same Christmas Eve as this book. Then Ford got Merc involved in another scheme in *Taut*. Merc was also mentioned, though not present, in *Come Back* with Sasha, Harper, and James. And he had his biggest role yet in *Coming For You*.

I went into *Slack* knowing I wanted to write some twisty suspense about this dude and that he was "on a list" of killers being used by high and powerful people. I didn't invent "the Company" until I wrote *Come* for the *BEND Anthology* in May 2014, but I knew in *Slack* there would be a secret organization in a future book to explain what Merc was doing that night. In fact, thinking back, I had written out some scenes where Ford actually went with Merc to that job, but I deleted them all, and left Ford out of it to keep *Slack* on track.

I also knew Merc's book would be a long time coming because I had a lot of other projects planned, but *Slack* was my initial set-up for what would become *Meet Me In The Dark*. So by the time I started writing MMITD, Merc was real to me. I know him pretty well. I knew the book started with him saving Sasha on Christmas Eve and ended with him being fucked over by the girl he left behind. And I had already set up this mind control stuff in the *Come* books. James was insane, Harper was on weird drugs, Sasha might be a sleeper assassin.

All that stuff was there.

But I tell you what—this Sydney girl surprised the hell out of me in this book. She was the only one I didn't know. I knew her father, he's been mentioned before. But the only thing I knew about Sydney going in was that at the end of *Guns* (oh yeah, Merc was in that too) Merc is watching her coming out of a bar in Cheyenne with a guy… ("I watch the girl hanging on her piece of shit boyfriend outside the bar.")

That was it. That's all I had about Sydney. So her story unfolded as the plot progressed. I knew she was gonna have secrets and I knew she was going to get the better of Merc. She did that twice, so that made me happy. I knew Merc was an asshole and that he would walk away. That's all I had. So I don't know where I get these ideas. I do remember about a month ago, walking into the gym and telling my trainer, James, that I was writing some fucked up shit. That was during "research week".

I find this book disturbing, but not for the same reasons that most people will. I don't find Merc disturbing at all. I know him intimately. I see past what others can't because I created him. So even though he is a violent asshole in the first half of the book, I know *why* he's like that. I'm fine with Merc.

But all this mind control stuff really affected me in a negative way. I spent about a week researching it online. I read articles and watched videos. (And FYI, this MKUltra stuff was real. The really did these experiments on people back in the day by pumping them up with drugs without their knowledge. They admitted to it, and then the CIA, under the Nixon administration, promptly destroyed all the records) I looked for specific drugs to use, but ended up keeping it simple and leaving most of those brand names out. And it took me a while (Julie time – like a week) to put this plot together so that it made sense and could still be something people might like.

It was a difficult book for me in a lot of ways.

But I remember watching the commentary video on the Director's Cut version of that Tom Hank's movie, *Castaway*, and the one thing that stuck out was that they came up with the plot after they randomly put objects inside the Fed Ex boxes. And then they consulted survivalists to determine how Tam Hank's character might use those things to stay alive on that deserted island.

So I kinda felt like that's what I was doing in MMITD. I had these objects in the form of Merc's past roles in other books, and I needed to figure out how I can use them to survive. It was fun (now that my mind control paranoia has waned) and challenging. But I'm really happy with how the book turned out.

There is also a lot of set-up for Sasha's book in here, which will hopefully release a month from now. May 20, 2015 is my plan, but release week usually puts me behind schedule, so I might not make it. I'm trying hard though. Sasha's book will be the "end of" book. Meaning—end of these Company plotlines. I think she is the last character who needs to deal with them. But who knows, maybe someone who survived in *Coming For You* will be back? ;)

Anyway, I know I write twisted thrillers. And sometimes people ask me why I don't stop writing romance and just write thrillers. I have a really good plot for one just waiting for the time to write it. But I *like* romances. I don't want to write thrillers with no romance. I think the romance is the best part. I like the way my characters are all so unlikable by themselves, but putting them together makes them complete. It softens their edges and makes them companionate. I almost never finish reading a book if the characters are too perfect. I like them to be damaged and ugly inside. I like the men to be mean and/or unlovable until that one special girl comes along who can tame them. And I like the women to find their own strength. These twisted plots give them the opportunity to overcome seemingly insurmountable obstacles. So I'm gonna keep writing romantic suspense as long as I have plot ideas.

I hope you enjoyed this story. Merc and Sydney are messed up by themselves, but they are complete when they are together. I guess that's my aim when I write. Take two fucked up people and make them better once they fall in love. :)

|||||||||||||

If you read Three, Two, One (321) and didn't see that I posted a bonus ending scene between Ark and Blue online, you can read that scene here: http://us5.campaign-archive1.com/?u=9313bfe0e0713e135eac00c60&id=9d38ba0879

The Street Team and Shrike Bikes people teamed up for a contest I ran to promote MMITD on release week and I gave them five different tasks to do. Some of the amazing ideas they came up—I'm blown away. And one of the tasks was to spell out the title of the book using household objects. One of these images in particular stood out in my mind, because she used her husband's guns and hunting gear to do this. I asked her if I could use these images in the official book trailer and she said yes. So I'd just like to say thank you to Lauren and Matt Duncan. Love your guns, man. Love them!

I have one more thing to say, and this is about my editor. I get a lot of messages from people telling me how to edit. Why, I don't know. I have an editor. Her name is RJ. I am *never*, as long as she keeps taking my manuscripts, going to ditch her. She is the only editor I've ever used, she's been working with me since my first book, *Clutch*, and she has been a major contributor to my success. She is the only person who read this book before the ARC's went out and so I owe her a huge thank you for all her guidance.

After writing thirty books I know what an editor is. And it's *not* a proofreader. I still get typos, everyone does. Editing is not about typos or grammar. Editing is about plot and characterization. Editing is about sentence structure and flow. It's about knowing what part of the book is my "true story" and what part needs to be cut. She also knows my style. Fiction is not bound by grammar or spelling. The point of a good story is not to have perfect grammar. That's silly. I take some liberties in this area and those liberties create my "voice". People seem to like my voice, so I'm gonna keep doing it.

We do our best to find stray typos after the editing is done, but that's not why I hire RJ. I hire her to take what I write and tell me how to improve it. That does include grammar and stuff. She has a master's degree in publishing — she knows what she's doing. But what RJ does is something most people can*not* do. She sees my story arc. She knows what works and what doesn't. She calls me on all the parts I try to half-ass my way through. She knows what I'm capable of and never lets it slide.

She's invaluable to me. *She is the reason* why my books are so consistent and why you keep coming back for more. She makes me better.

So big huge thank you to RJ.

(By the way, the EOBS is never edited!) :)

OK, I'm done here. If you enjoyed this story please take a moment to leave a simple review over at Amazon, even if you didn't buy the book there. It really, really, really helps me sell more books. I cannot stress that enough.

Thank you for reading and reviewing. Thank you for all your support and love. And thank you for making my work so fulfilling. *You* are the reason I keep doing it.

See you in the next book!

Julie

||||||||||||

I have a really great Street Team. The best, in fact. They are awesome and we are like a family in there. I'm not taking new members, we are closed. But I do run a fan group on Facebook called Shrike Bikes. They are in there all the time, as am I. So if you'd like to hang out with us, just click the link and ask to join the group. One of us will approve you as soon as we see the request.

I also run Release Day Share Contests. If you sign up to help me spread the word about my books on Facebook and/or Twitter, you will be automatically entered to win a free copy of the book on release day. If you have already purchased the book when you are notified that you are a winner, you may choose an advanced release copy of an upcoming book instead. The next book (as I write this) is Sasha's story, and her sign-up form can be found here: http://iamjustjunco.us5.list-manage.com/subscribe?u=9313bfe0e0713e135eac00c60&id=c1e04e3840

If you want to be notified of upcoming books, sign-up forms for advanced release copies (ARC's), special pre-release teasers, or how to order a signed copy of this book, you can sign up for my newsletter here: http://jahuss.us5.list-manage1.com/subscribe?u=9313bfe0e0713e135eac00c60&id=0fb0896cf5

ABOUT THE AUTHOR

JA Huss is the New York Times and USA Today bestselling author of more than twenty romances. She likes stories about family, loyalty, and extraordinary characters who struggle with basic human emotions while dealing with bigger than life problems. JA loves writing heroes who make you swoon, heroines who makes you jealous, and the perfect Happily Ever After ending.

You can chat with her on Facebook (www.facebook.com/AuthorJAHuss), Twitter (@jahuss), and her kick-ass romance blog, New Adult Addiction (www.newadultaddiction.com).

If you're interested in getting your hands on an advanced release copy of her upcoming books, sneak peek teasers, or information on her upcoming personal appearances, you can join her newsletter list (http://eepurl.com/JVhAr) and get those details delivered right to your inbox.